NIGHTFALL

AMERICAN MIDNIGHT - BOOK 2

DAVID KAZZIE

GRUB CLUB PUBLISHING

ISBN-13: 978-1735010502

ISBN-10: 1735010502

❀ Created with Vellum

As Always, For My Kids

ALSO BY DAVID KAZZIE

PROLOGUE

The man sat hunched over the steering wheel, his foot a little heavier on the gas than was probably safe. It was late, nearly two in the morning, and the George Washington Parkway was empty. He absently punched the preset radio buttons, switching from station to station, looking for a familiar tune to soothe his roiling soul. Strange how you fell back to the familiar for comfort. But not one song caught his ear. Not one damn song he liked. Not one that could calm him down. No matter. He was almost there.

Up ahead lay a quarter-mile stretch of road that was not under video surveillance. For whatever reason, the traffic engineers hadn't bothered with a camera here. He had checked the public camera feeds dozens of times to be certain. The road bent sharply ahead of a rocky outcropping. The speed limit here dropped to twenty-five miles an hour. On the far side of the rock formation began a curved guardrail. It was a tricky curve. A moment of inattention here might put you right over the side.

He eased his foot off the accelerator as his destination came into view. It was a cool night, but sweat slicked his body. His shirt was glued to his back and even his boxer shorts felt damp. He was crazed with fear; he had never been so afraid in his life. He pulled into the breakdown lane about thirty yards shy of the guardrail and killed the engine. It hissed and ticked loudly in the silence.

His breathing was shallow and rapid. He took a deep breath, and then let out a long shaky sigh. He still had work to do tonight, not to mention a long walk home in the dark. After confirming that he was in the camera's blind spot, he got out of the car. His legs buckled; he steadied himself with a hand against the window. The fresh air was crisp and clean and tinged with a hint of pine. It made him feel a little better.

His name was Solomon Tigner. He was forty-six years old, divorced, no kids. He worked as a climate scientist. And what he knew quite possibly could get him killed.

He unlocked the trunk with a press of his key fob. The beep preceding the disengagement of the lock startled him, and he nearly jumped out of his skin.

"Come on, Tigner," he whispered. He frequently talked to himself. At work, at home, sitting in traffic. If he was really lost in thought, it sometimes happened when he was alone in public. "Almost home."

He stepped toward the trunk, still in disbelief at what he was planning to do. If he had been stopped by police, if he'd been involved in a traffic accident, there were a thousand ways this little gambit could have gone off the rails. But none of those things had happened, and he was close now, so close.

Good thing, because it would have been very difficult to explain the corpse in his trunk.

No one would have believed him.

He wasn't responsible for the death of the man. He had never even met him. He'd purchased the body from a technician from the office of the chief medical examiner, a shady sort who knew how to make the paperwork on a dead homeless guy disappear. It had cost Solomon ten thousand dollars, but that didn't matter. Ten thousand dollars wasn't going to mean much in the very near future. But the technician didn't need to know that. Besides, he knew better than to ask questions of someone who'd handed him one hundred hundred-dollar bills for a dead body.

Solomon just needed a body whose build matched his own, someone who had died of natural causes. Black, like he was. No gunshot wounds or blunt force trauma. Fortunately for Solomon, he had been blessed with the most average body of all time. Five-foot ten on the nose, a hundred and ninety pounds.

He leaned down into the trunk, slid his forearms under the man's armpits, and hoisted him over the lip. The technician had helped him load the body into the trunk; this was the first time Solomon was moving the corpse by himself. And they called it dead weight for a reason. After a few false starts, his legs and arms burning underneath him, he knelt down and hoisted the body over his shoulder in a fireman's carry.

He stumbled and staggered into the thankfully empty roadway like a man carting his drunk drinking buddy out of a bar. He regained his balance and tottered back toward the car. He lined up the shot and deposited the man right into the driver's seat. The dead man's head banged solidly against the door frame, but he did not seem to mind.

Solomon adjusted the corpse in the seat, buckling him in, placing his hands on the steering wheel and wrapping his stiff fingers around it. Ordinarily, this sort of thing would have freaked Solomon the hell out, but not tonight. He was just too scared. When the man was properly situated in the driver's seat, he returned to the trunk and removed the final three pieces of the puzzle before slamming it shut.

A bottle of bourbon.

A pack of cigarettes.

A lighter.

He shook a cigarette loose from the pack, lit it, took a few puffs. It trembled in his hand, but it calmed his nerves. It made him feel like he was in charge of his destiny.

In the distance, the white sodium glow of headlights appeared over the crest of a hill about a mile to the south. It was a clear night, and he could see a long way.

"Shit," he said, dropping the cigarette to the ground and crushing it under his shoe.

He slipped into the backseat and slammed the door behind him. He reached around the driver's seat and unbuckled the seatbelt. The corpse tipped over on its side, across the console and under the window line. Solomon ensured the car was turned off, the lights extinguished.

The Doppler effect of the approaching vehicle grew

stronger. Solomon held his breath and shut his eyes tight, as though that would make any difference. Unless it was a state trooper, he really didn't think the car would pay him any mind. Most folks did not stop to assist stranded motorists, especially at two in the morning on a desolate stretch of road such as this. The car blew by without so much as a second look. Solomon's car rocked slightly as the other vehicle rocketed past him toward its unknown destination. After a quick check of the road behind him, he leaned into the front seat, repositioned the corpse at the wheel, and buckled him back in.

It was time.

He got out of the car and said a little prayer for the deceased man. Other than the fact that he had been homeless and that he was now dead, Solomon knew virtually nothing about him. It was a shame, really, because he was about to become an important player in a grand game. In some ways, he was as important as Solomon himself.

This wasn't self-aggrandizement on Solomon's part.

It was a combination of fate, brains, and bad, bad luck.

He was a brilliant scientist. Beginning at a young age, he had demonstrated remarkable aptitude for the physical sciences. He graduated from high school a year early, finished college in two years, and had completed his first doctorate by the age of twenty-one in environmental science. He went to work for the NOAA, the National Oceanic and Atmospheric Association, the government agency dedicated to studying and improving the health of the planet's oceans and atmosphere.

He added a second doctorate in climatology by the time he was twenty-five. He loved his work; it was all he cared about. It had cost him his marriage, but that was okay with him because his heart had never been in it in the first place. Georgane was a lovely woman, and she had deserved so much better than him. Fortunately, she had found it and was now mother to twin high school freshmen. She was a beloved elementary school teacher. Perhaps he should warn her.

His work had drawn the attention of a powerful think tank, which hired him shortly after the ink on that second doctorate had dried. He worked on cutting-edge science, all geared toward averting the certain climate catastrophe awaiting all of them. Reducing carbon emissions, protecting the Arctic sea ice, optimizing renewable energy sources. It was incredibly intoxicating work. This group of a dozen scientists drawn from multiple disciplines.

Then it had taken a turn. A very dark turn.

If they found him, they would kill him.

He had tried going to the FBI. But they had had someone on the inside, someone waiting for a leak. They had been waiting for him. That night, he slept in a motel room he'd paid for with cash and woke up the next morning to discover his house had exploded. According to the news, the cause had been an unexplained gas leak.

Right.

That was when he had run.

And now he was here.

He opened the bottle of bourbon and took a long swig. It was good bourbon. Looking back, he wasn't sure why he hadn't simply bought the bottom-shelf swill, which would have been thirty dollars cheaper. Ah well, at least it was smooth going down. He took a second swig, smaller this time, savoring it. Hell, if ever he had earned a stiff drink, it was right now.

He tipped the bottle over and splashed the corpse with the rest of the liquor. Now he did feel badly. It was a shame to spill such good bourbon, even in furtherance of such an important mission. The car reeked of the oakiness of the whiskey.

He leaned over the corpse's lap and shifted the vehicle into neutral. Positioned as it was on a slight grade, the car began to roll.

Shit, he should have had the cigarette lit already.

Using one hand to steer the car as he jogged alongside it, he deftly plucked a cigarette from the pack in his shirt pocket and slid it between his lips. Then he quickly lit it with tremorous hands. He took a long drag, ensuring the tip had ignited, and tossed the smoldering cigarette into the dead man's lap.

The fire bloomed instantly as the car continued rolling toward its date with destiny. Luckily, the grade of the road wasn't particularly steep, and a healthy jog kept Solomon alongside the rolling vehicle. Just a few more yards now to the gap between the rock formation and guardrail.

Like threading a needle.

Just a few more seconds.

The car slipped right through the gap. Solomon's forward momentum jostled him against the guardrail, but he was able to grip the metal railing before tumbling over. The car, however, cleared the unprotected shoulder. The undercarriage scraped the edge of the roadway as it toppled over and gravity took over.

The bloom of fire had already engulfed the passenger compartment. It was just a matter of time now. The car bounced along the steep hill, which dropped sharply before shearing off into a vertical cliff. The car plunged one hundred feet and, much to Solomon's delight, exploded on impact.

The fireball was so intense, the heat radiated against Solomon's face.

He watched the conflagration for a moment and said another prayer for the dead man. As a scientist, he struggled with the faith that had been instilled in him as a child by his grandmother, the churchiest woman he had ever known. But tonight, he felt the strength and sincerity of the prayer deep in his bones. In death, this anonymous man had saved Solomon's life.

He followed the prayer with an expression of thanks.

The plan had worked.

He just might stay alive.

As the fire burned at the bottom of the ravine, he turned and jogged away into the darkness.

1

FIVE YEARS LATER

I t was time to make bread.

Two cups of newly milled flour sat atop the kitchen island while Lucy Goodwin studied the no-knead bread recipe. Although she did not normally work in the kitchen, she'd had a hankering for fresh bread she'd seen to herself. And the community encouraged its citizens to cross-pollinate their skill sets. You never knew when you might be called on to work in an area unfamiliar to you. She was a good enough cook, but baking had always been her Achilles' heel. Just the thought of the aroma of baking bread was enough to make her mouth water. Today was her off day, and so she had decided to spend it honing her culinary skills. It was a rare opportunity, as her days were normally full. She would not exit today without bread.

She mixed the flour, yeast, and salt in a plastic bowl, her eyes darting from bowl to recipe. After mixing the dry ingredients, she added most of the water and began stirring the solution, swirling it into a viscous paste. She was left with a thick, sticky ball of dough. Around her, the kitchen staff hustled to and fro, preparing the day's breakfast for the community's nearly two hundred residents.

Lucy's eyes darted to the next line in the recipe.

Cover bowl with plastic wrap and let rest in a warm place for twelve to eighteen hours

Twelve to eighteen hours?

Her heart sank. She briefly considered dumping the entire thing in the trash, but finally, at forty-four, she'd managed to grab a hold of her temper. She had not read the recipe in its entirety before beginning her work. She would just have to wait until the next day for her fresh bread. It would be worth it though, she reminded herself. It would be so worth it. Baked up in the brick oven, slathered with a little jam. So good. Nothing came easy these days. Anything worth having was hard. Every meal, every drink of water, every good night's sleep came at a price.

"How's that bread coming along?" asked Taylor Rutschmann, a bespectacled brunette woman about Lucy's age. She'd been assigned to the kitchen since the community's inception. She was quite adept at taking the community's bounty and stretching it to feed dozens of mouths.

"Think I'm done," Lucy said. "Just need to let it rise."

"Leave it on that table over there," Taylor said, pointing to a sunny corner of the kitchen. "It stays warm there. Good for the dough."

Lucy set the bowl on a small table and fixed a cup of tea before taking her leave of the kitchen. Impatient as she was, she stole a glance at the bowl on her way out the door, wishing she didn't have to wait until the next day for fresh bread. Damn unfair. These days, tomorrow was not at all guaranteed. You just never knew anymore. If you had fresh bread, you ate it today.

It was a nice but chilly morning. It was early, a little past seven. Now that the bread was done and set to proof, the day was open in front of her. She was still on call, of course. As the community's chief medical officer, she never had a true day off. But she still liked to take advantage of her pseudo-break. A book. A book would be nice. It had been a long time since she'd gotten lost in a book. A long talk with a book was often what she needed to soothe her soul.

She made the short walk from the kitchen to the cottage she shared with two dozen women. The cottage was quiet. Most of her housemates were still asleep on this Sunday morning. She lingered at the bookcase in the foyer, the small library they had pieced together over the past four years, unable to decide on something to read. Her free time was so sparse she couldn't afford to get into it with a book she didn't love.

Just pick one. Give it ten pages, and if you don't love it, move on to the next one.

She finally selected a Stephen King novel, *11/22/63*, which she'd long been meaning to get to. She went back outside, set a blaze going in the outdoor fire pit, and began to read. Instantly, she was swept up in it. Thirty minutes passed as she sank deeper and deeper into the story. So engrossed was she that she did not hear her visitor approaching. Terri Packard, one of the nurse aides, was within arm's reach before Lucy sensed someone was there. It startled her so badly, she dropped the book.

"Sorry, Luce," Terri said. "Didn't mean to scare you."

"You got me good," she said, laughing.

But Terri, normally possessed of a cheery disposition, did not join in the chuckle. Her face was tight and severe. She shifted her weight from one foot to the other.

"Something wrong?"

"Two new patients overnight," she said, her voice shaky. "Fever, chills, dry cough."

Lucy tensed up.

"You think it's corona?"

Terri was a good diagnostician, and if she suspected the virus that caused Covid-19, the bizarre respiratory illness that swept the globe nearly a decade ago, then that was probably what it was. She'd worked for a long-term care community in the old days and had absorbed a fair amount of medical knowledge from the experience. Strangely, the pandemic, which had killed around three million people worldwide before being wrestled under control like an angry steer, sometimes felt more frightening than the Pulse and its aftermath, which had killed many times that. Something about an invisible killer like a virus had messed with your mind in a way that even their civilization-ending blackout did not.

The prospect of disease loomed large in their community. Any outbreak was potentially disastrous, especially since the Pulse had boomeranged them all into a new Stone Age. Although she was not a medical doctor by training, she was an experienced registered nurse, and well, there were no physicians in their community. The census four months earlier had put the population of their community at one hundred and ninety souls. Just bad luck. She kept hoping a licensed physician would show up at their gates, but so far, that hadn't happened.

"Maybe," she said. "I don't want it to be."

"But you think it is."

"Yeah."

"Masks?"

"Took care of it."

"Good," Lucy said. "Let's go take a look."

Terri waited on the porch while Lucy went inside to change. She was anxious to get to the clinic and check on the new patients. It had been a while since the last outbreak; two years earlier, cholera had claimed five lives. A bubble of anxiety pushed against her sternum. Anxiety had become a new friend these past few years.

Before exiting the bedroom, Lucy dry swallowed a Xanax tablet. She would just as soon go without the medication, but anxiety negatively affected her ability to focus on her work. She had developed a dependency on the pills, she was sorry to say, but the good news was that all controlled medication was in very short supply, and she had no choice but to ration the tablets she had.

"How high are the fevers?" asked Lucy.

"One-oh-one, one-oh-two, in that range."

Lucy chewed on that bit of information as they finished the walk to the clinic in silence. If it was coronavirus, it was hard to say where it had come from. Folks were free to come and go as they pleased and frequently intermingled with other communities, especially at the various market days where they bartered for supplies they needed. Outbreaks cropped up from time to time. The wildly contagious pathogen was always out there, looking to buy its way back into the game.

The trip to the clinic wound through a copse of trees. A wooden bridge spanned the narrow creek, which was running low today. Trees were still barren as they edged toward the end of winter.

They called their community Promise.

Promise sat upon five hundred square acres, the former home of a Boy Scout camp, along the James River in Goochland County, Virginia, about twenty miles west of the former capital city, Richmond. At its center sat Lake Dillon, which provided much of the community's freshwater supply. To the south, about a mile as the crow flew, the James River snaked lazily toward the city of Richmond.

Lucy and her brother Jack had moved here a year after the Pulse. They had never intended to abandon the farm that had been in their family for four generations, but circumstances had left them no choice. Things had deteriorated much more quickly than either of them had anticipated, and neither of them had been all that optimistic to begin with. Their reserves were deep, but in the urban areas, food and medicine ran dry in less than two weeks. Water lasted a bit longer, as municipal systems relied more on gravity to deliver it from the reservoirs. But with so much demand for water, the supply ran out about a month into the crisis and without power, there was no way to replenish it.

The incident was still burned in Lucy's brain. It happened about two weeks after returning home from her harrowing rescue of Norah and subsequent escape from a dangerous criminal named Simon. It had been a pleasant morning, low humidity, the skies a fierce blue, and they were taking their breakfast on the country porch of the farmhouse she, Norah, and Jack shared.

They were hungry, desperate, a middle-aged couple from the suburbs.

Norah had spotted them first, skulking about the growing fields.

"Hey, someone's out there," she said, gesturing toward the screen overlooking the crops.

A thin, bedraggled woman was pulling baby potatoes right out of the ground, alternating between shoving them into a backpack and into her mouth. Her partner, a middle-aged man wearing dirty khaki shorts and a grimy T-shirt, was filling a plastic grocery bag with them.

They'd heard about scavengers from their neighbors, but this was their first experience with one. Lucy and Jack had already considered the prospect and had decided to take on newcomers into their homestead. More bodies meant more hands to work the fields. These two could help them scale their growing and farming operations, make sure they had enough to get through the coming fall and winter.

"Let's go talk to them," Lucy had said. "They look nice enough."

"These two?" Jack asked.

"We have to start somewhere," Lucy said. "Strength in numbers, right?"

Jack let out a frustrated sigh.

"I guess."

Armed with sidearms, Lucy and Jack had gone out
the back, only to be greeted by a hail of gunfire. A round
nicked Jack in the arm; Lucy dove off the porch and took
cover at its base. Her enraged brother followed her. A
quick check of his arm revealed the good news; the bullet
had grazed him. Another inch to the left and it could
have hit an artery. Their assailants were unskilled and
stayed in the open, wildly discharging their weapons.
Still taking cover behind the brick porch, Jack drew a
bead on each of them, muttering under his breath about
their stupidity, and then killed each of them with a shot
to their chests.

That afternoon, she and Jack had buried the bodies in
a remote tract of land at the edge of their property. In
death, the couple looked painfully normal. Just a couple
from the suburbs. But there were signs of other things
frozen in their dead faces. Hunger. Desperation. Terror.
The things that had brought them to Lucy's doorstep that
morning.

That night, after Norah was asleep, she and Jack had
sat on the porch, discussing the implications of the day's
events.

Abandoning the farm was not an option.

"We have to defend this place," Lucy had said.

Her mind was on Norah, the girl Lucy had rescued in
Washington, D.C., on the day of the Pulse, the day the
world had changed forever, and keeping her safe. A farm
like theirs was a critical step in achieving that mission.

"We'll be fine," Jack had said.

"Those two could've killed us," she said.

"They didn't."

"But they could have."

"But they didn't."

"You're missing the point."

"I know," he said, sighing. "We'll have to be more careful. I'll start working on more fencing."

She suggested allying with their neighbors, forming a collective. Jack was opposed to the idea; in fact, he abhorred it.

And she wasn't sure he would ever have come around if it hadn't been for that one night in October.

"Who else is inpatient?" Lucy asked as they drew close to the clinic.

"Sammy Boston and Frances Statler."

Boston was in end-stage kidney failure; all they could do was keep him comfortable. Frances was recovering from a badly broken leg she'd suffered when her horse had thrown her.

"Nothing we can do for Boston," Lucy said. "We'll move Frances to the isolation tent."

Thick cloud cover had settled over the area by the time they reached the clinic. This was not unwelcome news; bad weather would keep people indoors and limit the spread of the pathogen.

The clinic made its home in a small health lodge. There wasn't much to it — a six-bed patient ward and her small office where she stored rudimentary patient records. After moving Frances to the isolation tent, they'd have three beds for additional coronavirus cases. She hoped they wouldn't need more.

After masking and gowning up, they made their way to the patient ward. Lucy herself had contracted Covid during the pandemic, but she wasn't certain if she still carried any immunity to the disease.

Lucy's first patient was a wiry middle-aged woman named Natalie. Lucy did not know her well. She made soap and candles, two of Promise's biggest trading commodities. She was coughing and wore the bright shine of fever.

"Good morning, Natalie." She nodded. Her breathing was labored, and it took a minute for her to find the wind to respond.

"Started feeling sick during the night," Natalie replied before pausing to draw a slow breath. The simple reply took a lot out of her. "I didn't want to take any chances exposing anyone else.

Terri handed Lucy a thermometer; she placed the metal tip under Natalie's tongue. Two minutes later, Lucy had her answer. The woman's fever had spiked to a hundred and four. If she had been sick for two days, she was likely contagious for several days before that. She had a potential outbreak on her hands. They needed to start tracing Natalie's contacts immediately.

She made a few notes in her chart and directed Terri to give her Tylenol to control the fever. The story was the same with the other patient. High fever, coughing, short-ness of breath. Classic symptoms of Covid-19. Both patients provided their contacts over the past ten days as best they could remember. Tracing the contacts was a key step in preventing a larger outbreak. The problem was that without testing, there was no way to know if this was Covid. Several respiratory diseases presented in similar fashion.

Lucy and Terri spent the rest of the morning interviewing the patients and establishing their contacts over the past week. Then they checked the pharmacy; they were extremely low on the antiviral medication that had been proven to treat Covid-19. It wasn't a silver bullet, but it did reduce mortality significantly. As she eyed the empty cupboard, she made a clicking sound with her tongue.

"We're going to have to make a trip to the Falls," she said.

"Yeah, I guess so."

The Falls was Promise's chief ally along this section of the James River watershed. It drew its name from a small waterfall near a short jog in the river that served as the community's centerpiece and fresh water source. It was an odd place led by a perplexing former nun named Julianne; its population was exclusively female. No men were allowed. But the two communities had co-existed peacefully for years.

Despite the fifteen-mile gap between them, the communities traded frequently. The Falls produced paper products, clothing, and, in addition to its stockpile of pharmaceuticals, had developed an expertise in producing herbal medication; in exchange, Promise provided produce and dairy to the Falls. A year ago, they had signed a mutual defense agreement. An attack on one community would be viewed as an attack on both.

It was about a three-hour ride on horseback; she would need to leave shortly to return by dark. Lucy was already working on her preflight checklist, as it were, all the boxes she would need to check off to ensure safe passage to and from the Falls. She didn't like the idea of leaving the patients, but given that they'd be trading for medication, she needed to see their offerings with her own eyes.

"You start tracking the contacts," Lucy said, making notes in each of the charts. "Tell everyone to mask up. No exceptions. Don't give the oxygen unless you have no choice. If it's Covid, we're gonna need to make it last until we get back."

LUCY LEFT Terri to begin contact tracing and made her way to Jack's tent. He eschewed living in the communal quarters in favor of a solitary existence on the fringes of the campground. No one gave him grief about it; he worked harder and longer than virtually anyone and was left to his own devices. If he wanted to sleep in the multiple personality disorder that was the central Virginia climate, which swung wildly between extreme winter cold and oppressive summer heat, spiced with as many tropical storms as snowstorms, he was free to do so.

His tent, a big six-person job, was empty, so she rerouted north toward the large maintenance shed where Jack spent his free time dithering with some electronic component or another. Even all this time after the world's electricity had gone out, Jack remained convinced they could jerry-rig their way around the devastating effects of the Pulse. The rain picked up as she jogged, the precipitation dully spattering the green nylon shell of her rain parka. On a drizzly Sunday morning, there was little activity. Smoke curled from most of the lodges' chimneys. People would be hunkered down in their cottages, lying in bed, sitting around the blazing hearths, drinking their bitter coffee.

She found Jack sitting under the overhang, smoking a cigarette.

"Where we headed?" he asked when she had drawn within earshot of his position. His voice was thick and gravelly from years of smoking. She kept pushing him to quit, but he never would. She didn't bother anymore. He was well aware of the risks; he didn't particularly expect to live long enough to develop lung cancer.

"How'd you know?"

"The look on your face," he replied.

"The Falls," she said. "We need meds. Possible Covid outbreak."

He pitched the half-smoked cigarette to the ground, where a droplet of rain extinguished it with a hiss.

"Let's get moving then."

2

The journey to the Falls cut southeast through green Virginia countryside, running largely parallel to the river, curling north, before bending southeast to the James again. Lucy sat astride Pancake, a twelve-year-old American quarter horse that she adored. He was fourteen hands high, his coat a deep, burnished copper. He was a bit skittish around men, perhaps the byproduct of an abusive former handler. Lucy took the point while Jack brought up the rear aboard another quarter horse, this one named Egg Drop. Despite the rain, they were making good time; they would be at the Falls within the hour.

They rode in silence until the road narrowed, harkening their final approach to the Falls. The horses' hooves clocked softly on the pavement, damp and overrun with weeds. The road was still in decent shape, but she didn't know for how much longer. Each cycle of the seasons brought extreme heat and bitter cold, swelling and shrinking the asphalt until it began to ripple and crack.

Lucy was cold and tired. She hoped Sister Julienne was in a decent mood; it lubricated the gears of commerce between the two communities. She needed as much of the medication as Julienne was willing to barter. They had brought prime goods to trade; their saddlebags were heavy with meats, eggs, and cheese. It would be an expensive day, but she was willing to pay. If it was coronavirus, and it caught hold in the general population, they had a rough month ahead of them. It wasn't particularly deadly, killing about one out of every two hundred people it infected, but it could put dozens on ice as they recovered from the nasty respiratory illness.

Jack pulled up next to her as they made the final turn for the entrance to the Falls. Ahead, about a hundred yards distant, a sentinel stood guard before two sawhorses blocking the road. The blockades were largely symbolic, telling bandits and highwaymen that this community would be more trouble than it was worth. The same reason having a dog had been the best defense against burglars. You hear a dog barking, you're probably gonna mosey on to the next house.

"Can you behave yourself this time?" she asked.

Jack loved flirting with Sister Julienne, much to the conservative woman's chagrin. Lucy got the impression that the woman enjoyed and abhorred his attention. The Falls sat on the campus of a defunct wilderness school for troubled teens, a sister school to the Catholic school where Julienne had taught. Julienne had come here after the Pulse, evacuating the city with several coworkers in the aftermath of the disaster. There wasn't much to the ten-acre campus, a few buildings dotting the property. The wilderness beyond it, however, was vast and full of game.

"Do I have to?" he said with a smirk and a twinkle in his eye.

She sighed.

"If she's in the mood, fine," Lucy said. "If she's in one of her moods, back off. We need these meds."

"Whatever you say, boss."

Lucy didn't push it; there wasn't much point. If he wanted to behave, he would. If not, then she would have to deal with the fallout. It was just the way her brother was, and these long years since the Pulse hadn't softened him at all.

He did have a soft spot for Norah. Norah visited him often at his tent, where they played chess, a game he had taught her; she had taken to the game quickly and won as many as she lost. She had helped fill the void in his life carved out by the passing of his niece, Lucy's daughter, Emma.

They donned their facemasks. If they came in looking for antiviral without them, they were likely to be shown the door in due haste. Lucy recognized the guard, a lean young woman named Vikki Kelner. It was a good omen. She was friendly and enjoyed the alliance with Promise; she often represented the Falls at the Market, a monthly swap meet that drew a dozen communities to trade goods, services, and gossip.

"Howdy," Lucy said, keeping her distance.

"Lucy," she said, nodding her head. She paid Jack

little attention; the woman was not a fan of her brother. "What brings you by on this rainy day?"

"We need some meds for a possible Covid case," she said. "Julienne around?"

"She's in her office," Vikki replied, taking a step backward.

There was little risk of coronavirus transmission outdoors and at a distance, but Lucy did not want to poison the well.

"Wait here."

Vikki signaled to someone inside the gate; she relayed the message to a courier who scampered off to find Julienne. As they waited, Lucy and Jack dismounted and led the animals to a small creek running parallel to the road. The horses set to drinking, rehydrating after the long journey. Lucy soothed herself by stroking Pancake's mane. He was a good horse; the stress of the morning drained away, if only briefly.

It had been a while since she'd worn the mask in public; it was uncomfortable and itchy, but they had proven to be quite effective in slowing down the virus during the pandemic.

Julienne did not keep them waiting long. Lucy recognized her footfalls on the gravel road feeding onto the campus from the main road. Accompanying Julienne was Marie-Anne Clarke, her second-in-command. Julienne was a formidable woman; she ran the Falls with an iron fist. She was in her sixties now; her eyes were a bright sky blue, the centerpiece of a fair face that had begun to show its age.

"Y'all must be in a bad way with bags that heavy," she

said. She had a lilting southern accent; her family was old Richmond, which was a fancy way of saying her ancestors owned slaves once upon a time.

"Need some medicine," Lucy said. She didn't need to say which one.

Julienne shook her head and scoffed.

"That cursed virus," Julienne said. "Every time I think we've stamped it out, it comes back."

"You don't have to tell me."

"Are you sure it's corona?"

"The symptoms suggest it is," Lucy replied. "Obviously, without testing, we're flying blind."

"Hmm."

She turned her attention to Jack.

"You're awful quiet today, cowboy."

Lucy smiled behind the mask. Julienne was in a good mood. Okay, maybe not good, but better than usual.

"Oh, Julienne, your beauty just leaves me speechless."

Julienne blushed, her cheeks reddening sharply against the white habit framing her face. Lucy had to bite her lip to keep from laughing; she could only imagine the penance Julienne would be seeking during her daily prayers after they'd left.

"We're looking for fifteen doses," she said. "We've got plenty of meat and produce to trade."

Julienne coughed sharply and looked back at Lucy.

"Sorry, Lucy," she said. "None to spare today."

Lucy's stomach flipped.

This was unexpected. The Falls was well known throughout the region for its deep repository of medicines; Julienne was one of the primary producers and suppliers of nightcress, an herbal medication that had proven very effective in managing the disease. And Julienne was always looking to deal.

"Nothing?" Lucy said. "Julienne, I've got a possible outbreak on my hands."

"I wish I could help you," Julienne said, her voice tight and low. "Believe me, if I had it to trade, I would."

A ripple of fear flashed across Julienne's face. It was quick, gone as soon as it had appeared, but it was there.

"Come on," Jack said. "It's us. You're a fair woman."

"I really wish I could help," she said, patting a hand to her chest. "I'm afraid today is not your lucky day."

She turned to leave; Lucy reached out and grabbed her by the elbow, a violation of social distancing etiquette. The former nun glanced over her shoulder, her face blank as stone. Whatever she was afraid of she feared more than coronavirus.

"Have we done something wrong?"

"It's not that," Julienne replied.

"Then what?"

Julienne wrenched her elbow free and turned toward Marie-Anne.

"Have a safe trip home."

The women left Lucy and Jack standing alone at the entrance to the Falls.

3

The exchange with Julienne left Lucy filled with unease as they made their way back home. That was not the Julienne she was used to dealing with. Her tone, her demeanor, it was all very unlike the woman she'd come to know. And Lucy did not know what was driving it. Perhaps they were entering a new phase of this post-Pulse world, a world where scarce resources had become scarcer still.

It wasn't like things had been easy in the five years since that terrible day in May. Even after forming their collective, it had been a struggle. There had been long days and nights with not enough food to go around. Nights they had lain down with empty, rumbling bellies, determined to make their winter stash last a bit longer. The toughest stretch was from the New Year through mid-March, when they had all but exhausted the fruits of their summer canning. When they were eating moldy onions and mealy potatoes lousy with sprouts.

But they were alive. They had figured out how to stay that way. Those who had not adapted had perished, she was sorry to say. And the loss of life had been catastrophic, almost unimaginable. Although the true casualty toll would never be known, Lucy would not be surprised if it were north of one hundred million in the United States alone. Worldwide, assuming the effects of the Pulse had been global, and that was something they still did not know, it would be in the billions.

Staying alive was a full-time job, and it required all their guile, their intelligence, their hard work. A life of barter and isolation had become their new status quo. But maybe the status quo was changing again.

Jack, who had taken the point, snapped his fingers twice and pulled back on his horse's reins, breaking Lucy out of her rumination on the failed trade with the Falls. The finger snap was used to signal the presence of possible danger. They were still about eight miles from home. Off to the left was a faded billboard advertising a distributor of recreational vehicles. The road curled west here before beginning turning north toward Promise.

Blocking the road ahead was a horse-drawn wagon, flanked by two men on horseback. Lucy's heart began to race, but she did not panic; this was not her first rodeo with highwaymen. Jack would be calm as well. He feared nothing and no one. It was a good attribute to have in an older brother hellbent on keeping you safe.

Lucy drew up abreast of Jack, and together, they stared down the three strangers. Although they were too far away to get a good look at the men, she did not recognize the wagon. She wondered where they had come from; Promise was not far from several trading routes that had evolved in the intervening years.

Crossing paths with other travelers was not an uncommon occurrence. These encounters usually passed uneventfully. People normally kept to themselves on the road, exchanging simple pleasantries. It was a big thing these days, telling a stranger that you meant them no harm. But Lucy's alarm was blaring right now. As though these men had been waiting on them. She couldn't shake the nagging feeling that they were in for a fight. If these men had meant to pass by, they would have fallen into a single line. These three had blocked the road intentionally.

It was a hell of a thing, facing your own mortality on a regular basis. Every trip beyond the borders of Promise was fraught with danger. There was always the possibility that you would not make it back alive. It was just how it was.

They'd lost a few folks over the years at Promise; folks who'd left for the Market or on a day trip and had never made it back. The one that still chilled Lucy to her core was the murder of a young woman named Abby. A marathoner before the Pulse, she had gone for a long run one chilly winter morning. When she didn't return that afternoon, Lucy and Chris Dobson had gone looking for her. A cluster of vultures circling a meadow about ten miles away from Promise led them to the grisly find—the poor woman's head at the base of an old oak tree. They had never found her body, much less the person responsible.

"Y'all blocking the road," Jack called out.

In the immense silence, his voice carried, echoing off the asphalt, bouncing off the trees lining the road.

"Ain't you the observant one?" called out the man in the middle, presumably the leader of this merry band. His voice was deep and flat, no accent that Lucy could detect. He was white, his features ruddy and weathered, almost Nordic. A thin layer of straw-blonde hair covered his head.

"We don't want any trouble," Jack said. "Just passing through."

Jack liked playing it soft. Playing possum. Let the others think that he would be quick to roll over. Lull a potential attacker into a false sense of security.

"Well, it's gonna cost you today," the man said. "Think of it as a toll."

Jack cut his eyes to Lucy. He had no intention of paying any toll to these men. The trio approached slowly, the two flankers leveling their weapons at Jack and Lucy. The one on the left was tall and thin. His teeth were extremely white, which was unusual these days. He looked like a lawyer or a banker. The third member of the crew was African American, heavier set.

"How much is the toll?" Jack asked.

"How much you got?"

"Well, that doesn't seem very fair," Jack replied.

As Jack engaged the group, Lucy reached inside her denim jacket and rested her hand on the butt of her gun. Many firearms were still functioning in the aftermath of the Pulse, particularly older ones. Newer weapons, especially heavier armaments that relied on advanced circuitry, however, had been rendered useless. Lucy was careful to keep her movements concealed behind her horse's large head. She had always been a quick draw and had become more so over the years; she spent time each day working on her draw, honing it until it was a single flash of movement. Her weapon could go from safely holstered to being open for business in less than a second.

"Who said anything about fair?" the man replied. "These here times are anything but fair as I'm sure you've noticed."

Lucy was ready to fire, but she held back for the moment. It was still two versus three, and it was unlikely she could pick off all three before taking return fire. She needed more time to find an advantage to exploit. The three men had drawn within thirty yards. The leader was about Lucy's age. He looked relatively healthy; his face was full, and his eyes were bright. His comrades looked equally robust. These were not men who went hungry.

"Trust me," the Nordic man said. "It's in your best interest to cooperate today."

"Why is that?" Jack asked.

"The winds of change are blowing," the man said.

"Meaning what?"

"Let's just say this area is under new management."

Jack fell silent as Lucy continued to assess the situation. If these men had wanted to kill them, they easily could have ambushed them in the curve in the road. Which meant there was a longer game at play here. This was more than a quick hijacking; their assailants would be interested in the source. So these weren't your ordinary smash-and-grab highwaymen. Maybe not the brains behind the operation, but a step up from your basic street mugger. That said, they weren't terribly bright. Their first priority should have been to disarm their prey. Perhaps they had gotten lazy in their skullduggery. Perhaps they had gotten used to people folding at the first sign of force.

"And if you're good boys and girls," he went on, "we'll put a nice gold star in your file."

While Jack engaged the men, Lucy settled on a plan to extricate themselves from their situation. Sadly, all the viable solutions required a certain level of violence.

"Okay," she called out. "You promise to let us pass?"

"Oh, you betcha."

"I'll get the stuff out for you," she said. "We've got salted meat and some produce."

The man rubbed his belly in an exaggerated show of appreciation.

"Untie the bags and leave them by the side of the road," he said. "Show me what's inside first though. Real slow like."

Lucy gently tapped the horse's left side three times, a sign to Jack that it was time to make their move. She dismounted, keeping her left foot in the stirrup, swinging her right leg over the saddle and shimmying down to the ground. She was standing in between the animals now, the air ripe with their scent. As she rifled through the saddlebags, Jack dismounted as well, remaining on the far side of his horse, where the three men could see him.

The bandits would be focused on him, of course;

invariably, men were always perceived to be a bigger threat than women. They would assume that Lucy was a dutiful little woman posing little danger to them. The two flankers had lowered their weapons, seemingly confident that they had the situation well in hand. Another successful hijack. Probably thinking about the war story they'd be telling later. She detached the saddlebags and carried them to the side of the road; then she removed the contents and held them aloft for the men to see. They had chard, kale, and strawberries along with a few pounds of salted pork and beef jerky. Items that traveled well. The leader clapped his hands slowly, which only served to piss Lucy off.

She retreated to the cover of her horse, gently rubbing his flank, hoping he'd still be alive a few minutes from now. As she set one foot in the stirrup, using the horse's mass for cover, she drew her weapon and came up firing. The assault took the men by surprise. Before they could execute a defensive action, Lucy's opening fusillade caught the man on the right full in the chest, blowing him off his horse and sending his body cascading to the ground. A second wave missed the leader. She slid back down to the ground, anticipating the horses' panicked reaction to the gunfire. The man on the right returned fire. His rounds whizzed past Lucy's ear, close enough to send her heart into her throat.

Her horse whinnied, rearing back on his hind legs, and then ran directly toward their attackers. Jack's horse had bolted for the woods lining the road, leaving her exposed. She ran for the trees, the gunfire chewing up bits of asphalt as she fled for their cover. So focused on her attack had the men been, however, that they appeared to have forgotten about Jack. He had moved west along the tree line and then burst forth on their left flank.

He circled behind the bandits' spooked horses and killed the leader, the Nordic man, with a close-range shot to the back of the head. The third man, still astride his thrashing horse, raised his arms in surrender.

"Throw your gun down," ordered Jack.

The man tossed the weapon to the ground. It hit the grassy shoulder with a heavy thud. Jack grabbed the man by the arm and wrenched him down off the horse. He crashed to the ground in a heap, lucky to avoid a head or spinal injury. Jack, virtually steaming with fury, violently yanked him into a seated position. His nostrils were flaring, and a sharp crease had formed in the middle of his forehead. Lucy stepped toward him and placed a hand on his back, silently reminding him not to execute their prisoner.

She knelt down next to the man, taking his chin in her hand. Jack trained the gun on the man's head, his finger gently massaging the trigger guard.

"Now you listen to me good," she said. "My friend here wants to shoot you very badly. Very badly. And I know him pretty well. So I suggest you answer the questions we're going to ask you."

"Fuck you, bitch."

He reared his head back and spat at her; he'd telegraphed it enough to give her time to duck out of the way of the massive loogie. Lucy eyed him for a moment and then delivered a right cross to his cheek. The punch flattened the man on his back. This stage of the interrogation had come to an end.

"Guess what, chief?" Jack asked.

The man looked up at Jack with hate in his eyes.

"You're going on a little field trip."

4

L ucy was up before dawn.

She was not a great sleeper, and this night had been no different. She normally fell asleep quickly, but she was often up two or three times a night. Her mind would race, careening between days behind her, the days ahead, thinking about Emma, thinking about all the dangers that surrounded them. And her accommodations were not particularly conducive to deep rest. The acoustics in the cottage were not great, even though each woman had her own private cubicle they had retrofitted the lodge with. There were a few heavy snorers, and depending on the airflow, it could sound like they were right in bed next to you. And rue the nights punctuated with romantic encounters, couples trying hard not to make noise, which somehow made it that much louder. It wasn't frequent, but it did happen.

She climbed out of bed, rubbing the sleep from her eyes as she got moving. It was awkward, but it wasn't like they had many options, especially in the colder months.

She dressed in jeans, a long-sleeve T-shirt, and a fleece pullover. Spring was in the offing, but the mornings were still quite chilly.

She had agreed to meet Jack for another interrogation session with their prisoner before reporting for her shift at the clinic. It had been three days since they had returned with him, and he had not said a single word. That was frustrating, but they had gleaned quite a bit of intelligence in the aftermath of the short but fierce battle with the three bandits.

After the man had made clear his intent not to cooperate, Lucy inventoried their supplies while Jack watched over the prisoner. The sheer quantity suggested the men must have been on some kind of long-range patrol. They were carrying nuts, dried fruits, beef jerky, and a few canned goods. They had a tent, matches, cooking fuel. Even some ground coffee. Coffee! Coffee was a luxury these days. Altogether, it was enough to keep them fed for at least a week. The men were healthy and well fed. Heavily armed. Four nine-millimeter pistols and two semi-automatic M4 rifles. Military grade. Their horses looked healthy, their coats shiny, their bodies sleek and strong.

Depending on how deep into their patrol they were, they may have been carrying quite a bit more at the outset of their journey. When she'd finished loading the supplies into their saddlebags, Lucy examined the bodies of the two men they'd killed. No identification, which wasn't surprising. The white man had a tattoo of a bald eagle on his left forearm. Not terribly instructive.

It all begged a very important question.

Who were they?

Most folks didn't see this much food in a month. These men were obviously part of a larger community, and a well-to-do one at that. Unlike anything they had encountered in the years since the Pulse.

While Lucy worked, Jack sat cross-legged across from the man, leveling his gun at his face. Typical Jack. He wanted their prisoner to know that they had stirred up a hornet's nest, that not everyone out here in the big, scary world just rolled over. But the man sat stone still, looking off into the distance. He was a brawny-looking fellow sporting a thick beard. His cheeks bore the gin blossoms of a man who had spent a lifetime enjoying the hooch. His eyes were a deep blue, set in a face dark and leathery from the sun.

When she'd finished securing their supplies, Lucy looped the reins of the horses together with a short length of rope; Jack blindfolded the man and secured his hands behind back with a pair of zip ties they carried in their supplies. They set the man in the wagon, stopping every little while to ensure the man's bindings remained true. Jack drove the wagon, Lucy bringing up the rear to keep an eye on the prisoner. They left three of the horses behind; it was too complicated logistically. Jack would return the next day to retrieve them. They likely wouldn't wander far.

They took a few detours to keep their prisoner geographically disoriented, reaching the outskirts of Promise as the sun touched the horizon. Lucy was exhausted, the stress and trauma of the day bleeding into her muscles, into her very core. It had been a long time since she'd seen live fire. It had only happened a few times since the Pulse. She'd forgotten how intense, terrifying, even a little exciting the experience could be. Her heart was still racing; she was alert, fired up. Eventually, her body would crash, and sleep would follow, but for now, there was work to be done.

They took him down to the dank, dark basement of the administration building. They had converted it into a holding cell several years earlier, adding steel bars and a heavy door they had stripped from the sheriff's office in the nearby town of Maidens. To date, they'd only used it for drunks and domestic abusers; usually, the two things went hand in hand. This was their first time using it for an outsider. They'd been fortunate in that respect. But as time went by, this kind of entanglement had probably been inevitable.

Word of the captive spread quickly, and the three members of Promise's governing council met them at the door to the basement when they arrived with the prisoner in tow. She and Jack ignored them as they tended to the prisoner, escorting him down the outdoor steps and into the basement, the Council in tow. Candles threw dashing, flickering light; the inmate painted a ghastly silhouette against its cold stone walls.

Jack shoved the man inside the cell and locked it. He retreated to the corner of the cell and sat down, pulling his knees up to his chest. He seemed resigned to his fate, whatever it proved to be. After ensuring the cell was secure, she, Jack, and the Council members returned upstairs. Lucy lit a cigarette; it was homemade and harsh, but it granted her a brief moment of relief.

"So it's true," said Carol Ridyard, one of the Council members. She was young, a graduate student working on her dissertation at the time of the Pulse. But she was incredibly bright and worked nonstop in her role as one of Promise's leaders.

"Indeed," Lucy said, blowing a thin stream of smoke into the mist.

"Where's he from?" asked Jon Schlosser, the second Council member.

"He isn't talking yet," Jack said. "But he will."

Lucy hoped the man would talk before too long; Jack wasn't afraid to take unusual steps to elicit information. He'd been an intelligence officer in the Army many years earlier. College had not been in the cards for Jack Goodwin, and so he had enlisted in the military. He scored highly on aptitude tests, drawing attention from a counterintelligence unit, a field in which he had thrived for several years. But the work had taken its toll, and his military career had come to an ignominious end when he had decked a superior officer who had caught Jack in bed with the man's wife.

"Were there others?" she asked.

"Yes," Lucy replied. "Two others. We took care of them. They were pretty well outfitted. If I had to guess, they were on a long-range patrol."

A silence fell across the group. The prospect unnerved the Council as much as it bothered Lucy. They all worried about a new threat rising to undo all they had worked to build. It was always out there. While they worked to keep the gears of Promise turning, it was impossible to know what was happening outside their little bubble. News was scarce and often unreliable. Rumors, gossip, and myth came and went with the wind.

She had often lain awake worrying about such a threat. There was just no way to know when trouble would arrive on your doorstep. And that's how it was these days. If your number was up, it was up.

That first night, they put two guards on him, one immediately outside the cell and one at the top of the basement stairs. Two of their strongest and most reliable men. Perhaps it was overkill, expending two men for guard duty, but the Council did not like taking chances. A single guard could be overpowered, tricked, taken in by a charming prisoner.

Twice a day, they fed the prisoner flatbread, a little salted meat, and some water, just enough to keep him going, but not enough to make him happy. He ate it robotically; he was not one of these types to throw it back in your face. He seemed to understand that displays of rebellion would hurt no one but him.

But for those first three days in captivity, he did not make a sound.

Lucy stopped by the kitchen on her way to meet Jack for a piece of the bread she had seen to that Sunday morning, smeared with a little jam. She'd been too busy to bake it herself, but it tasted damn good. It was chilly and dank, leading her to pull her jacket tightly around her body on the walk to the administration building. A light wind was blowing, making it feel even colder. She hoped the man would break soon; the more she thought about the ambush, the more worried she had become.

The irony of it all was that Lucy no longer suspected

that coronavirus had been responsible for the respiratory illness that had sent her to the Falls in the first place. No additional cases appeared in the four days since the first patient had arrived at the clinic; both index patients were recovering rapidly. That had been the sneaky thing about coronavirus; it often looked like other far less severe illnesses. Terri had done a good job tracing the two ill patients' contacts, eight in total, and all were self-quarantining in tents on the perimeter of their community. None of them were showing symptoms of illness; besides, there were worse things than fourteen days alone in a tent, excused from your chores, nothing to do but sit, sleep, and read.

Jack was already there when she arrived, sharing a smoke with the guard, Danny Bowen.

"Morning, Danny," she said.

Danny nodded. He wasn't much of a talker. He was a strapping guy, about thirty years old, well over six feet tall. He'd been a roofer before the Pulse, but as he liked to say, his favorite thing to do was drink and get into fights. But he was a skilled worker, and since joining Promise, he'd been instrumental in the constant maintenance work the community needed. He was fiercely loyal to Promise, which made him an easy choice to guard the prisoner. Jack dropped his cigarette to the ground and crushed it under his boot.

"Tired of waiting, Luce," Jack said.

She'd been expecting this. Jack was ready to begin using enhanced interrogation techniques that he had honed during his time in the military. They needed the man to talk. They needed to know what he knew.

"Let's see how today goes," she replied noncommittally. The idea of torture made her skin crawl. It was usually ineffective because most people did not know how to properly question a detainee. But even when the interrogator was skilled, as Jack was, it was awful. Most people broke quickly, and their intelligence was quickly corroborated. Every once in a while, you'd get someone who wouldn't break. Someone who was cobbled together with steel and anger and purpose. True believers. The ones who didn't break and ultimately suffered the most.

She suspected their captive might fall into the second category.

"I can only stay a little while," she said.

When they got down to the basement, the captive was standing in the middle of his cell, as though he'd been expecting them. The guard, a middle-aged Colombian immigrant named Ernesto, was watching him like a hawk.

"He been behaving?" asked Jack.

"More or less," Ernesto replied. He'd only been in the U.S. for a few years when the Pulse hit. He was one of Lucy's favorite people in the community. His English was quite good but heavily accented.

"Put these on him," Jack said, handing Ernesto a pair of zip ties.

"Turn around and put your hands through the bars," ordered Jack.

The man didn't comply immediately, instead taking the time to size Jack up. He tilted his head one way, then the other, as though to take the full measure of his adversary. Finally, he shrugged and complied with Jack's instruction. Jack slapped the restraints on the man and pulled the cords taut. When the man was secure, Jack and Lucy entered the cell, each carrying a stool with them.

"Why don't we try this again?" Lucy asked, taking a seat on the stool. "What's your name?"

No response.

"Where are you from?"

Nothing.

"Why did you attack us?"

Silence.

"You obviously don't need our supplies," Lucy said. "So why did you do it?"

The man smiled. Jack punched the man in the gut. He didn't put everything he had into it, but he did spice it with a little sauce. The man grunted in pain.

"I'm warning you," Jack said. "I don't know what kind of soft targets you've been hitting out there, but you don't want to mess with us."

The man turned his head and spat on the ground, then he smiled that shit-eating grin once more. But then he spoke.

"You have no idea what you've done," the man said.

"Enlighten me," replied Jack.

"My team and I are due back tonight," he said. "When we don't show up, they'll move heaven and earth to find us."

"It's good to have friends," Jack said. "So who's this *they* you're talking about? Maybe I want to get to know them."

"Oh, they'll find you soon enough," he said. "You left more evidence than bin fucking Laden after 9/11."

"Why don't you tell me now and we can speed the process along?"

"I don't want to ruin the surprise," the man whispered.

Jack delivered a second blow to the man's midsection, this one harder and direct to the kidneys. He would probably piss blood later. Lucy winced at the violence, wishing to hell it wasn't necessary, understanding that sometimes it was. This was a brutal world they lived in. It demanded things of them that she had never dreamed of. Even in the height of the Covid-19 pandemic, people had looked out for each other. Food banks were stocked to overflowing. People had food on their tables, people had roofs over their heads. It was humanity's last great display of unity.

Because then the lights had gone out, and they had stayed out. The aftermath had been terrible, and not just due to the battle for resources that sprung up in the wake of the Pulse. There was that nagging belief that the power would come back, that any moment, the lights would come back on and they could rebuild and move on. You started hearing things. A gust of wind could be a power line starting to hum again. And the world had gone dark in more ways than one. People went insane waiting, waiting, waiting for something that had never come. It wasn't just the physical darkness, the absence of lamps and streetlights and traffic signals, and the blue light of laptops and phones and tablets. It was deeper than that, a darkness of the soul that had spread.

The man grimaced and grunted through the pain until his breathing stabilized.

"You can do whatever you want to me," he said between shallow gasps. "I'm not saying another word."

"We'll see about that."

She placed a hand on Jack's forearm, a gentle touch designed to throttle him down. He flinched at first, but then his muscles relaxed. Sometimes, she knew exactly when and how to calm him down. The session had been extraordinarily productive, more so than she had expected. There was definitely a new threat out there.

"You've been very helpful."

Lucy had seen enough for now. The narrow concourse outside the cell had started to brighten with the coming dawn. She needed to get to work.

5

The hanging was scheduled for midday.

Alexander hoped he could change his father's mind before then.

He was sitting in the cafeteria, finishing his breakfast. Well, that wasn't entirely accurate, as he had barely touched his food to begin with. His stomach was unsettled, and he was having a hard time catching his breath. Each of the few bites he had taken was threatening to make a reappearance. He was a tall boy, six feet tall, rangy, still growing as he neared adulthood. He was seventeen years old. Acne had done a number on him, and he'd developed a bad habit of picking at his pimples, leaving his face in perpetual relief.

Alexander had not slept a wink, tossing and turning all night. He normally slept like the dead; he worked hard all day, every day, as did all those of able body in the Haven. But the place had been atwitter since lunchtime yesterday when a nice man named Oliver had been caught stealing a loaf of bread and four slices of salted meat. Alexander liked Oliver; he knew dozens of magic tricks that had enthralled Alexander many times over the years.

Oliver's guilt was not in dispute. Over the past few weeks, the kitchen staff had noticed the bread and salted meat on hand was not matching the daily written inventory they kept. Suspecting that a thief was walking among them, they had set up a sting and caught Oliver red-handed. He readily admitted to the crime. A search of his room turned up half a pound of cured meat.

And there had been no question of Oliver's ultimate punishment.

The penalty for theft in the Haven was death.

Alexander pushed back from the table and emptied the contents of his tray into the trash. Wasting food was frowned upon, but he didn't care. Normally, he was a stickler for the rules and did not defy them for any reason. But this was too important.

It had been a long time since the last execution. At least two years. Alexander had borne witness to the sentence being carried out, as did all Haven residents over the age of ten. It had been a double execution, a man and woman carrying on in an adulterous affair. Adultery was another of the Haven's many capital offenses. Alexander had watched with horrified interest, covering his eyes with his hand but keeping his fingers spread apart just so. The pair, Lilith and Sheldon, had swung from a large tree in a large hayfield about a quarter-mile from the Haven. It was a medieval affair, the townsfolk escorting the condemned from cell to noose.

Initially, the then-fifteen-year-old had found it to be

very exciting and just. These people had broken the rules, and if you broke the rules, they punished you. It was just how things worked. But watching the condemned prisoners stand helplessly on those wooden stools, the thick nooses lassoed around their necks, as his father had conducted the execution ceremony had profoundly affected him.

A burning desire to call out, to stop this terrible thing, had flooded his veins, but the cry died in his throat just as the hooded executioner kicked the stools out from under the trembling legs of the prisoners. The woman's noose had worked flawlessly, snapping her neck and instantly killing her. Sheldon's noose, however, failed to sever his spinal cord, and he spent nearly five horrifying minutes thrashing and flailing as the rope slowly suffocated him, his eyes bulging so hard Alexander feared they would literally pop out of his skull. At one point, Alexander felt the man staring right at him, as though there was no one else standing around that giant, ancient oak, just the two of them. Staring at Alexander and judging him while the life ebbed out of him.

But he was almost eighteen now, nearly a man, and he had his own thoughts on things. Thoughts that diverged from those of his father. There was no need to execute this man for an offense that amounted to shoplifting. And he was going to let his father know about it.

He crossed the grounds, his mind focused on winning Oliver a commutation of his sentence. Of course, he had committed a crime, and he should be punished. But the punishment had to fit the crime. It had to be proportional. He had read that in a book from the library. A book about criminal justice reform. He loved to read and had often spent hours wandering the darkened library like a troubled spirit. The book had been sitting on a return cart, presumably placed there on the day of the Pulse and still awaiting re-shelving five years later.

The Haven made its home at an abandoned golf resort. Firethorn Country Club sat atop nearly one hundred acres of once-pristine land. Before the Pulse, its championship course had drawn golfers from around the world and had been scheduled to host one of golf's major championships that summer. For the past four years, however, it had been Alexander's home. He lived with his father in the six-story resort hotel that served as the club's centerpiece. Until recently, he had shared the penthouse with his old man; several months ago, his father had approved his request to move into his own suite one floor down.

Some five hundred people called the Haven home, many of whom had been with Alexander's father since the early days. The ones closest to him, his top advisers, he'd known for years. Alexander did not know what his father had done for a living before the Pulse; any time Alexander asked him about it, he was cagey and evasive. Eventually, Alexander had come to understand that his father had spent much of his adult life on the wrong side of the law. He had stopped asking.

Alexander found his father in the first-floor conference room of the hotel, sitting alone at a long oak table. Alexander recognized the leather folio laying open in front of him. These would be the written protocols governing the execution ceremony. The man took his work very seriously, down to the last *i* to be dotted, the last *t* to be crossed. His lips moved silently as he read through the material.

"Father?"

That was another thing. As a boy, Alexander had referred to him as "Dad" like any normal kid. But a few years ago, he'd instructed Alexander to refer to him as Father. He didn't know why, but he had done it. It sounded ridiculous, and his stomach clenched with annoyance whenever he said it. Just the cheesiest thing ever.

His father looked up. He was a good-looking man. He was in his forties, but he looked ten years younger. One of those men who would always be handsome.

"What is it?" he asked coldly.

"I want to talk to you."

"Can it wait?" his father said. "I'm preparing for the ceremony."

"It's about the ceremony."

His father raised an eyebrow. He motioned for Alexander to sit down. Suddenly, Alexander's mouth had dried up, all the moisture that made it possible to speak evaporating in the heat of his father's gaze. He hated the way the man made him feel. He never seemed to be good enough for his father, not since Alexander had gone to live with him as a young boy. His mother had been raising him on her own, but then she had become sick with the cancer that ultimately took her life. Alexander had only met his father a few times before going to live with him full-time.

"Well?" his father said after a few awkward moments of silence.

Beads of sweat trailed down Alexander's flank. He became aware of his own body odor.

"You shouldn't kill Oliver," he said as firmly as he could.

His father leaned back in his chair and tented his fingers to his lips.

"I am not killing him," he said. "He is being punished in accordance with the laws of our community."

"I know," Alexander said, the words getting stuck in his throat. His entire argument had abandoned him. "It's just that..."

The words hung in the air as he struggled to get back on track.

"It's just that it doesn't seem fair."

"Alexander, what is the punishment for stealing from the community?"

"Death."

"Is this punishment a secret?"

Alexander's heart sank. There was no question. There was a reason there had been no executions in the last two years. People knew the score. Initially, they had tried an eye-for-an-eye approach to justice. But that had proven impractical. In the early days of the Haven, they had taken the hand of a thief, but he had developed sepsis and died anyway. The Haven had adopted the single sanction approach shortly thereafter.

"No."

"Alexander, I take no joy in what we are about to do today. But it is a necessary thing. It is an important thing.

Keeping everyone at the Haven safe is my duty. The best way to do that is to make sure we have rules and that those rules are followed.

"But..."

His father held up a hand.

"You didn't see how bad things got after the Fall," he said. "I did my best to shield you from it."

"Yeah, but Oliver is a good person," Alexander said. "He made a mistake. He should get another chance."

His father pushed his chair back from the table and stood up.

"Another chance," he said, echoing his son's words. "Another chance."

He began pacing the room, the heels of his shiny, black shoes clocking along the tile floor.

"Yes, perhaps we should."

Alexander's heart soared, but he didn't understand what was happening. His father almost always rejected his arguments out of hand.

"Maybe we just give him a stern talking to. Put him in the cell for a little while."

Alexander's mood brightened. His father was listening to him. For once, his father was really hearing him.

"After all, it's not like he murdered someone."

"Exactly!" Alexander said, slapping the table with his hand.

"I'll tell you what," his father said, now stalking the room with a weird energy emanating from him. "I will do you one better."

"One better?" Alexander said, his stomach fluttering suddenly.

"Yes! We will make it legal for people to steal food!"

Uh, oh.

"If someone is hungry, and it isn't mealtime, they can just help themselves to anything they want from the kitchen."

Embarrassment and shame flooded through Alexander. He'd been stupid to think he could change his father's mind. He lay his hands on the table and stared down at them while his father continued his performance.

"In fact," he said, wagging a finger in the air, "we will get rid of all our rules. It certainly will be easier."

Alexander searched for an off-ramp; it was way past time to end this summit. His father's back was to him as he made his way toward the far side of the room. Alexander would leave, and later this morning, he would join the other residents of the Haven as they escorted Oliver to his death.

"No, wait, we will let, no, encourage people to rape and rob and kill one another!"

As Alexander pushed back from the table, his father spun around and slammed both his fists into the table.

"Sit down!" his father bellowed.

Alexander complied. His eyes welled with tears.

"Listen to me very carefully, son."

Alexander nodded.

"Without rules there is chaos," he said, his voice back down in volume. "And without consequence, there is no reason to follow the rules. What we do today keeps the chaos at bay."

It keeps the chaos at bay.

"Do you understand?"

"Yes, sir."

"Now leave me," he said. "I have work to do."

THE WORDS ECHOED in Alexander's head as he joined nearly five hundred Haven residents on the terrible walk to the majestic oak tree from which Oliver would hang. It was a beautiful old tree guarding the green of the long, par-five third hole.

His father made him stand alongside him at the hanging tree. Oliver locked in on Alexander, sensing, perhaps, an ally here. But Alexander simply stared emptily back at him, focusing instead on the mole above Oliver's eye and thinking about the card tricks Oliver had dazzled the Haven with. They were so good. Alexander's favorite trick had been one in which a member of the crowd tore up a playing card that he'd marked with a red pen and sealed it in an envelope. After setting the envelope on fire, Oliver would direct the audience member to his or her own pocket, where they would find the unmolested playing card. He had begged Oliver to teach him his tricks, but the man had always demurred. And now, it seemed, his secret would die with him.

Two sentinels stepped forward, each taking Oliver by an elbow. He resisted, flinging elbows this way and that, but with his hands bound tightly behind his back, his efforts were futile. They lifted him onto the stool and encircled his neck with the noose dangling from the thick branch.

Alexander's father read the sentence of death as Oliver's head hung low.

"Stands here, the accused, Oliver Grimm, who has been found guilty of the capital offense of larceny against the Haven, and who shall now be put to death by hanging."

It was simple and to the point.

He nodded to the two hooded guards. They kicked the stool out from under Oliver's feet.

~

EVENING.

The execution had gone smoothly. Oliver's neck snapped like a twig breaking, and in a perverse sort of way, that was about the best anyone could have hoped for.

After the hanging, Oliver's lifeless body was dumped into a previously excavated grave unceremoniously. The people returned to the Haven and quietly went back to their day. A sullen silence dropped over the place. Alexander skipped dinner, which made up for the food he had discarded that morning. At least he was square with the house on that issue.

He spent the evening in his room on the fifth floor of the Firethorn hotel trying to write in his journal. The words would not come, however, and he secreted the journal in its hiding place under his mattress. He drifted over to the window overlooking the resort. The day's last light had all but leaked out of the sky. A campfire was burning somewhere, its orange glow flickering against the darkness.

Journaling was an activity he shared with no one; his father would not approve. He was not one to share his innermost hopes, fears, and dreams to anyone in person, much less commit them into writing. Most of the people here were like his dad.

Rough folks.

Survivalist types.

Lots of guns.

Most were nice enough. They treated Alexander well. But he hated this place. He hated their lives here. He missed school so terribly. He had loved English and history class, the math and science not so much. His father steered him away from his books, instead teaching him the trades, the skills that would be useful in this post-Pulse world.

He missed his mother. She'd been gone more than a decade now, but sometimes the grief would rear up and run over him like a runaway freight train. His specific memories of her were fading. He had a few photographs of her from when he was small, but only a precious few. He remembered the way she made him feel though. Safe and loved. She sang to him. They took walks on the nature trail in the wooded park near their apartment. She made him eat his vegetables. On this point, she had been very stern. He regretted giving her a hard time about it now. He regretted it because he had wasted some of the little time he'd had with her on petty matters like being angry with her about vegetables.

Then she had gotten sick and died, and the strange little man from Child Protective Services had taken him down to the hospital cafeteria for lunch. There, the man explained that Alexander would be going to live with his father now. He had been right at the age where he understood death without understanding it. For some time after he'd gone to live with his father, part of him kept expecting her to show up and whisk him back home.

But, of course, she never had.

Then the Pulse had hit.

It had been lunchtime at McDowell-Markey Middle School in Arlington, Virginia. As the scope of the disaster became apparent, people around him had panicked. Even the teachers. It was because of the phones. It was one thing for the electricity to go out. Losing the phones, their lifelines, had been the thing that had driven folks over the edge. But he had not panicked. Amid the chaos, he told a teacher he'd seen his father in the crowd. A little lie, perhaps, but a necessary one. He walked the two miles home, his mouth agape. Fires burning, abandoned cars, even an airplane.

His father was gone often that first week, leaving Alexander to his own devices. For the most part, he stayed close to home, as his father had directed. He read books, played D&D with the boy across the street. Occasionally, they would venture out exploring, as any preteen boys would do. But days stretched into weeks, and still the power had not returned. Although his dad always returned with food for the two of them, the neighbors had started running out, and things started to get weird. People began abandoning their homes. Gunfire became constant background music.

About a month after the Pulse, Alexander's father told him they were moving and ordered him to pack a bag. They met up with a handful of his father's friends, men who had come to the house often while Alexander was growing up. Ten of them hit the road around the first of July, and they began the journey south. They walked for days, finally arriving at the golf resort after a two-week trek. It had been a fun trip. Camping every night, cooking meat on the fire. It felt like a family.

Alexander was never quite sure why they'd selected this place as their new home, but after a few months, he stopped thinking about it. There was too much to do, and his father had worked him hard. The men were always out on supply runs, bringing stuff back, bringing people back. He worked the new farmland, converting the fairways into growing fields, sowing the seeds, helping construct the irrigation systems.

Sometimes, he would lay awake at night, stunned by how quickly his world had changed, his life had changed. With each passing season, his old life drifted farther and farther away, a junk satellite lost in space. He kept hoping, probably longer than many others, that the lights would magically kick back on, and they could go back to their old lives.

But they never did.

And he began to understand what the Haven really was.

He had started to wonder what it would be like to be

dead. Strange metaphysical questions began shooting through him. Would he be with his mother again? That prospect alone made the idea mildly attractive. And he wouldn't have to be here in this godforsaken hellscape anymore. It certainly couldn't be any worse than being here. Could it?

In fact, even if he hadn't been seriously considering it now, he could see a pathway there. That scared him. Just *thinking about* thinking about it was frightening enough. And if things hadn't changed, he could see himself walking down that dark path through a dark wood.

But then he had met the girl.

They had met at the Market. At the table of the resident tarot card reader. He often found himself drawn to her because she reminded him of Oliver. Not because he believed in her pseudoscience, but because he had loved the cards themselves. It was like a grownup version of the role-playing games he loved so much, like *Dungeons & Dragons* or *Magic: The Gathering*.

He didn't know how long she had been standing next to him when he noticed her. Just out of the corner of his eye, this glorious creature appeared. She was tall, almost as tall as he was. Her hair was cropped short, close to her head. Her eyes were deep brown, almost black.

"You believe in this stuff?" she asked him.

The reader ignored them, laying out her cards across the table and then sweeping them back up like she was playing solitaire.

"No," he replied, laughing nervously. "I don't know."

"What's your name?" she asked.

"Alexander."

"Cool."

He drifted away from the table; the girl followed him. They walked in silence for a while, making loops around the Market. He was incredibly nervous. He was inexperienced with girls. There was a handful about his age in the Haven, but they paid him little mind. Eventually, his nerves got the best of him, and he began chattering like a bird. He couldn't help himself.

At one point, she slipped her hand into his own. This he couldn't believe. He was embarrassed by how sweaty his palm was, the way he kept losing his grip on her hand, but she did not seem to mind.

"What do you do for fun?" she asked.

"I like to read."

"Me, too," she said. "What kind of books do you like?"

He prattled on about the fantasy and science fiction novels he loved, the ones he'd read and re-read until the bindings fell apart. He told her about the board games he liked to play, even the video games. It was as if he could only think of the things that would drive a pretty girl like her away. Still, she stayed with him. Just walking and talking with her, holding her hand, her listening. It was the best afternoon of his life.

She led him into the woods, just outside the perimeter of the Market, and kissed him. More than anything, he remembered the way her lips had tasted on his, cherry lip balm, maybe. His body buzzed like electricity flowed through it, but he was embarrassed she might feel the tent he'd pitched in his pants. She said nothing, though, and they kissed for a few minutes, and he never wanted it to end.

Then she pulled away from him, a big smile on her beautiful face. He had done it! He hadn't screwed it up!

"I have to go," she said. "Maybe I'll see you next time?"

He nodded.

She turned to leave. Panic flooded through him. A sudden realization.

"Hey!" he called out to her.

She turned toward him, a wry smile on her face.

"You never told me your name."

"It's Norah."

6

Lucy left the clinic as the sun dipped below the foothills to the west, bathing the land in purple shadows. It had been another chilly day, and the temperature was dropping as evening fell. She pulled her jacket tight against the cold wind blowing in from the north. She stopped by the woodshop on her way home, but Kasandra, Promise's carpenter, was alone in the shop.

"Hey," she called out.

Kasandra looked up from her project, a lovely chair she had been working on. Her strawberry-blonde hair was pulled back in a ponytail. Despite the chill, sawdust clung to her sweaty face. She was about thirty years old, mother to a little boy named Harlan. Her table would fetch a good price at the next Market, which was less than a week away.

"It's looking good," Lucy said.

Kasandra tapped her knuckles on the armrest.

"Yeah, thanks."

"Have you seen Norah?"

"She left an hour ago," replied Kasandra.

"Any idea where she was headed?"

Kasandra shrugged.

"Sorry."

Kasandra turned her attention toward shutting down her shop for the night. Carpentry was difficult, exacting work, and it was virtually impossible once twilight arrived. Lucy bid her farewell and continued her journey home.

Norah was sixteen years old, well on the way to adulthood. She came and went as she pleased. The only rule was that she had to be home by full dark. Norah was normally a dutiful kid, a joy to raise since fate had thrown them together five years ago. Her grandmother had died in the crash of the train they'd been riding when the Pulse hit. The shock and the grief of her loss had caught up with her several weeks after they'd made it back to Lucy's farmhouse. Once the adrenaline and the rush of their escape faded, post-traumatic stress began to take hold of Norah. It had been insidious, a slow-moving emotional cancer.

PTSD was different for everyone, as Lucy had learned in the Army. She'd already been down that road once before, having dealt with her own bout of it after her discharge from the Army. Even with her coping mechanism, Lucy had had her bad moments in the aftermath of their escape. Sometimes, she would bolt awake, drenched in sweat, the image of the burning mall she and Norah had escaped so vivid, so real, the acrid tang of smoke filled her nostrils.

Norah began spending more time alone, shut up in

her room unless she had chores. Her introversion deepened, and she began drifting out of her own life like an old clock winding down. Norah was going through the motions, eating, sleeping, doing her chores. She didn't complain, she didn't experience joy. She simply existed.

But she and Jack had been patient and careful. A book about the treatment of PTSD helped her guide Norah out of it. It took time, several months, but eventually, they found Norah underneath that scarred shell. She emerged from it stronger, tougher. It was a little sad, though, because she was no longer the child Lucy had met on the train that fateful May morning, engrossed in a Harry Potter novel. She was not quite an adult either, but she wasn't the carefree tween she had been. Even the decision to leave the farm behind had not rattled her. She took it in stride and offered her own valuable input as to how the three of them should proceed.

But that said, she was still a teenager, bright, determined, and oh-so-stubborn. Lucy herself had been an obedient child; her father, Kurt Goodwin, an auto mechanic, drank a lot and tended to become belligerent when he'd had too much, so it was easier to toe the line and stay out of his way. Not like Jack, who had waged terrible war against their father. He had the scars to prove it. When their father had drunk himself into his grave before the age of sixty, she was more relieved than anything.

A group of Promise residents was sitting around a blazing fire at the facility's primary campsite. Kicking back in front of a fire was popular on chilly days. A modern-day equivalent of meeting up with friends for happy hour after work. And the work never stopped— farming, hunting, food preservation, cooking, waste management, and water treatment — everything that went along with the operation of a society that had unexpectedly found itself in colonial times.

"Luce!" someone called out. "Grab a chair!"

"Thanks, but it's been a long day," she replied. "I'm gonna hit the sack. Anyone seen Norah?"

Some murmurs from the group, but no one knew where she was. At sixteen, Norah still attended school for four hours each day. The balance of her day was dedicated to working with Kasandra in the woodshop. Norah was a hands-on kind of kid. She enjoyed the attention to detail that woodworking demanded. She spotted a couple of the teens Norah sometimes hung out with, but they did not know where the girl was.

Lucy lit a lantern and entered the lodge. It was still chilly, even with the windows closed; this was the best sleeping weather of the year. Before long, the hot, humid weather would arrive, and many residents would decamp for tents in the shade of the trees. Lucy and Norah normally did so as well, at least through September, right when the leaves started to change color.

The lodge housed twenty-four women and girls. In addition to its six double rooms, they had retrofitted the living space into an additional twelve small cubicles. Lucy poked her head inside Norah's room, which was next to hers, but surprisingly, it was empty. It was about six-by-six square, just enough for a twin mattress and a small bureau, one that she had built herself. There were no clothes strewn on the ground. She had hung a few pieces of art in cheap frames on the wall.

Lucy continued to her room, conscious of the fact that it was well past Norah's curfew and growing simultaneously annoyed and worried. She changed into shorts and a T-shirt and sat on the floor, her back against the wall. Despite her physical exhaustion, she was too amped up to sleep. That morning's interrogation session combined with Norah's flouting of the rules had her heart racing. The Stephen King novel she'd been reading lay on the pillow; she set the lantern next to her and began to read. But she was unable to focus as her worry and annoyance grew. There was no point in trying to look for her in the dark. It would be like looking for an invisible needle in an invisible haystack.

Outside, the party continued for another hour before people began making their way to bed, but Norah had not returned. Eventually, silence. And still no Norah. Lucy pulled on a sweatshirt before heading outside, debating the addition of another log to the fire. Although the blaze had largely died down, the embers were still holding enough heat to keep Lucy warm. And still she continued to wait.

The fire pit had finally gone cold when the sound of crunching gravel reached Lucy's ears. Norah's silhouette appeared in the darkness, illuminated by the faintest of moonlight reflecting off the clouds. She did not appear to see Lucy as she crept toward the door of the lodge. Lucy briefly considered letting things be for the night and talking it out with her in the morning. But she wanted Norah to know that she knew, that she had caught her red-handed. She was at least two hours late. And Lucy would just stew about it all night if she didn't address it now. It was an itch that demanded to be scratched.

"Evening," Lucy said, her voice breaking the night silence like glass.

Norah yelped, nearly jumping out of her skin. She turned toward Lucy, her hand pressed against her chest.

"You scared me!" Norah said.

"I could say the same for you."

This silenced Norah.

"You're late," Lucy said. "Very."

"Yeah, sorry about that."

"Where were you?"

"Out."

"I'm aware of that."

Norah didn't elaborate, which just served to annoy Lucy further. Lucy took a long, deep breath and released it slowly, a valve releasing the anger and displeasure rising in her chest. She didn't like getting angry, particularly at Norah, but the child had crossed a line here. And sixteen was still a child, even if Norah was as tall as Lucy now. She had experienced a dramatic growth spurt when she was thirteen, rocketing skyward until she was virtually eye to eye with Lucy. She hadn't grown much since, maybe half an inch, but it was still disorienting to look her in the eye. Much different from the gangly eleven-year-old she'd been when they first met.

But still a child.

"I'm going to bed," Norah said.

"Sit down."

Norah scoffed.

"I don't feel like hearing a lecture," she replied. "I'm tired."

"I'm tired, too," snapped Lucy. "I should've been asleep hours ago, but you decided to break curfew. So where were you?"

"With friends."

"No, you weren't."

"Oh, are you checking on me now?"

"Yes, when you're supposed to be home and you're not, I check."

"It's not a big deal."

"It is to me."

"Why?" she said. "You're not my mom."

Lucy winced. It was a punch in the face. The nuclear weapon in Norah's limited arsenal, one that she did not deploy often. But when she did, it was devastating; Norah knew how badly it stung Lucy. No, Lucy was not Norah's biological mother, who had died in a drive-by shooting some years before the Pulse, but she treated the girl like her flesh and blood. She loved Norah deeply and made sure the girl knew it.

Lucy worked very hard to treat Norah as the unique individual she was and not a proxy for her own daughter, Emma, lost to cancer more than a decade ago. But sometimes it was hard to keep the two separate and not wonder what might have been had Emma lived. Hell, if Emma had lived, Lucy's entire life might be different now. She may not have been on the train at all and, thus, may never have crossed paths with Norah.

Norah's jaw was tight; her arms were crossed defiantly at her chest. Lucy searched for the right words as her heart throbbed with sadness. Norah did not know about Emma. She had made the decision long ago not to tell her that once upon a time there had been a beautiful little girl named Emma, a girl who had stolen Lucy's whole heart. She was going to tell her on Emma's birthday. She would take Norah out onto the porch, and they would sit together, and she would tell her about her.

"It's a bad idea," Jack told her after Lucy had confessed her plans.

Lucy flinched like he had slapped her in the face. She started to argue with him, but Jack had held up a hand.

"Hear me out."

"Okay."

"You know I loved that kid more than anything," Jack said. "I think about her every single day. I'm never gonna get over losing her. And I'm just her uncle. I can't imagine what it's like for you. I won't even try to imagine."

Lucy's throat tightened as her brother spoke. Jack had indeed adored his niece. They had a special relationship, more like father-daughter than uncle-niece. He took her fishing often, which she loved. They would sit in his canoe for hours, and she would talk and talk. Even after she had gotten sick, on her good days, he would pick her up on Saturday mornings and they would be gone all day. Even when she wasn't feeling great, she would insist on going, and sometimes Lucy had to step in. Then Emma would be mad all day, even when it was clear she just wasn't up to a day on the river.

"But Norah is here now," Jack continued. "And it's gonna be hard on her. No family, rug pulled out from under her, stuck with strangers. You talk about Emma, you're gonna give her a ghost to compete with."

"But--"

"You want her to feel loved, to feel at home, right?"

"Of course," replied Lucy.

"Then we need to keep Emma here," he said, gently tapping his heart. "Otherwise, Norah will think you're comparing her to Emma, even when you're not. And let's be honest, you probably will. At least sometimes."

"I wouldn't, I swear," she said, although her words didn't have much heft to them. Her brother was an astute observer of the human condition. She wanted to tell Norah stories about the sister she would never know. And they were sisters who would never know one another, sisters who would never even know *about* one another, she was understanding in the harsh light of Jack's advice.

Jack smiled.

"Give Norah a chance," he said. "It hurts, I know. A few times, I've almost slipped up myself, start to tell her a funny story about Emma, but then I catch myself. It's better this way. Let Norah know that she's our number one. And she is."

Lucy nodded, understanding finally that Emma would have to stay locked away in her heart. Norah would compete with no one. They would help her heal, even if, by not telling, it hurt Jack.

Even if it hurt Lucy.

And here, tonight, Norah still knew nothing about Emma. She did not know that her fiercely devoted guardian had been a mother once upon a time. This was what it meant to be the adult in the room. To jump on the grenade to protect the ones you loved.

"You're right," she said to Norah. "I'm not your mother."

"So stop acting like it," she said, her voice dripping with contempt. "I don't need your help."

It was a heavyweight fight, one that she was losing badly. She couldn't recall a time Norah had attacked her like this; it was only a matter of time, of course. She was a teenager, after all, and this is what they did. To be honest, Lucy was surprised that it hadn't already happened.

"I'm going to bed," Norah said. She stomped off without another word, taking very little care to keep the noise down. A teenager in full.

Lucy sat before the cold fire pit for a long time.

7

L ucy was dreaming a lovely dream when Jack shook her awake the next morning. It had been about Emma. They had been at the park having a picnic, but she kept hearing a voice in her head. Even in the dream, she had begun to fear that it was a dream. This happened often, as though her subconscious would never stop reminding her that all this, sitting with Emma under this picture-perfect blue sky, so blue it hurt your eyes to look at it, was too good to be true. She desperately tried ignoring the voice because if it was a dream, that meant she wasn't here at all, and neither was Emma.

But the voice persisted, and soon reality shattered the dome of the dream; it cracked and splintered like a film reel coming apart. Then she was awake in her bed, and the memory of the dream began to fade as well. First, the vivid details dissolved and then even the hazy edges shimmered into nothingness. To make matters worse, she hadn't been asleep long, her fight with Norah keeping her awake for hours. She blinked the sleep away and blew out a noisy sigh. Her eyes felt gritty and heavy.

"He got out," Jack was saying.

"What?" she asked blearily, even as she grasped the import of his words.

"He got out," Jack repeated.

Now she was awake and fully aware. Jack didn't need to elaborate. Their captive had escaped.

"How?"

"Don't know," he said. His voice was low and raspy. His eyes looked heavy and sunken. "Ernesto's dead."

"Oh, shit. When?"

"Not sure," he said.

She needed to examine the body to ascertain an approximate time of death. It would give them an idea of how big a head start the man had gotten.

"Let me get dressed."

Jack left, leaving her alone. She bolted out of bed, threw on a pair of pants, and pulled on her trail running shoes while conducting a damage assessment. If he made it back to his camp, it would be difficult for him to find his way back, but it would not be impossible. They needed to find him. She grabbed a small medical kit she kept in her bottom drawer and followed Jack outside.

Together they sprinted toward the administration building. It was early morning, a little after dawn. Danny was waiting for them at the top of the basement steps, holding a cigarette with trembling hands. There was a large bloody welt over his left eye. So much for the man's size and strength.

"What happened?" she asked.

"I'm sorry, Luce," Danny said. "He got the drop on me. I didn't hear him coming."

"How long ago?"

"I don't know," he said. "He knocked me out cold. I just woke up a few minutes ago."

"You're lucky he didn't kill you. How the hell did he get out?"

"Ernesto had the key downstairs."

She sighed.

"Danny," she said, exasperated.

That was a huge violation of their security protocol. The cell door key was to remain with the perimeter guard, not the cell guard, for this very reason. When they switched off, the key stayed with the perimeter guard.

"I know, I know," he said dejectedly.

She wanted to scream, tear him a new one. But that would be pointless. The man was gone. As she collected herself, two of the Council members, Carol and Jon, arrived on the scene.

"I need to look at the body."

The others nodded.

Taking a lantern from Carol, Lucy went downstairs first, Jack close behind. The quiet struck her first, the absence of life. She approached the cell, its door ajar, with the lantern held high. Orange light spilled across the barren cell. Even knowing the prisoner was gone, it was still a gut punch. They'd had him. They'd had this valuable asset here, and now he was gone.

Ernesto's body lay just beyond the cell door, up against the wall. His head was twisted at a grotesque angle. She knelt down and held the light over his head;

the skin was purplish black. It didn't take a genius to deduce what had happened. For whatever reason, Ernesto had gotten too close to the cell, and the inmate had choked the life out of him. The sight was ghastly and depressing. It must have been a terrible way to die, feeling the life choked out of you. Ernesto was nice, kind-hearted. Maybe the inmate had faked a medical emergency, tricked Ernesto into drawing within arm's length, even though they had specifically instructed the guards to get help for any claims of medical distress. If the inmate had been convincing enough, that might have tipped the scales. So sad. She pressed a hand to the back of Ernesto's neck; the skin had cooled some.

"Help me get his pants down," she said.

"What?" Jack asked in disbelief.

"I need to take his temperature," she said, already working to loosen his belt. "The body loses about one-point-five degrees in temp each hour after death. Come on!"

His sister's admonishment spurred him into action. It took a couple of minutes, but they finally wrenched his pants down far enough to give Lucy the unfortunate access she needed. She inserted the thermometer and waited. Two minutes later, she removed the instrument.

"Hold the lantern up," she said. "Not too closely."

She held the thermometer against the backdrop of yellow light. Ninety-seven degrees. She breathed a sigh of relief.

"He's been dead an hour, give or take," she said. "We may still be able to find him. Can you track him?"

"Maybe."

They went back outside, and Jack began studying the ground. While he searched for the killer's trail, she directed Danny to get help in removing the body from the scene. They would have a burial for him later.

"Anything?" she asked after Danny had skulked off, his tail between his legs.

"Partial footprint here," he said, pointing at the muddy ground. They had removed his shoes so he couldn't hang himself. Lucy could just make out the impression in the soft ground. More prints lay ahead, spaced out about three yards apart. The alternating footsteps of a man on the run.

"He's probably still on foot," Lucy said. "These lead away from the stables."

"Good point," Jack said. They made it to the stables, saddled up, and were on the move within minutes.

A light rain had begun to fall as they reached the border of Promise. The prints were starting to wash away in the rain. Lucy was growing increasingly worried that the man would get away.

They reached some thick brush, forcing them to slow down. Here, the man had made no attempt to conceal his tracks; the trail was lit up with markers of his passage. Flattened brush and snapped twigs and branches were left in his wake as he careened through this part of the woods.

"Look there!" Lucy called out.

A spot of dark liquid had drawn her attention. It looked like blood. She dismounted her horse and stepped up to a tangle of vines. It was definitely blood.

The unmistakable teardrop-shaped splatters of dark crimson liquid stained the leaves and wet grasses.

The trail of droplets veered off from the main pass into much thicker and thornier terrain. They would not be able to continue on horseback. Jack dismounted the horse, and they secured the two animals to a thick, low-hanging branch of a large oak tree.

Lucy and Jack drew their weapons as they left the well-marked trail. They moved slowly and in tandem; the rain had largely let up. Any precipitation still falling was largely captured by the trees' thick canopy overhead.

"Let's split up," he said.

She nodded.

"Stay frosty," she said in a whisper.

The escapee had left the faintest trail ahead. She moved slowly but not too slowly, as the forest was often quick to revert to its original shape and swallow up any sign of interlopers. She kept an eye on Jack, who was blazing his own trail just to her west.

Although Lucy knew these woods well, they seemed particularly ominous as she picked her way through. Tree branches and thorny vines pulled and tugged at her shirt-sleeves and pantlegs. Every minute or so, she would pause and listen, hoping to catch the sound of the prisoner on the move. His escape was nothing short of a disaster. She was second-guessing every decision they made regarding the prisoner. Perhaps if they had put someone else on the cell, this wouldn't have happened. It certainly wouldn't have happened if Jack had been on guard.

Perhaps it was a sign that they had grown soft. After

all, they'd had a pretty good run of luck in the last couple of years. Food, shelter, clean water, reliable trading partners. It wasn't easy, not by a long shot. It wasn't like life before the Pulse. That life was probably over forever. But even now, you still had your haves and your have-nots. And this prisoner posed a threat to all of that. A harbinger of trouble that lay ahead. The canary in the coal mine.

A gunshot rang out, breaking her out of her reverie. She dropped into a crouch and skittered behind the cover of a large oak tree. Here, she was well-concealed by the underbrush, but she was unable to see the shooter. A second bullet struck her tree fairly high up. The sound of splintering bark was close by. She froze, holding her breath, careful not to make a sound.

She made herself small, dropping into a deep crouch, pressing up against the ancient tree's sturdy trunk. As frightening as it was, the good news was that they had caught up to their prey. They still had a chance to recapture him. And the odds were in their favor.

Another burst of gunfire pierced the morning calm. These were different rounds; perhaps Jack had a bead on the prisoner. Several minutes passed without any additional activity. She edged her way around the base of the trunk, keeping her sidearm raised. She saw no sign of Jack or the prisoner.

They were about fifty yards off the primary trail in a section of the forest bracketed on the east by a two-lane highway. If the fugitive made it to the highway, his chances of escape would increase exponentially.

The unmistakable crack of snapping branches nearby

drove Lucy's heart rate sky high. The second twig breaking let her triangulate the source of the noise on the far side of the tree. She reared up to her full height, kept her back pressed against the trunk. She edged around, keeping the gun up and preparing to fire.

There was a small clearing on the far side of the tree in between the exposed roots in another curtain of tangled lines just ahead. The brush rippled as a figure made his way through it. She slid her finger onto the trigger, prepared to fire. She could just make out a figure crouched low in the underbrush. There was a gap between the branches, revealing a man's arm bearing a tattoo of a playing card with skulls in each of its four corners.

She exhaled a sigh of relief, recognizing the tattoo instantly.

It was Jack's.

"Psst," she hissed. "It's me."

He emerged slowly from the brush, his face and arms scratched to hell.

"Did we lose him?" she asked, lowering her weapon.

"I could hear him a bit farther east," Jack replied. "I think he made it to the highway."

Lucy's heart sank.

"Dammit," she said. "We can follow on horseback."

They crashed through the brush back to the trail where they had parked the horses. They rode hard, but it still took fifteen minutes to make it to the main road. An old blue Cadillac that had died on the day of the Pulse kept its lonely watch on four flat tires on this stretch of Route 726. The car was an old friend by this point, getting a little older and rustier with each passing year. The road itself was covered with dead leaves and twigs. It was still in good shape mostly, but it was starting to show signs of inattention. Lucy gazed east while her brother turned his eyes to the west. The highway was empty in either direction.

"Let's split up," Jack said. "If you see him, you take him out," he said.

Lucy nodded. That had been her plan, much as she hated it. They could not take any chances. They exchanged a fist bump; Lucy headed west, and Jack went east. They agreed to search until dark before meeting back at home.

"Be careful," he said.

"You know it."

Lucy kept her horse at a brisk pace, pausing for water breaks at familiar creeks and streams in the area. She had covered five miles by early afternoon, but there was nary a sign of their fugitive. She kept her eye on the shoulders of the road, looking for any clue as to his presence. At one point, a rustling in the trees caught her eye, and she froze. She drew her weapon and aimed it at the rippling brush. It turned out to be a small deer making her way through the day.

It was the only sign of life she detected. Two miles farther up, she turned back for home.

The edge of twilight was upon her by the time she reached home. Her inbound trip proved to be no more fruitful than the outbound. She was exhausted and starving. She stabled Pancake, making sure to give him an extra serving of oats and water before leaving him for the night.

Jack had not returned, so she waited for him at his tent. Pogo, Jack's dog, lay obediently at her feet, seeming to sense her troubled soul. Finally, just before the final light of the day had drained off, Jack appeared in the gloom. The dejected look on his face told Lucy all she needed to know.

The man had gotten away.

8

The June Market day was the biggest of the year. Like all Market days, it was held on the fifteenth of the month, in that sweet spot between the last of the winter root vegetables and the bumper crop of summer produce that was in full swing right now. Promise sent half a dozen people on horse-drawn wagons loaded down with goods to trade; they came back with wagons just as heavy.

The Market was held in the town square fronting the Goochland County Courthouse. The square featured a large, open plaza with ample room for multiple vendors. The Market had been held each month for nearly four years now. It was the brainchild of Sean Paling, a small dairy farmer in Caroline County, a rural community about thirty miles north of Richmond. In the days following the Pulse, he quickly realized the coming food security calamity awaiting virtually every man, woman, and child in the country. As a dairy farmer, he needed feed to keep the milk flowing and his animals alive. He began cutting deals with nearby farms for produce, meats, and medicine.

Soon, a new mini economy featuring many small communities had formed, necessitating a more central location. All were welcome to trade at the open market. It operated on the barter system, as cash had become virtually useless within weeks of the Pulse. The Market was ruled by a seven-member governing body, one person from each of the seven different permanent communities. Terms lasted for a single year, and no one could serve more than two terms consecutively.

There were at least two dozen booths today. It had been a good spring, and the selection was plentiful. Goods would be cheap. The basic principles of supply and demand still applied in their post-apocalyptic economy. There were fruits, vegetables, meats, cheeses, candles, soaps, ammunition, and medical supplies. Herbs in particular had grown in value with each passing year as the supply of manufactured pharmaceuticals continued to dwindle and people began to rely on herbal remedies. Lucy had been studying this subject intently; she had stacks of books on them in her clinic office. Mark Ellis was an amateur botanist and manager of the Promise farm, and he was quite adept at identifying plants that they could repurpose as medicines.

It had been three weeks since the bandit's escape from Promise. The other shoe had yet to drop. They had detected no unusual activity near Promise. Lucy wanted to believe that they were safe, that in the chaos of his escape, the man had lost his bearings and had been unable to find them again. It would be nice to have something go their way. Their worst fears didn't always have to be realized.

But they were still concerned. Shoring up their defenses had become a priority for the Council. As Promise's head of security, Jack spent much of his free time patrolling the area, on the hunt for scouts or other malcontents who might wish them harm. He often came to the Market but had not made the trip this time. He wanted to stay close to home. This was fine with Lucy; she trusted him to keep them safe. It let her focus on her work in the clinic.

Nancy Hankle led their caravan to their pre-appointed spot, wide enough for a dozen tables. They spent an hour setting up their wares. Six people were assigned to man the tables; the rest would stalk the market, looking to make deals. Ideally, they would unload their entire stock and return home with all new goods. If they brought it to trade, they had plenty back home. It wasn't a perfect loop at Market, but it often worked out that way. Each community was usually able to offer something the others couldn't.

For the first year, Lucy's medical expertise had been in high demand. Her medical skills returned a bumper crop of supplies. But then a community called Eastborough had found itself a physician in a recent wave of arrivals, sending the price of her services down. Plus, as people had become more comfortable with DIY medicine, they were less likely to seek out trained medical professionals. Sure, it led to a few more negative outcomes, but not so many that it warranted trading a week's worth of supplies for a day with a nurse.

Today, Lucy was on the hunt for ammunition. In the wake of the ambush, they wanted to build up Promise's stores. Everton had developed a method to manufacture ammunition, a skill that was in high demand; the community was small but poured all its efforts into its production lines. Its factory was hidden. Barrett Cash, a former newspaper reporter, was its leader. He had long carried a torch for Lucy, but she had rebuffed his advances. She told him the distance between their communities made it more trouble than it was worth, but that wasn't the complete story. For now, she wasn't interested in a relationship. He was quite handsome, she had to admit. He had gorgeous, shoulder-length black hair and high cheekbones. His father had been Japanese, his mother, an American teaching English in Tokyo. It had been a brief fling near the end of her tour of duty; his mother did not even know she was pregnant until she had returned to America.

She waited until Barrett had finished setting up before making her way toward his booth. He was sitting on a storage crate, reading a book. He was a big reader. It had been one of his most endearing attributes. Noticing her approach, he looked up from his book. He smiled broadly when he saw her.

"Hey, stranger," he said.

It had been some months since they'd last seen each other. He still looked good, perhaps a little thinner than the last time they'd crossed paths. A few lines had formed at the corners of his eyes. He was a few years younger than her, so it pleased her that he was finally showing a little age. Despite turning him down with no regrets, she still felt butterflies in her stomach. It annoyed her that he had any kind of grip on her. She didn't like being beholden to anyone, especially emotionally.

"Hey," she said.

"What's happening?"

She hoped he was as uncomfortable as she was, but she doubted it. He certainly wasn't showing it. He had a cool confidence about him. He rolled with the punches. It was what she liked most about him. He was a sharp contrast to her brother, who was quick to fly off the handle. Barrett never lost his cool.

"Fine," she said, realizing her discordant reply a moment too late. "Not much, I mean. Our usual deal?"

"Sorry, Lucy," he said. "I don't have it today."

"What do you mean you don't have it today?"

"I just don't have it today," he said. "We've had some manufacturing problems."

Barrett had never come to Market without ammunition. As valuable a commodity as it was, it was his only commodity. If he really didn't have it, he wouldn't have bothered making the long and dangerous trip here.

"So what's in the crates?" she asked, gesturing at the three grey containers behind him.

He paused before replying, as though to come up with an answer she would find palatable.

"Some other odds and ends."

"What happened to your factory?"

"We had a bit of a fire."

He said it unconvincingly. Then he looked around furtively, as though to check if anyone was listening in. He motioned to her with two fingers, drawing her close to him. At first, she thought he was going to try to kiss her, but the vibe was all wrong. The look on his face was not of a man getting ready for romance.

"My shop is fine," he said softly. "Not about the shop."

"Then what is it?" she asked.

A rustling sound behind her broke the intimate conversation. A big smile washed across his face. A big phony smile. Mari Hermansky, who lived at the Falls, approached Barrett carrying a small crate of peaches. She set them on his table.

"How are you, Mari?" He asked.

"Doing fine," Mari replied. She was about Lucy's height, straight, brown hair. She wore glasses; one of the lenses sported a hairline crack down the middle. These days, there was no eyeglass shop. She and Lucy weren't exactly friends, but they never had a cross word before. It was surprising, then, to Lucy that Mari did not even acknowledge her presence.

Barrett turned away from the table and retrieved the small package from one of his containers. It was wrapped in coarse, brown paper, secured with string.

"The peaches are very good this week," Mari said.

Barrett grabbed a peach and took a bite. Its juices stained his face.

"Mmm," he said. "Delicious."

"See you next time, handsome," she said, taking the package with her.

"You're terrible," he said with another flash of that phony smile.

Mari left, leaving Lucy alone with Barrett once more. Lucy was boiling mad now, but she was careful not to show it. Something was going on, and she needed to find out what it was. Barrett could be very sensitive, and if she came on too strong, he would fold.

"Peach?" he asked, holding one up.

She ignored his weak attempt to skirt the subject.

Barrett returned the peach to the crate and set to work tidying his booth, humming a tune as he did so. She stood at his table, tapping it with her fingertips. She let him attend to his busywork, knowing that he was burning off nervous energy. There was something he wanted to tell her. The key was to let him tell her in his own time. After he had straightened the booth for the umpteenth time, he returned to his position at the table.

"What's going on?" she asked as gently as she could.

"I don't really know," he said. "But there's a new player in town. Some rough folks."

"Go on," she said, immediately recalling the trio of bandits she and Jack had tussled with.

"Not sure where they're from," he said. "But they're bad news. You remember that guy Phineas?"

She did. He was a nomad, enjoyed life on the road. He made his living as a traveling musician, drifting around the state with his guitar. He put on live shows in exchange for food and medicine.

"He'd scheduled a gig at some community down near the airport," he said. "When he showed up, everyone was dead. Just slaughtered."

A chill ran up Lucy's spine.

He seemed to be trembling. She lay a hand on top of his. His hand was cold and clammy. "Are they here today?"

"I don't think so," he said. "I haven't seen them."

"What else?"

"I don't know much else," he said. "It's a big group. They may be trying to expand their territory."

Lucy twirled a lock of her hair as she considered this new information. While troubling, the news wasn't terribly surprising. Eventually, someone was going to make a move like this.

"Did they tell you not to trade with us?"

He nodded subtly.

"Thanks for the info," she said.

She eased back into the crowd without another word. As she made her way back to her team, a sense of unease grew inside her. She became very aware of how the others were looking at her, acknowledging her. Were they shunning her? Were they ignoring her? Normally, people were happy to see one another at the Market. It was a welcome break in their routine, an injection of variety into their day-to-day lives.

Instantly, she felt like she wasn't welcome. It was a bizarre feeling. One that she had never felt before.

Promise was one of the charter members of the Market, and all of a sudden, she felt like an outsider. She made a loop of the entire market, keeping to herself, avoiding any interaction with others. She didn't want any more awkward exchanges like the one she'd had with Barrett. Back at the kiosk, Becky Alsen, Rowena Mills, and her sister, Heather Statler, were deep in discussion. Their tables were still loaded with the goods they'd brought to trade. Business was at a standstill. They typically saw steady business throughout the day. It confirmed what Barrett had told her. They were being blackballed. It confirmed her suspicion that the man they'd captured was one of them. And now they were being punished.

"Guys?" she said, startling them.

"No one will trade with us," Heather said gloomily.

"Something's not right, Luce," Rowena said.

Something was terribly wrong. Around them, the Market was proceeding normally. Trading was in full swing. There were loud arguments, boisterous laughter. The air was redolent with the warm aroma of pipe smoke and marijuana. It was like having an out-of-body experience. Like they had died and were watching it all unfold from the spirit world.

Something fundamental had changed.

"Let's get home," Lucy said.

9

The Council called the meeting to order. It had been a week since the debacle at the Market. They had increased patrols. Each night, a dozen sentinels stood guard, roaming the property, looking for any uninvited guests. A perimeter fence or wall had not been feasible given the size of Promise, but Lucy sure wished they had one now. The Council had been meeting daily, discussing their options, coming up with a plan. Now the nearly two hundred residents of Promise had piled into the cafeteria, demanding answers. The room was loud, boisterous, ripe with anxiety.

Word of the incident at the Market had spread quickly, and tensions were running high. They were okay for now, but the idea of being isolated from the larger world had left everyone unsettled. Lucy felt it too. She had asked Norah to stay close to home, although she was not sure how compliant she was being with her requests. Kids that age, you couldn't watch them twenty-four hours a day.

"I still can't believe he got away," Jack said. He thumped a closed fist against the arm of his chair. He was still fired up, the escape of the prisoner burning at his core. He had anger he needed to discharge, but for the moment, there was no place to unload it. Although Lucy wasn't fond of his quick temper, she had to admit he was right. The blackball was in some way related to the mysterious man who'd gotten away.

They still did not know much about the new threat. Either this newcomer indeed did wield a good deal of power, or they had convinced others that they had a good deal of power, which was just as concerning. Someone that could control a narrative was not to be underestimated.

Acquiring good intelligence on the world beyond was a constant challenge. Communities rose and fell, either dissolving or merging with others. People came and went; someone you'd known for months or years and saw frequently would disappear, never to be seen again. Every now and again, you'd hear stories of someone full of piss and vinegar, trying to establish themselves as some kind of warlord.

Certainly there had been bloodshed the dark days following the Pulse, though the violence had largely been limited to the urban areas once supplies began to dry up. Many had perished during that first terrifying summer. It had been ironically cruel. Millions had starved not because there wasn't enough food but because of the total collapse of the American food supply chain in which that food had become hopelessly clogged. Somehow in their nation of plenty, millions had gone hungry while countless tons of fruits and vegetables rotted on farms and livestock died because there was no way to get it to the market.

If Lucy had still been living in the city, if she had not inherited the small farm, she would have likely seen a similar fate. But she had been one of the lucky ones.

"When's the next market?" asked Betsy Marden. She was one of the farmhands; very few worked as hard as she did. Her battery never seemed to run dry.

"Two weeks," Lucy replied.

"We need to find who this new player is," Jack said.

"Any ideas?" Carol, the chair of the Council, asked.

Silence fell across the group.

Jack chewed on his lower lip, a habit of his when he was deep in thought.

"I've got an idea," Lucy said.

"Go on," said Jon Schlosser, another Council member.

"We send in a spy," she said.

"What do you mean?"

"We pick someone who hasn't been to Market before," she said. "Pretend to be an outsider. Ask questions. Eavesdrop."

"I don't like this cloak and dagger business," Jack said.

"What a surprise," Lucy said, annoyed with her brother. Patience was not one of his virtues.

"I say we just go in there and rattle some cages until we get the information we need."

"And expose us to even more danger?"

Jack let out a noisy sigh.

"There is no danger," he said. "This is just a bully.

Trying to scare everyone. It's probably four guys jerking off in a tent."

"I hope you're right," Lucy said. "But until we know for sure, we're not taking any chances."

THEY ASKED RAY HOFSTETTER. Ray was a quiet man who kept to himself but was never afraid to volunteer for dirty work. He'd been a software engineer, brainy, thoughtful. He didn't socialize much, happy to work alone and be alone. The kind of face you forgot just a few minutes after meeting. He would be perfect to send in.

They left at midday on the day before the Market, making the ten-mile journey on foot and forgoing the horses. It would be easier to stay hidden. They spent a quiet night in the woods a mile from the town square; they did not build a fire for obvious reasons. It was a chilly night, but they had packed heavy clothing. After a cold meal of bread and salted meats, they retired with little chitchat. It took Lucy a long time to fall asleep, but once she did, she slept hard. She woke with the sun, her muscles stiff but feeling refreshed. Jack was already up, a cigarette dangling from his lips. Ray was awake, reading a book. They enjoyed a quiet breakfast. Little was said. All understood the importance of the mission.

"Ray, you ready to do this?"

He nodded, his face a cipher. He was hard to read. If he was nervous about his mission, he was hiding it well.

"What's your name?" Jack asked, running through the cover story they'd constructed for him.

"Bill Dixon."

"Where you from?"

"Boston."

"What are you doing here?"

"Headed north for the summer," he said. "Gonna spend the summer in Maine."

"What've you been up to since the Pulse?"

"On the road," he said. "I don't like being in one place too long."

He and Lucy exchanged a glance. He delivered the story without hesitation. He was ready.

"We'll meet you at the rendezvous point," Lucy said. "You're gonna do fine."

"Remember," Jack said. "Just listen and learn."

"Got it," he said.

After a handshake from Jack and a quick hug from Lucy, Ray was on his way, leaving the siblings alone at the campsite. It felt eerily quiet as they packed up the campsite, even though Ray himself rarely said a word. When the gear was secure, they followed Ray's trail through the woods east toward the Market; they would remain in the woods overlooking the town square. It was a chilly day, cloudy. She was glad she'd worn her heavy parka. They secreted themselves at the edge of a long tree line on a grassy hillside. Beyond the trees, a wide hill sloped gently toward the town square. In the winter, after a good snow, it made for great sliding for the kids.

Lucy and Jack took position about fifty feet from one another. Each had a pair of binoculars. They agreed to keep watch until the Market closed for the day, after which they would meet Ray near a large grain silo on the outskirts of town.

Lucy took the easternmost position; Jack covered the western flank. A light rain began to fall from the low, grey skies overhead. On the plus side, they didn't have to worry about the glint of sunshine on their binoculars.

The Market opened on schedule. It was weird watching it from afar. From their vantage point, it looked like a child's playset come to life. Tiny figurines moving to and fro. It was familiar and alien at the same time. It felt like she was watching a home movie, a relic of days gone by. But even seeing the familiar faces that she had grown to know over the last few years, she was filled with a kind of dread. The sensation that things had changed right under your feet.

Change was hard, especially in this new world. Just when you thought things had stabilized, this world threw you a curveball and you had to learn to lay off a bit, just a fraction of a second before taking your swing, to make sure you put wood on the ball.

The surveillance mission was difficult and tedious. It demanded all of her attention.

The morning ticked by slowly. Around midday, the sun near its peak, Lucy's stomach rumbled. She ate the flatbread in her pack mechanically, never removing her eyes from the field glasses. She did not want to miss a thing. But for all her careful attention, she saw nothing out of the ordinary. Ray entered the Market without issue, drifting from booth to booth. They'd given him a few odds and ends to trade so he could fit in. She saw unfamiliar faces, which was not uncommon. Immigration and emigration were common in any community. The appearance of new faces and disappearance of familiar ones was forever a constant in their lives. There were always rumors of the grass being greener elsewhere. Rumors of places where the power was on again. Rumors of heat and air conditioning flowing through the vents, of stocked grocery stores. Even in a world absent of social media, the rumor mill was always churning.

But she'd never known anyone who'd actually seen one of these Valhallas with their own eyes. It was always a friend of a friend who had told them about it.

Traffic entering and exiting the Market was steady all day. It warmed Lucy's heart to see so many communities coming together. Maybe one day, they could get back to something resembling normalcy. Activity began to slow down as the sun began its final slide to the horizon. With the crowd dwindling, Ray made his way to the exit, joining a steady flow of people making their way home. A core group would stay the night and party. A bonfire, charcoal grills, booze, drugs, sex, fights, it had it all. Anything and everything went. She'd stayed for an after-party once before. Although it was too much for her, it gave folks a chance to blow off steam.

Lucy packed up her belongings and withdrew from her post. She silently moved through the woods. It was cool here, quiet but for the babble of a nearby brook. She loved the woods. The solitude eased her troubled mind, gave her a chance to think. She hoped Ray had gleaned some useful intelligence.

The forest thinned out after about two hundred yards, opening up on a highway running east and west. The little town of Bronco lay about a quarter-mile to the west. A trio of silos rose up like giant guardians on the town's outskirts. She was nervous, keeping her hand on the butt of her weapon and staying close to the trees, staking out a serpentine path around the trees on the edge.

She heard nothing and saw no one. This town was mostly abandoned, although a few free-love squatters had made their home here. She'd met them once at one of the Market afterparties. Weird bunch. Lucy had no plans to enter the town proper anyway, keeping to the large tract of land once owned by a grain company. She opened the perimeter fence, the hasp squeaky and rusty with age. The fence itself was rusted, bowed in spots, broken in others. Like so much of their world, it was run down.

The rendezvous point was just ahead. Behind her, a flicker of movement. Her hand dropped to her holster before she recognized Jack's gait. Not a saunter, not a stroll, some combination of the two from a man who was not afraid of this world, who was not afraid to meet it head-on. She paused, waiting for him to close the gap between them.

"Any sign of Ray?" he asked, a nervous hitch in his voice.

"I saw him leave the Market," she said. "Lost him in the crowd."

"Same," Jack said.

She scanned the area carefully, keeping her eyes on shadows and corners. Jack did not rattle easily, and if something had tickled his gut, it was to be taken seriously.

"Let's have a look around," Lucy said.

Jack looked a bit manic and a lot pissed. He was itching for a fight. Recent events were building up on him, and he was liable to blow soon. But she needed him to remain calm. His skills were considerable, but they deteriorated rapidly when his temper got the best of him.

"Stay calm," she said.

She now shared his assessment that something was amiss. Ray had not arrived at the rendezvous point. This was deeply troubling. Lucy was engulfed with dread about their fate.

Moving in tandem, Lucy and Jack moved deeper onto the grain company's land. There were three silos on the property, the largest about sixty feet in diameter and roughly two hundred feet tall. The other two were about half the height and diameter. The rally point was the far side of the southernmost silo. Lucy and her brother kept close to the wall of the big silo as they snaked their way through shadows.

A flash of color on the ground caught Lucy's eye. She held up a fist, signaling Jack to stop behind her. She knelt down to the ground, which was carpeted with shriveled and dry, brown grass, stained with fresh, crimson liquid.

Blood.

Her heart sank.

She and Jack exchanged knowing glances.

She held her breath, primed her ears, but the place was dead silent.

The trail of blood continued around the perimeter of the silo, increasing in quantity as they neared the backside of the large building. Lucy and Jack slowed their pace, keeping their backs pressed against the cool metal. Both had their weapons drawn. They were near the back of the property now, less than twenty yards from its northern perimeter fencing.

The trail of blood had metastasized into large puddles. Long shadows stretched out, obscuring their view. The shadows kept them largely hidden from any malicious actors who might have been lingering here. But Lucy didn't need a perfect line of sight to see what had happened. Ray lay face up near the fencing; his throat was slashed.

He was dead.

As Lucy approached the body, Jack covered the area with his gun, ensuring that they were alone. But no one else was here. Whoever had killed Ray wanted them to see this. Otherwise, they would've just ambushed all three of them at once. She knelt next to Ray, this fine, quiet man.

Their world was a risky one, and tomorrow was never guaranteed. But it didn't make this any easier to swallow. Ray was a good man with a great deal to offer, and his life had been snuffed out like it was nothing.

Jack tapped her on the shoulder and gestured toward the side of the silo. Lucy turned slowly, dreading what she was about to see. Jack's face had flushed with rage.

There was a message written on the silo. In giant, capital letters, the words "SEE YOU SOON" had been hastily and sloppily slapped on the wall.

The message had been written in blood.

R ay's murder escalated the unease following the blackball from the Market into palpable fear. The new threat looming just beyond their borders was all anyone could talk about. In the dining hall, in the lodges and cottages, around the fire pits. Who? How? And why?

Over the next few days, Lucy treated several people for anxiety attacks.

A few confided in her that it was the most worried they'd been since the early days after the Pulse. Back when nobody's survival had been guaranteed. But they'd moved into a new status quo, a new normal.

The day after Jack and Lucy's return, a brief memorial service for Ray was held in the open plaza at the center of their community. Farid, a refugee from Syria who arrived in the U.S. the day before the Pulse, eulogized their fallen brother. By the time he finished his words, there was not a dry eye left.

The Council moved Promise to its highest level of

readiness. They had three dozen people on patrol twenty-four hours a day. As head of security, Jack continued to lead scouting missions in the immediate vicinity. But no one else was permitted to leave the compound. All they could do was wait for the other shoe to drop.

The shoe dropped two days later. Lucy was in the clinic, midway through a sixteen-hour shift. There had been no additional cases of coronavirus since the initial cluster. The irony was not lost on her. Her search for antiviral medication had put them on a collision course with this new threat. The sisters at the Falls had had the medicine she was looking for. Like Barrett, however, they made a tactical decision not to trade with Promise.

Lucy was in the middle of charting when Terri came bursting through the door. She endeavored to keep thorough records of the medical care that she provided to Promise's residents. In the absence of the computerized electronic medical records she become accustomed to in the last few years before the Pulse, it was extremely challenging. But she did her best; it helped that Promise was relatively small. Even with a population of a couple hundred, it wasn't impossible to keep good records on her patients.

"We've got visitors," she said.

Lucy's heart started racing.

She pushed back from her desk, carefully stacking the papers to review later. Terri looked frazzled, so Lucy avoided peppering her with questions about their visitors. She checked on her patients one more time before turning their care over to Terri. She had proven to be a quick study. Lucy had grown increasingly comfortable with her at the helm. Others worked in the clinic too, but none had shown the same level of aptitude.

Before leaving, she exchanged one final look with Terri.

"It's gonna be okay," Lucy said reassuringly.

Although she really didn't know that.

She went outside into the heat of the day. It was a warm spring day, the sun burning a bronze hole into the cobalt sky.

Her breathing was shallow as she made her way to the front gate. She was nervous of course; it was a fool's errand to underestimate any new threat. She took everyone seriously from the outset. It was safer that way. But she was not panicked, at least not yet. A lot of nerve, these newcomers must've had. Their murder of Ray was monstrous, but did they really think they could just march in here and scare them?

If they expected Promise to simply roll over, well, they had another thing coming. Promise was strong, well-armed. Their only disadvantage had been not finding their harassers first. It was never a good idea to show weakness in this world. You couldn't let people think that you had no spine, no backbone. Unless you showed that you were willing to defend what you had with force if necessary, then any old Tom, Dick or Harry could just come in and take what was rightfully yours.

Three men were waiting for them just inside the signs marking the entrance to Promise. Jack and Jon Schlosser were already there. Both were holding rifles, but the muzzles were pointed at the ground. The three men were unarmed, which Lucy found very curious. The leader was a tall, white man of average build. A thick, bushy, salt-and-pepper mustache danced above his upper lip. His face was leathery and wrinkled. It was like the scene back on the road, but also nothing like it at all. They were here on their doorstep.

As Lucy approached, he raised his arm in friendly acknowledgment. Lucy did not return the gesture. She didn't trust gestures of goodwill from strangers.

She came abreast Jack and the other Council members.

"How you folks doing?" the man asked.

"Can we help you with something?" Lucy asked.

The man looked at each of his compatriots in turn. Then he looked back at Lucy, a big smile breaking across his face.

"Just trying to be neighborly," he replied.

"How about we just skip to the end, and you tell us what you want?" Jack said.

The man nodded slowly in mock approval of Jack's demand.

"I like you," he said, wagging a gnarled finger at him. "You don't mess around. Down to business as they say."

"Give me one reason I shouldn't blow your head off," Jack said.

"Oh, aren't you Mr. Tough Guy?"

Jack raised his shotgun, and Lucy thought he was going to shoot the man. Lucy wouldn't have minded such a fate for this jackass, but she was getting the feeling that this was not in their long-term interest.

"All these guns," he replied.

He waved away Jack's weapon dismissively as though

it were a water balloon. He did not seem the least bit intimidated by Jack's threat to execute him. Lucy began to feel very uneasy.

"You can do what you want to me," he said. "But please keep in mind that if any harm befalls me or my friends, every single one of you will be dead by tomorrow."

Silence.

"Anyway, my name is Joshua. We are representatives of the Haven, a community like this one not too far from here. We are looking to expand our footprint. Bring in some smaller communities. There is safety in numbers, after all."

The Haven. Well, now they had a name to go with the face. A stupid clichéd name from post-apocalyptic books and movies, but a name, nevertheless.

"Not interested," Lucy said.

He chuckled.

"Oh, I am sorry if there was any confusion," Joshua said. "We're not really asking."

"You've got some nerve," Jack said. "You are barking up the wrong tree, friend."

"Look, we hate unnecessary violence," Joshua said. "But we need you to understand how very serious we are. We know that you're a formidable group and that you have a lot to offer. But we don't want you getting any ideas. If you try to resist, the penalties will be, shall we say, severe."

"Did you not hear me, dickweed?" Jack asked angrily. "The answer is no."

Joshua's mouth scrunched up in disappointment,

making a *tsking* sound as he did so. Then he held up a single finger. A shot rang out; before Lucy could process what had happened, Kyle slumped to the ground. A large caliber bullet had blown his head apart. The poor man was dead before he hit the ground.

"We have you surrounded by a dozen snipers," he said. "We will just keep killing you until you agree to our terms."

Jack raised his weapon again, and this time he really was going to fire. Lucy stepped in and placed a hand on the barrel.

"Jack, don't."

Lucy was boiling with rage, and she wanted nothing more than to kill these three men where they stood. But for now, they had the upper hand. Better to live to fight another day. The day she had long feared was at hand. Outnumbered, outgunned, outsmarted. Putting up any additional resistance today would simply cost them more lives. There were times when you put up, and there were times when you shut up. Unfortunately, now was the time for the latter.

"What do you want?" she asked

"Simple, my dear," he said. "We want you to contribute."

"To what?"

"To the good of the order," he said.

"What does that mean?" she said.

"We want half," he said.

"You must be out of your goddamned mind," Jack said.

"Jack, no!"

Joshua held up a finger again, and another shot rang out. From somewhere deeper in the compound, a scream. Another life snuffed out.

"Do I have your complete attention now?"

Lucy gripped Jack's elbow and squeezed it in an attempt to keep him quiet.

"Yes."

"We want half of everything you produce each week," Joshua said. "We've been watching you, and we have a pretty good sense of what you've got here. We'll send couriers every Friday at noon to collect. We'll do an inventory now so we can get a sense of what we'll be expecting every week. And God help you if you miss your quota."

Lucy didn't bother informing him that such a tax on their resources would leave them precious little to stretch across two hundred mouths. The cruelty, after all, was the point. To keep them working, producing more so that they could meet their quota and feed their community. A dominated group would be less likely to cause a ruckus.

The crowd behind them began murmuring to one another, stunned by the ultimatum and terrible violence that had been unleashed on their community.

Joshua held up a finger once more, a single, terrible finger.

One final shot rang out.

A thud behind her.

The crowd scattered.

11

It was their first day of tribute. Everyone was up early to ensure everything was ready. The previous week had been spent in the fields, harvesting the kale, chard, lettuce, rutabagas, radishes, and carrots that were coming up. These vegetables, along with eggs and cheese, constituted a large portion of Promise's early spring diet. Lucy was happy to have food regardless of the form it came in, but if she were being honest, the early spring vegetables had been her least favorite. Now, though, they seemed so precious.

Since dawn, wheelbarrows had been running back and forth from the field to the barn, where workers wrapped the produce in thin cheesecloth to keep it dry. They would easily meet the first quota. Better to focus on the positives. Thinking about a time they might not meet it was a one-way ticket to despair. The community was terrified. Joshua's snipers had killed three people that day without so much as blinking. Sophie, Kyle, and Peter joined Ray as the latest victims of their occupiers.

The visitors were expected at midday when the sun was at its peak. Without clocks and watches and smartphones to measure the time of day, though, that was more of a guidepost rather than a specific appointment time. It was still strange, not being able to look at a clock or smartphone to check the time. Lucy had been obsessed with keeping the time. Upon her return to the farm five years earlier, she had taught herself how to read a sundial with a reference book from the library. It was a link to the old world.

They finished the work late in the morning, around two hours before the arrival of the couriers. Lucy checked in on her two inpatients at the clinic and did some paperwork. One with a broken leg and one complaining of chest pains. As she was finishing up, Jack arrived with two stainless steel mugs of coffee.

They sat on camping chairs just outside the clinic, waiting for their date with destiny. She didn't know where this path would lead. She just hoped they could adjust to this new reality. It reminded her vaguely of the lockdowns in the early weeks and months of the coronavirus pandemic. Just like that, *boom*. Sports, schools, restaurants had shut down. It was a stark reminder that your entire world could change without warning.

"Should be an easy week," she said.

"Hooray for us," he said, holding up his mug in a sarcastic toast. Normally sullen and morose on a good day, Jack had become even more so in the days following the takeover of Promise.

"Look, I don't like this either," she said. "But we have to be patient."

"This is bullshit."

He was ornery this morning, so she didn't reply. Nothing good would come of it, at least not right now. His left eyebrow twitched once and then a second time. It was the canary in the coal mine of Jack Goodwin's legendary temper, his reactor core melting down.

When Lucy had been in the eleventh grade, she had briefly dated a boy named Jeff Powell. Like Jack, Jeff was a senior, a fine lacrosse player on his way to the University of Maryland on an athletic scholarship. He was handsome and charming and intelligent, and that was why it had been so surprising when he had hit Lucy the first time. They had been fooling around, and he had wanted her to go down on him, which she did not want to do.

She was only sixteen years old and was inexperienced with boys generally. She was aware that sometimes men hit women, and sometimes it happened to girls her age, even with boys they had known since they were little. But she never imagined it would happen to her.

After gently denying his request, she had laid her head on his chest because she did not understand that things had changed, irrevocably so. But then he had smacked her on the top of the head. Nothing too hard, just an expression of his displeasure. When she reared up, though, he had delivered a runaway fist to her eye, splitting the skin over her eyebrow.

She got up and rushed out of his house, skittering down the stairs like a startled deer escaping a hunter. She zipped past his father, a federal district court judge, reading in his easy chair, out onto their expansive front porch with the columns and fancy Adirondack chairs.

She ran home, blood trickling down her cheek. She tried sneaking into the house through the back door, hoping to avoid running into her parents or brother. But she stumbled across Jack on the porch steps, sneaking an illicit cigarette. When he saw her standing in the spill of the backyard floodlight, he reared back in surprise.

"What happened to your face?" he asked.

The adrenaline of her flight from Jeff's bedroom had faded from her, and now a dull, heavy throb had settled around her eye.

"What do you mean?"

"You're fucking bleeding, Luce."

He got up and gently tilted her cheek toward the light.

"I tripped while I was walking home."

He scoffed.

"Bullshit," he snapped. "Tim do this to you?"

"Jack, please."

It was the wrong thing to say because it confirmed Jack's suspicions. She had intended to keep lying to Jack. But somewhere, deep inside, she didn't want to keep lying. Deep down, she understood Jeff Powell did not deserve her protection.

"That asshole."

He was on his feet now, the cigarette pitched to the ground and crushed under his black Doc Martens. There had been rumors that Jeff Powell was rough on girls, but Jack had never verified them. It was always a friend of a friend who'd heard from someone that had seen him smack a girl he was dating.

As he stood there, quivering with rage, his eyebrow had started twitching, rippling like a coked-up caterpillar.

The fuse had been lit. He bolted from the yard, leaving Lucy alone. She chased after him, telling herself that she wanted to stop him from doing anything rash, but understanding years later that she had simply wanted to see what he would do.

According to the police report filed early the next morning, Jack had kicked down the Powells' door and beaten Hunter into unconsciousness, leaving him with two broken ribs, a detached retina, and a lacerated kidney. Hunter, who was no slouch physically, had made the mistake of believing he was any kind of match for Lucy's angry brother. He was not. He spent three weeks in the hospital after which he was advised to never play lacrosse again.

Jack was charged with malicious wounding and aggravated assault. He spent six months in a juvenile detention facility, extremely fortunate that he had been eight months shy of his eighteenth birthday at the time of the attack. He then enrolled in a military school for the balance of his high school career before enlisting in the Army.

His eyebrow was twitching now.

They were silent but for her brother's heavy, ragged breathing. The respiration of an angry, cornered animal. She agreed that the current status quo couldn't last, but they were not ready to mount a counteroffensive yet. They just did not have enough intelligence on their opponent. They had been so busy working to meet the quota that there had been little time to focus on forming a resistance. Sure, they had talked about it with gusto, from killing the next group of couriers to poisoning their share. But so far, it had been just talk. If they misplayed their hand, the Haven could slaughter all of them.

"We need to figure out where they're from," Lucy said. "It can't be too far."

The Haven's base of operations remained a carefully hidden secret. Their territory was large. According to reports from other communities, the couriers' wagons were loaded down with booty from multiple locations, including items from outside their trading circle. They may have come from as far west as Charlottesville or from Fredericksburg to the north. They may have had interests in the city of Richmond, a dozen miles to the east.

"That'll take too long," her brother replied. "We need to act now. I say we kill anyone who shows up today."

"No," she said. "If we make a move now, it could blow up in our face."

He got up and stormed off. She lingered a minute in her chair, trying to find the words that would settle him down. They couldn't afford a misstep at this point. It was too soon. She joined Jack outside; he was looking up at the sky. He often looked to the heavens for comfort, as she did. A reminder that they were just a bit of the big picture, a few grains of self-aware dust in the great big nowhere.

"Promise me," she said. "You won't do anything rash. We'll come up with a plan."

"I promise," he said.

She wanted to believe him.

She wasn't sure she did.

THEY ARRIVED RIGHT ON SCHEDULE.

Four on horseback, one of the animals pulling the bed of a pickup truck that had been retrofitted into a bizarre horse-drawn carriage. All men, all fearsome looking. Many of Promise's residents were on hand, curious as to how this day would play out. They all stood in a light drizzle while the men dismounted. One approached Lucy, brushing dirt and grime from his hands. He wore jeans and a denim jacket. Thick stubble covered his face. He reeked of body odor.

"Let's make this quick," he said. "We got everything?"

He lacked any of Joshua's charm or wit. He looked healthy and well-fed. More evidence that their enemy was powerful and not to be underestimated.

"Yep."

The team responsible for collecting the loot had stored the haul on large tarps, which made it easy to slide the week's share to the entrance. It looked like a splendid farmer's market, hundreds of pounds of leafy green and root vegetables making up the season's first bounty.

She did her best to ignore Jack, who stood seething next to her. She could almost feel the rage radiating from his body. The sound of the ligaments and tendons popping in his hands as he tightened and unfurled his fists were audible in the silent afternoon air.

"We've got a large produce scale in the pickup," the man said. "Start loading."

The collection team stepped forward. The four of them had worked hard to itemize the harvest. It was important to know what was coming in from the fields, and more importantly, what was headed out the door.

Esther, one of the farmhands, began filling the weighing bowl with as much produce as it could hold. One of the men wrote down the weight of each load onto a clipboard. Then Esther loaded the goods into large plastic bags the Haven had brought with them. It was a lengthy, tedious process and took the better part of an hour. Lucy's heart ached as their conqueror's wagon grew heavier with the fruits of their labor.

"Everything looks good," he said as they finished tallying up the day's take. "The boss will be happy."

"Your boss can go fuck himself," Jack said quietly but firmly.

The man looked up from his clipboard with a bemused look on his face.

"What the hell did you just say?"

"You heard me."

Jack had a strange, little smirk on his face.

The man grabbed Jack by his shirt collar and pulled him close. Jack did not react. He simply continued smirking at the man. For a moment, she worried the man might kill Jack, but as the scene played out, it was clear that he would not. Jack had pushed his luck right to its razor's edge but no farther.

The man did rear back and slam a fist directly into Jack's ribcage. Jack doubled over, wheezing, coughing, gagging. While he was bent over, the man brought up a knee into Jack's chin, which sent him staggering back to the seat of his pants. The man was much bigger than Jack, and the blows had done some damage. Jack lay writhing quietly, but Lucy knew her brother would have no regrets. He'd taken this opportunity to vent his frustrations in a way that hadn't gotten him killed.

While Lucy checked on Jack, the other residents finished loading the last bit into the trailer. Without another word, the men climbed back into their saddles while the wagon driver made a wide U-turn before pulling away from Promise. Everyone retreated gingerly to the cottages and lodges while Lucy watched them pull away, kicking up a fine cloud of dust as they did so.

It was so goddamned frustrating. Watching them take what did not belong to them had been much harder than she had anticipated. It wasn't fair, and it wasn't right.

Well, little lady, life is rarely fair and right.

This would not be sustainable. Her mind was racing ahead to the end of the season, when they would be turning to the fruits and vegetables they had canned for the winter ahead. They also would miss out on the late-season trading activity, when they normally acquired a decent supply of commercially canned goods that were still floating around.

At some point, they would have to make a stand.

True, it might cost them everything.

But some things were worth risking everything for.

12

Life went on.

That was the strangest part of this for Lucy.

Life went on.

Winter had finally receded after stubbornly hanging on, even surprising them with a little freezing rain not long after the Haven had taken its first delivery. Now they were into early May, the time of year when the air smelled fresh and clear and warm. Pleasant breezes swirled across Promise. Some mornings were still brisk and chilly, but often the sweatshirts and coats were shed by late morning.

Lucy returned home after a long day, first, a full day in the clinic, capped off with a few hours in the fields assisting with the harvest. There was so much coming in from the farm that they needed all hands on deck to pick, sort, and organize. And of course, set aside the Haven's share. She was bone tired, too exhausted to even eat. Skipping meals was not a great strategy, but the idea of expending energy to eat dinner seemed too much to bear right now. She stripped off her wet and dirty clothes, exchanging them for shorts and a t-shirt, and lay on her bunk. A brief thunderstorm had broken a shell of humidity while they were picking vegetables, and it had felt good to be in the rain, brief as it was.

And yet for all her exhaustion, she could not sleep.

There was too much on her mind.

It had been nearly a month since the spasm of violence that had brought them to this terrible point in their lives. Yet for all the fear and loathing that accompanied this new life under the thumb of the Haven, it was something they slowly became accustomed to. They buried their dead, and within these past few weeks, the violence had become a distant, albeit terrible, memory. After all, this world was about survival and doing what you needed to do to ensure such survival.

They still had not come up with a plan to deal with the Haven. For now, they had no choice but to comply. Otherwise, they would kill more Promise residents and then just take what they wanted anyway. It was self-defeating to raise a fuss. They would just be hurting themselves.

The odd thing was how quickly you became used to it. People still came and went, lived like they had been living. They had easily met the weekly quota, and they still had enough to eat. But they were robbing Peter to pay Paul. Food that would be headed for canning and pickling for the coming winter was being redirected toward the Haven. If you put that out of mind, then it was easy to fall into a sense of security. They had to remember. Initially, it didn't seem too bad, even though your gut told you otherwise. Even when they told you that you were part of something bigger.

"We look out for each other," Joshua had said.

It wasn't out of the goodness of their hearts, of course. Promise was a valuable producer, and they intended to keep the supply lines open. And did they ever produce that spring. The rains were plentiful. Slow-moving showers every few days kept the crops fat and happy.

But she could see and hear it in the others. Resigned acceptance of their new fate. Excuses made, rationalizations given.

After all, it wasn't like they had to become best friends with the people from the Haven. They came every week, collected their cut, and they were on their way. There was plenty for the rest of them to eat. They didn't need the Market anymore. If they needed something they didn't have, they went through the Haven. It was more expensive, of course, but that's what happened when a new competitor cornered the market.

But through the balance of the spring and as they rounded the turn for summer, things were copacetic. The field hands returned each day loaded down with tomatoes, cucumbers, squash, peppers, zucchini. Eggs and meat were plentiful, and in the absence of refrigeration, they stored preserved food in large zeer pots, an ancient form of refrigeration dating back thousands of years. The technology was simple enough. A smaller pot sat nested inside a larger one that was lined with wet sand. The evaporation of the water from the sand pulled heat from the inner pot and kept its contents quite cold. For such a primitive design, it worked remarkably well.

At some point, they would have to deal with the Haven, but they weren't there yet. It was percolating in the back of her mind, something they would get to. She didn't want to be beholden to them forever, but she did not want to risk their lives to do so.

Plus, she had other things on her mind.

Norah.

Thoughts about Norah kept her awake on this night despite the fatigue deep in her bones.

Their relationship had remained chilly in the aftermath of their showdown at the fire pit. She tended to her chores quietly and efficiently without being told. Unfortunately, this removed one of the threads connecting the two of them, which was exactly what Norah wanted. Fewer opportunities to hassle her about her chores meant fewer opportunities to pry into her personal life.

Lucy's daughter, Emma, had never made it into her teens, and so this was an entirely new experience for Lucy. She could only draw on her own experience as a teenaged girl, and she had been so different from Norah that it provided no useful perspective. Norah was extraordinarily kind but very quiet, hard to reach. She was slow to trust others. To her detriment, Lucy had been quick to trust, as evidenced by her repeated mistakes with the boys prowling the hallways of Collegiate High School.

Lucy sat up in bed.

A boy.

It had to be a boy.

She had known it all along, she supposed. She simply did not want to accept that her little girl, her Norah, was a young woman now and would be doing the things that she herself had done at sixteen. When she finally accepted what she knew to be true, everything fell into place. Norah's day-dreaminess, her scattered brain, it all added up. She had a boy on the brain.

Solving this unsurprising mystery had dislodged one of the splinters keeping her awake, and she quickly fell into a deep, dreamless sleep.

It occupied much of her thoughts for the next week.

At work, in the fields, sitting around the fire with her friends, lying in bed. She couldn't help but want to know more, a protective instinct washing over her. The idea that a boy would hurt Norah, that he would break her heart was painful enough, and it hadn't even happened yet. She was already fired up, angry for Norah, hell, even for Emma, who would never have to endure heartbreak.

No, sweet girl, none for you. Your heart was pure and unbroken to the end.

Initially, Lucy assumed it was one of the boys from Promise. There were three who fit the bill. Norah had been friends with them for a long time, and it would not have been surprising if one of those friendships had blossomed into something more. And absconding into the woods for nighttime rendezvous would be just the thing teenaged lovers would do.

She watched her carefully for the next week or so, watched her interactions with the handful of teenaged boys who also called Promise home. The kids were a relatively tight group. Sure, they had their drama and their squabbles, but they seemed to get along, understanding that they alone had one another's backs. There were brief romances and hurt feelings from time to time, of course, but for the most part, they made up a happy little corner-stone of their community. But after a few days of observa-tion, it became obvious she had eyes for none of them. They were friends, and they joked and treated each other like brother and sister, but the spark simply was not there. No lingering eye contact, no hip squeezes, physical contact that continued a moment too long. No sneaking off after a meal together.

Eventually, Lucy concluded that the apple of Norah's eye was not local. Which meant Norah had found herself a long-distance beau. And the only place she would have met someone would have been the Market. She had always enjoyed making the trip, as all the youngsters did. It was their chance to break free of their cocoon, if just for a little while.

She continued watching Norah for another week, no longer calling her out on her late-night excursions. Instead, she used the opportunity to collect information. Clearly, telling her she was grounded had had no effect. Forbidden fruit tasted all the sweeter after all. It was diffi-cult discerning the patterns in Norah's movements, espe-cially with the constant work in the clinic. But eventually, she had found the needle in the haystack of Norah's life.

On a pleasant Sunday afternoon, Norah told Lucy she was going for a bike ride to clear her head. She wasn't asking was the thing. She was *telling* Lucy, and this was how it was going to be. Ordinarily, Lucy would have insisted she go with a friend because they worked on the buddy system. But she let it slide this time. After all, Norah would have a buddy on this trip. She just wouldn't know it.

"Be back before dark," Lucy said. "Long before dark."

"Fine," Norah said agreeably.

Perhaps she had been surprised by Lucy's quick agreement. She might have been spoiling for a fight. Well, she wasn't going to get one. Lucy had a longer game in mind.

NORAH LEFT Promise at noon on a bicycle, carrying a backpack. She had pilfered a few items from the kitchen, as though she were assembling a picnic. She pedaled north and then northeast for ten miles along State Route 522 to a little hamlet called Gum Spring. Following her had been tricky; Norah had developed a good set of instincts. It took all of Lucy's skills and abilities to successfully track the girl undetected.

Norah made her way to a small park on the edge of the town, bordered by a long rock wall. The park was choked with grassy weeds, neglected, but it was also home to a beautiful, large, and ancient oak tree at the wall's base. It was a clear day, the sunshine glinting off the quartz in the rocks. Norah leaned her bicycle against a bench and then set out a small blanket. She set out two plates and two sets of silverware. She was expecting company.

Lucy tucked herself behind a grove of trees just west of the park. She leaned her bike against the trunk of an old maple. Then she pulled out her binoculars to begin her surveillance. Norah was about a hundred yards distant.

"I know you're there," she called out suddenly.

Lucy chuckled to herself. She had not been as stealthy as she thought. She emerged from her hiding spot and approached Norah sheepishly. She felt like the most overbearing, pain-in-the-ass parent in the history of parenting.

"I need you to come home with me," Lucy said.

"I'm not leaving."

"Norah, dammit, I need you to understand something."

"Oh, I understand plenty."

"You're just a kid. What exactly do you understand?"

"Don't you trust me?"

Lucy could hear the hurt in her voice. The fight went right out of her.

"I do trust you," she said. "I just worry."

Norah did not reply as she continued setting out the picnic.

"You don't need to worry," she said after a few moments of awkward silence.

"Is he a good guy?" Lucy asked.

Norah set a loaf of bread down on the blanket and turned to face Lucy.

"Yes," she said. "He's the nicest person I've ever met."

Her voice was full of steel and resolve.

Norah chuckled softly.

"What?" Lucy asked.

"Probably too nice for this world."

They stood there in the quiet, neither saying a word. As it threatened to become awkward, the sounds of hooves clopping along the desolate road through the center of town reached her ears. Norah, all five-foot-seven of her, stood up as her guest approached. The smile on her face was apparent. Like a marvelous shooting star through a desolate, black sky.

"Just be home by dark," Lucy said.

"I will."

Lucy nodded and began making her way back to her bicycle. As she drew away from the park, she stole glances over her shoulder at the happy reunion unfolding. The boy aboard the approaching horse was about Norah's age, maybe a little older. He was fair-skinned, a shock of red hair atop his head. She hoped sunscreen was a regular part of his skincare regimen. He dismounted gracefully and looped the horse to the bench where Norah had left her bicycle.

Norah ran to him, throwing her arms around him. They kissed passionately but clumsily, the fumbling embrace of young people who had not been at it very long but were goddamned dedicated to getting it right. Lucy turned away, feeling quite embarrassed at this intrusion into Norah's life. She looked back when their chatter resumed. They had taken their seats on the blanket; Norah had begun serving their lunch. It wasn't much, just some flatbread and hard cheeses. Lucy's eyebrows rose in surprise when Norah withdrew a small plastic bottle containing a dark liquid.

A little wine for the happy couple.

Lucy watched a bit longer. Norah was positively beaming and did much of the talking. The boy listened attentively and seemed utterly enraptured by her. She had seen enough. As Norah and the boy lay on the

blanket looking up at the sky, pointing at cloud forma-
tions, Lucy elected to take her leave of the happy couple.

She walked her bicycle to a narrow road that paral-
leled Route 522 to stay out of Norah's line of sight. The
route was a bit more indirect, but it was more scenic, and
it would give her time to think. It was a lovely afternoon,
and she was looking forward to the ride home. Her mind
was at ease for the first time since that morning when she
had started reading the Stephen King novel in front of
the blazing fire pit. It felt like a million years ago.

It was true that you were only as happy as your
unhappiest child. For so many years, she could be only as
happy as Emma was as she fought the leukemia that ultimately took her life. And since she had died, Lucy's
happiness was a null function, an impossibility because
you could not divide by zero. The denominator of Lucy's
life was zero.

Until Norah.

And now, to see Norah so happy filled her with joy
unlike anything she could remember in a very long time.
Perhaps since before Emma had gotten sick.

She became so wrapped up in her thoughts that she
did not see the deer flashing in front of her until it was
almost too late. She veered sharply to right while
squeezing the bike's rear brake handle. The back tire
struck a patch of damp leaves, causing her to lose control.
She had been moving at a good clip, and the sudden act
of braking put her balance in jeopardy. Gravity took over,
and the bike skidded hard, tipping to the left as it ran off
the road.

Lucy gasped in surprise. The bike dumped her,

sending her rolling across the shoulder and down an embankment into a ditch, her arms and legs pinwheeling every which way. Before her body came to rest, her head struck a partially exposed rock. Fortunately, it was a glancing blow and not enough to cause permanent damage.

Unfortunately, it was a good enough smack to knock her out.

She watched a hawk fly overhead before she blacked out.

13

L ucy came to a few moments later.

She blinked hard a few times, clearing her field of vision. She breathed in slowly and exhaled, unsure how badly she was injured. It would be a good test whether she had suffered any internal injuries. Minimal pain. She finished emptying her lungs, rewarded with a cleansing if shaky breath. It felt good and probably meant she had not suffered any broken ribs or damage to her lungs. She pressed a hand to a particularly sore spot on the side of her head. Her hand came away tacky with a little blood, but the flow did not appear to be heavy.

The crash had left the lower half of her body submerged in about a foot of water standing in the ditch; the rest of her lay against the embankment. She had been lucky. If she had landed inverted, her head in the water, she could have drowned during her brief stint of unconsciousness.

She sat up, pushing off the arm pinned underneath

her. So far, so good. Using her hands to brace herself, she tried to stand up, but a sharp pain shot through her right ankle and brought her quickly back to her seat. The pain in her ankle became the center of her universe. If she put any weight on it, if she twisted it in any direction, fire shot through the muscles and the tendons. Already, it was swelling rapidly, the outer part of her ankle almost the size of a golf ball. She palpated the swollen tissue surrounding the bone. Her ankle was badly sprained, possibly fractured.

She was still nearly ten miles from home. She looked judgmentally at her crashed bike a bit higher up on the embankment. Hopefully, it was still in working condition. She didn't know if she could pedal right now, but it was a hell of a lot more appealing than trying to walk. Maybe with a little work, the ankle would loosen up long enough for her to get home.

Using the rock that had knocked her out for leverage, she pushed up to her feet, careful to keep the weight off her injured ankle. A wave of nausea washed over her and nearly sent her back to her seat. But she remained upright, closing her eyes as the swimminess passed. The embankment was steeper than she thought. Even when standing, she was barely level with the road. It would be difficult for anyone to see her, which, for now, was a good thing. Better to stay hidden.

She tested the ankle, gently adding some weight to it. But she abandoned the experiment as quickly as she had begun it. The piercing pain of a badly sprained ankle rocketed up her leg; she could feel the crunchiness of the torn tendons. She wanted to scream in frustration. A similar ankle sprain during a training exercise in the Army had laid her low for nearly a week.

The embankment sat on about a forty-five-degree angle; it would take some work, but she thought she could crawl to the top. She did not know what to do about the bicycle, however. There was no way she could move it up the hill to the roadway. Absent the bike, she did not know how she would get home.

She was in a bit of trouble here. She had some water in her pack, enough for a day or so. No food, but without water, she would die of thirst long before her hunger became an issue. Her best bet, much as she hated to admit it, would be to rest for the day, spend the night at the bottom of this hill, and test the ankle the next morning. It was a warm enough day, and although it would be an uncomfortably chilly night, exposure would not be a concern. Bears and bobcats were endemic in the area, but the odds that she would see one were low. Not zero, of course, but it would be an extraordinary stroke of bad luck stacked on top of her bad luck to have crashed in the first place.

Before committing to an overnight stay, however, she wanted to try one more attempt at resuming her journey. The prospect of spending the night here was not particularly appealing. Her absence would soon raise alarms back at Promise. Jack would be beside himself with worry. And for all their conflict, it would devastate Norah. She struggled with the fear of abandonment. It was something she had dealt with all her life up until the moment of the Pulse. And when her grandmother had died in the train crash that day, everyone she had known and trusted was gone. Even after their worst fights, she would do something to ensure that Lucy was still in her corner. After this past conflict, she had left Norah a note under her pillow telling her she loved her.

Lucy crawled across the embankment toward the bike, keeping the weight off her ankle, now swollen to the size of a baseball. She looped her arm in between the spokes of the front tire and turned toward the base of the hill. The bike was fairly lightweight, and with some elbow grease, she could tow it to the top of the embankment. There, she would decide whether to press on home today.

But for all of her willpower, her mental fortitude, her body simply was not able to perform. It was impossible to keep her purchase without bracing herself with her feet. That sent waves of excruciating pain radiating from her ankle. She wanted to gut it out, but she simply could not. She made it about a third of the way up the hill before she had to stop. She rolled onto her back, covered in sweat, grime, and mud. It had taken her the better part of an hour just to make it that far, every inch cloaked in agony.

The pain in her head had faded to a dull throb. Absently, she scraped blood that had dried around the wound and sighed. If she had just trusted Norah, she wouldn't have been in this mess. When was she going to learn? When would she be able to accept that Norah was no longer a child, particularly in a world that now cut childhoods short?

As the afternoon wound on, her eyelids grew heavy with fatigue. The sun beating down on her felt good.

Warm but not too hot. She retrieved the gun and the bottle of water from her pack and settled in for the afternoon, hoping the ankle would magically heal itself in the next hour or two.

She napped.

It was closing in on dark when she woke up again. She was surprised she'd slept for so long. Perhaps the smack to the head had been more serious than she initially realized. She felt a little better, more clear-headed, but the ankle was still useless. Given her positioning on the hill, with her ankle angled below her heart, the swelling had persisted. Attempts to put any weight on it were met with angry barking.

She had a little water in her pack, which had landed near her. She unscrewed the cap and allowed herself two swallows. Not knowing how long she would be here, she wanted it to last until tomorrow. By then, she would probably be able to put on enough weight to make it up the hill with the bicycle in tow. At dusk, biting flies emerged and left Lucy's arms and legs pockmarked with red welts. As night fell, the forest flanking either side of the narrow roadway came to life with croaking frogs and hooting owls.

The skies were clear and full of stars. It was her favorite thing about their new world. Absent the light pollution that had been a scourge of their pre-Pulse world, the night sky had become an astronomical wonderland. When sleep escaped her, a clear, starry night was just the thing to drain the stress and anxiety of the day. Eventually, the strain of the day caught up to her and she nodded off once more.

She slept poorly, the strong chill in the air and pain in her ankle waking her every little while. The hours crept by slowly. Of course, there was no way to get comfortable. It didn't get too cold, but it was definitely chilly. In the bottom of night, her body trembled, her teeth rattling together as her body fought off the chill. As dawn approached, her eyes were heavy with grit and exhaustion. She finally fell asleep just as the sun broke over the horizon, sliding into a deep sleep for the first time that night, but the clopping sound of approaching hooves woke her a few minutes later. Disoriented and confused, it took her a minute to remember where she was. Then a spike of pain in her ankle brought it all rushing back.

She held her breath, pressing her body against the embankment, willing them to pass her by. She tried to edge her way farther down the hill, hoping it would provide her greater cover, but the swishing of her movements through the grass was too loud to risk it. She froze again, but the hoofbeats above her had slowed.

Shit.

Indistinct chatter.

There were at least two of them.

Well, it was a good run, Luce.

If this was the end for her, she hoped they'd make it quick. She wouldn't beg for her life. If they were ungentlemanly, however, she wouldn't go quietly. If circumstances dictated it, biting their nuts off would be her last conscious act on this Earth.

The hoofbeats came to a complete stop, paired with the relaxed whinnying of two horses. This was followed by the distinct sound of boots hitting the ground and the slow saunter of her potential executioner. She rolled onto her side, curling her legs up under her, and propped herself up on an elbow. Two faces gazed down on her, one of an older woman and the second, rippling with acne, belonging to a teenage boy a little older than Norah.

The woman chuckled but this gave Lucy no comfort. These days people would smile just as soon as they would kill you. She nudged the boy and gestured toward Lucy's bicycle.

"You look like you could use a hand."

THE BOY COMMANDEERED the bike while Lucy and the woman rode the horses. They headed west with the rising sun at their backs. The horse was sweet and calm, the ride smooth. Lucy was just able to get her injured foot into the stirrup, which kept it relatively stable. It hurt like a mother and was impossible to stand on, but it would resolve with time and rest. Assuming she lived long enough.

"Where you from?" asked the woman.

They had turned off the main road and were crossing a clear-cut tract of land that had been in the early stages of development. A pair of bulldozers bracketed each side of the worksite. A backhoe lay on its side. It looked as though it had been in the middle of excavation when the Pulse hit. In the intervening years, the hole it had been digging had widened and tipped the large machine over.

On the far side of the tract, they entered a chilly tree

line ensconced with light fog. There seemed to be a trail the boy was following, but Lucy would be damned if she could find it. She really did not know where they were. They were traveling north now. She shivered in the chill.

She wondered what was happening back home. There was likely a search party out looking for her. The problem was that even when you weren't far from home, you were gone. The haystack was just too big. They would look for a day, maybe two, but in the absence of any actionable intelligence, they would have to hope that Lucy found her way home on her own. Taking the secondary route had been a mistake.

"Near the river. About ten miles from where you found me."

It was a way to answer her question without answering it.

The woman didn't inquire any further. Which was fine with Lucy, who spent much of the trip in a sleepy haze, maintaining just enough awareness to keep her balance on the horse. It wasn't a deep sleep, but by the time they reached their destination hours later, she felt a bit more refreshed. It was late afternoon; they had been on the road for several hours.

They had been traveling through a deep wood, along a trail that was only wide enough for them to ride single file. The woods thinned out as they approached a desolate four-lane highway. There weren't many vehicles abandoned here, suggesting it had been a low-traffic route even before the Pulse. Ahead, just to the right, was a large warehouse surrounded by a long stretch of perimeter fencing. An access road connected the main road and the warehouse entrance.

If these people planned to kill her, she hoped they would get on with it. Given how tired she was, even execution seemed preferable to waiting in exhaustion-cloaked darkness. But the woman showed her no malice. There seemed to be no imminent threat to Lucy's life. A sentinel at the perimeter gate waved them through. The woman seemed to be trusted enough to bring in a stranger without further inquiry.

"My name is Beatrice, by the way," she said.

She was a tall woman, about fifty years old. She was quite striking. Her auburn hair was tied in a long braid hanging down her back.

"Lucy."

"Nice to meet you."

Lucy nodded as they entered the outskirts of the warehouse complex. The large building at the center was bracketed by three smaller buildings. A dozen ghost trailers were still parked at the loading docks, the same spot they'd been sitting for five years. It was always weird to see a snapshot of the Time Before. It whipsawed you right back to a world that no longer existed. And although you'd become used to this new world, it was hard to see the way things used to be. For all its flaws and blemishes, life had been a hell of a lot easier back then.

They stabled the horses at a trailer that had been retrofitted as equine accommodations. Beatrice directed one of the stable hands to fetch a pair of crutches. Lucy sat with the woman on the edge of the loading dock while they waited for the crutches. Lucy kept her leg up on the dock to rest it. It was fiery with pain. The place was quiet but humming with activity.

"We use the trailers for lodging, medical, that kind of thing," she said. "We'll set you up in the medical trailer, get that ankle checked out."

"Thanks," Lucy replied. "What is this place?"

"We call it Westerberg."

The name rang a bell for Lucy, but she could not recall why. It gnawed at her while Beatrice accompanied her to the medical trailer. It was primitive but well-stocked. She was impressed with their setup. Beatrice helped her into the bed and set two pillows underneath Lucy's outstretched leg. The relief was immediate. While it had kept her off her feet, the long ride in the saddle had done little for her recovery. The ankle was now swollen larger than a baseball, and the slightest movement triggered waves of pain.

Unless they gave her one of their horses, she wasn't going anywhere anytime soon. Ideally, they would have simply escorted her home, but this wasn't an ideal world. That would have exposed them to unnecessary danger; on the flip side, Lucy would have to reveal the location of Promise to strangers. If nothing else, Promise did not deserve to suffer for her own run of bad luck.

The sun dropped behind the warehouses, enveloping this side of the complex in shade. A cool breeze was blowing, and it nudged her into her first true sleep in more than thirty hours. She slept.

She woke to the sound of her name.

Over and over.

She wanted to sleep, but the call was persistent.

Persistent and familiar.

A man's voice. A familiar voice.

This jarred her awake as her brain sorted through its voiceprint database, anxious to make a match.

She opened her eyes.

Staring back at her was a face she had not seen in five years.

Not since those frightening days immediately following the Pulse.

A broad smile spread across the man's face like a spring sunrise.

It was Tim Whitaker.

14

Tim Whitaker.

"Oh my God," she muttered.

"I can't believe it," he said, bursting into laughter. "Lucy, is that really you?"

She sat up as he leaned in to hug her.

"It's me," she said.

Tim Whitaker was a high school English teacher that she, Norah, and her late friend, Manny, had met in the harrowing hours following the Pulse. Single and childless, Tim had stayed at the school with the students whose parents had not collected them. He had offered Lucy's party refuge in his school while en route to their final destination, the residence of one of Manny's former coworkers, a troubled woman named Angela.

Westerberg had been the name of Tim's high school.

Tim had previously been romantically involved with Angela, an entanglement that nearly had cost him his life several days into their new reality. Still hung up on Angela, Tim had come to her house to check on her;

what he did not know was that Eric, Angela's boyfriend, had arranged to kidnap both Lucy and Norah and trade them to a human trafficker named Simon for supplies. In fact, Eric had already dispatched Norah to her captors. Due to her own stubbornness, Lucy had been with Eric on a supply run when Norah was taken. Only good fortune had placed Lucy in the right spot to discover his plot and thwart Eric's plan to kill Tim. It was, unfortunately, too late for her friend, Manny, whom Eric had murdered in cold blood. It was a stark reminder for Tim of how something from your past could climb out of the hazy yesterdays and still try to bring you down.

The past was not dead, as the saying went. It was not even past.

Lucy had killed Eric herself instead. Then, she and Tim had tracked Norah to Eric's employer's hideaway in a local mall; there, she had rescued Norah before he'd been able to sell her into a lifetime of horror. She had invited Tim to return to her farm to live, but he had declined, choosing instead to look after his students at the high school. She had hoped their paths would one day cross again, but so far, they had not.

He pulled a chair up next to her bed and took a seat.

"You made it," she said.

"Yeah, I'm still kicking," he replied with a heavy sigh. "Barely. What are you doing here?"

She gave him the Cliffs Notes version of her adventures, in disbelief that she had found Tim again. She had thought about him often in those early days. As the months and years slipped by, however, she had lost any hope that their paths would cross again.

"And Norah?" he said hopefully. The way he asked was telling. He didn't want to simply assume that they'd had a happy ending. You never even assumed anyone was still alive. "Is she...?"

"She's good," Lucy replied.

"Sixteen now," she continued, as though just that bit of information would tell Tim all he needed to know about how her putative daughter was doing. Their terrible fight loomed large in her mind. It reminded her of her own drag-out brawls with her mother when she had been Norah's age. Life was a circle. Everything came back around.

"Wow," he said softly.

He scoffed.

"Sometimes you forget how much time has gone by," he said wistfully.

"I know," she said.

He looked about the same as she remembered. Maybe a little grey around the temple.

"So she's sixteen, huh?" he said, anxious to change the subject.

"Going on thirty."

"Yeah, sixteen is a fun age," he said. "I taught my share of them."

"An age made even more fun by our dystopian environment."

"I'm sure."

"Anyway. Please thank your friends for helping me out," she said. "The ankle is a real mess. I would've been easy pickings out there."

"Will do," he said. He stared at her for another

moment before slapping his knees in joy. "It is so good to see you."

"You too," she said.

She was thrilled to see him. He was a good man. She hoped he was the same man she'd last seen all those years ago. This world, it had a funny way of changing you. Turning you into someone you weren't. In the name of survival.

"You hungry?" he asked.

"I could eat."

"Great," he said. "We can catch up."

"I really need to get back on the road," she said. "My folks will be out looking for me. I've been gone more than a day."

"Lucy, you said yourself the ankle was a mess," he said, wagging a finger at her. "Besides, it's not safe after dark. We have some bad seeds operating in the area. You don't want to be on the road too late. We lock the gates at dusk."

Bad seeds. She wondered if he was referring to their new overlords from the Haven. Or he had his hands full with some other terrible group of people. In every corner of the country, if not the world, stories just like theirs were playing out right now. And they wouldn't all have happy endings. In fact, not many of them would. It was a kill-or-be-killed world. If she were being honest, she was surprised that Tim had made it.

She worried he wouldn't have what it took to make it in this world. For his sake, for the sake of most decent people, she had kept hoping the power would return so they wouldn't sink into barbarism. The things she'd seen these last few years were enough to keep you on a steady diet of antidepressants.

"Look," he said, "you'll stay the night, and then if your ankle isn't up to it tomorrow, I will personally escort you home."

She wanted to object, but like discretion, prudence was another part of valor. The wise choice was to accept his offer. There was no need to take unnecessary risks. Back home, hope for her was likely at its nadir by now; another night away probably wouldn't move the needle in any statistically significant direction.

He handed her a pair of crutches leaning against the wall. Using the crutch to steady herself, she hoisted herself off the bed and began the metronomic shuffle of the invalid. He helped her down the ramp connecting the trailer to the loading dock; from there, she was able to manage on her own. Tim led her down the ramp and toward a small office on the edge of the loading dock. In the falling dusk, the windows glowed with lantern light.

"Have a seat," he said. "I'll get us some food."

She sat down, propping her injured foot on the adjacent chair. She did not think he would mind. The office was small, utilitarian. A desk, two chairs, and two beige filing cabinets. The windows were open, but it was stuffy. Her kingdom for an air-conditioned room.

Tim returned fifteen minutes later carrying two bowls, steam curling from the tops. He handed her a bowl and sat down across from her. It smelled delicious. As the aroma reached her nostrils, her stomach rumbled loudly. She had not eaten in a day.

"What is this place?" she asked, blowing the steam

from the surface of the bowl. It appeared to be a thick stew of meat and potatoes. She took a bite. It was delicious.

"It's a food distribution warehouse."

Her spoon froze in between her lips and her bowl. Tim was grinning at her. She took another bite, savoring the salty flavor of the stew. She could not remember the last time she had enjoyed a meal this much. Newfound appreciation for life and all that. She probably would have been fine if Beatrice had not found her lying in the ditch, but it was best not to tempt fate these days.

"Yeah, we hit the jackpot here."

"You're not kidding."

A food distribution warehouse was like gold. Better than gold, in fact. A full warehouse could hold many years' worth of nonperishable foods and other sundries. Canned goods, dry goods, salted meats, cleaning supplies. And in a way, things had come full circle. In the days following the Pulse, Lucy had made a trip to a distribution warehouse similar to this one to secure supplies; in that case, however, it had been a trap. One that had nearly cost Lucy her life. That warehouse had long been empty and had been the site of a planned ambush of Lucy and her friend, Manny.

"It was almost full when we found it," Tim said. "We hit it pretty hard in the early days, which was a mistake. Honestly, I kept thinking the lights would come back on, so there was no need to ration the supplies. Pretty dumb of me."

He said it with a wizened look on his face. The look of a man who had seen things, who had learned things.

"Eventually, we made the supplies our backup. Like a strategic reserve. So we got to farming, and we've done okay in that department. But the warehouse has pulled us through some dark times."

Lucy's head was spinning. A twinge of jealousy shot through her. At first, she felt bad about it, but she accepted it as natural. Tim had been very lucky to find this place; she could not think of someone who deserved it more.

"That's great," she said, and she meant it.

The stew had cooled enough to eat. She took three large bites, which settled the hunger pangs down. She took a break, wanting it to last; there was no guarantee she would be offered more, no matter how tight she had been with Tim.

"So what happened to you?" she asked. "I really thought one day you'd show up at my door."

His face darkened, and he set the bowl on his desk.

"You were right," he said. "Things got bad in the city really quickly. I guess I was pretty naïve."

Before they'd parted ways, she had warned him of the dark days that lay ahead if the power did not return.

"We held out at the school as long as we could," he said.

A somber look crossed his face. He took a deep breath before continuing.

"Most of the kids were gone within a day or so. Their parents finally made it. Never saw any of them again. There were eight of us left. Three teachers and five students. Don't know what happened to those kids' parents, but it probably wasn't anything good. It wasn't too bad at first. We moved to the science wing. Large classrooms, interior of the school, windows that looked over the quad. We could light candles without worrying about being spotted from the street. We had food, water, at least for a while. We lasted three weeks."

He paused for a moment, looked away, held a clenched fist to his lips.

"One day, I was out on a supply run, me and one of the kids. We always went out in pairs. There wasn't much left by then, there wasn't really anything left. Anyway, we made it back just before dark. That was our rule, we had to be back before dark because that's when things got really bad."

He shuddered.

"Anyway, we were cutting it close because we hadn't found anything, but we didn't want to come back empty-handed. Our supplies were starting to run low. I knew something was wrong right away. Just had a sense. Like the air had been sucked out of the place. The feeling that something terrible had happened. Maggie, the kid with me, went dead silent. Like she knew as well."

"They were all dead. All six of them. Two teachers and four students. I've never seen anything like it, never even imagined what something like that could look like. There was so much blood. I don't even think they stole anything. I think they just killed them because they *could*."

He traced his lower lip with the tip of his finger.

"Seeing something like that, man, it just changes you."

"I'm sorry," said Lucy.

"We hit the road after that," he said. "Maggie and me. She killed herself a month later."

"I'm really sorry," Lucy said. "I wish you'd made it down to the farm."

He chuckled.

"I lost the directions you gave me," he said, referring to the note she'd scratched out for him that last morning they'd been together. "I even came down to Goochland one time to find you. That is one big damn county. A lot of farms. I asked around, but I'm sorry to say that not a lot of folks were anxious to help a big black guy traveling by himself."

"Yeah, we were a bit behind on the Black Lives Matter movement, I am sorry to say," she said. "Things have improved in that department, though."

He flashed a mocking thumbs-up and paired it with an over-exaggerated smile, although her statement was laced with a good deal of truth to it. These days, you didn't trust anyone you didn't know, regardless of the color of their skin. And if you had someone you trusted, that bond was like gold, again, regardless of skin color. The foundations of white supremacy had collapsed in the wake of the Pulse, putting virtually everyone on equal footing.

"So you're the boss now," she said. It wasn't a question. He was clearly the leader here.

"If you want to call it that," he replied.

Just as she remembered. Humble. He would not have sought to lead. People had naturally looked at him to do that. As the folks at the school had.

"So how about you?" he asked.

"We made it a year at the farm," she said. "But it became clear we couldn't defend it by ourselves. There were just too many refugees from the cities. They were like locusts. My brother and I couldn't keep up."

After that first encounter with the suburban couple, Lucy had hoped that such a thing would be the exception and not the rule. But it wasn't. By the Fourth of July, just six weeks after the Pulse, America's pantries and cupboards were empty, and the supply chains had totally collapsed. By the first of August, starvation was a thing that was happening in the United States of America, or what was left of her.

Millions fled the cities, setting their sights on America's farms and hunting grounds. This triggered massive unrest and brutal violence. It couldn't even be described as war. It was elemental, not a fight over religion or politics, but a fight to simply exist. Once there were many more mouths to feed than there was food to put in those mouths, a spasm of violence and terror swept the nation from coast to coast until the new status quo settled in.

Lucy and Jack had merged their farm with the La'Moon family farm half a mile away. The La'Moons had two teenaged sons, and together they kept a twenty-four-hour armed watch over their land. Eventually, the two families combined with a group of homesteaders, friends of the La'Moons, and the seeds of Promise were planted.

"But you're doing okay now?"

She hitched for a moment, reluctant to tell him the truth. But she couldn't lie to him. And they needed allies.

"Yeah, we hooked up with a decent group. On an old

Boy Scout campground. It's been fairly copacetic. Until recently that is. We are having a bit of an issue."

His eyebrows went up.

"Bad?"

"Not great."

"Tell me more."

"You come across a group called the Haven?"

"Name doesn't ring a bell," he said. "But we've heard some chatter about a new player in the area. Up toward Fredericksburg. I've got scouts out every day looking for trouble. We haven't found anything. I'll ask around before you go. Could be your guys."

She placed a hand on his forearm.

"Stay frosty," she said. "These guys don't mess around. They've killed four of ours already."

"I will," he replied somberly.

THEY TALKED LATE into the evening, but eventually, the oxycodone that Lucy had accepted to control the pain in her ankle worked its magic, and she was unable to keep her eyes open. Tim took her back to the medical trailer, where she quickly fell fast asleep. She did not even remember him bidding her good night. She woke with the sun. A test of the ankle revealed continuing misery and limited mobility, but it would be enough to get her home.

After a quick breakfast of flatbread and jam, Tim put Lucy on a trusted horse and he paced them on her bicycle. He would return home on horseback. She was normally anxious about revealing their location, but she trusted Tim without hesitation. Forget the fact that she had saved his life on that very dark evening half a decade earlier. He was a good man, and it seemed like the years had not changed that part of him. It was like that old saying: adversity didn't build character. It revealed it.

The ride home passed quickly; she'd forgotten how easy he was to talk to. She found herself stealing unnecessary glances at the man. She remembered thinking that she was not particularly attracted to him when they first met. Now, however, she found herself dreading their arrival in Promise. It meant that they would part ways again, and there was no way to know when or if they would see each other again. She was already thinking of ways to keep him in her loop, a task made more difficult by their banishment from the Market.

Before she knew it, the outskirts of Promise came into view. The three-hour trip had flashed by in the blink of an eye. He would be on the road again soon, and she was already thinking of ways to delay his departure. Her heart fluttered.

What the actual hell is wrong with you, Lucy Goodwin?

There had been little time to think about personal relationships since the Pulse. Too much to do, too much to worry about. And any bond could easily be ripped away from you. Best to keep your distance and look out for yourself and those around you. It wasn't that the people of Promise weren't family. They were. But it was a collective love. And when you lost someone, it didn't hurt quite as badly because you loved the group, not any one person.

Harsh, perhaps.

But that was the way things were.

There were relationships, naturally, there always were. People often did things that were not in their best interest. After all, the apocalypse hadn't turned off human desire or the longing for family. A handful of children had been born in the community. Some relationships endured; most did not. But there had been no romantic entanglements for Lucy. She didn't want to risk it.

She took the lead near Promise's outer perimeter, waving to the sentinel on duty. It looked like Betsy.

Betsy waved back enthusiastically when she recognized Lucy. She hoisted her rifle back up onto her shoulder and clasped her hands in prayer, looking to the sky as she did so.

"Looks like you were missed," Tim said, chuckling.

"Well, I am the school nurse, so it's probably not my charming personality they miss."

"You haven't changed much," he said. "Good to see."

God, if you're out there, if I am blushing right now in front of this man, let this horse throw me and stomp me out of this embarrassment spiral.

"Lucy!" Betsy called out, jogging to meet them. "You're alive!"

"Yeah, I crashed on my bike two days ago and absolutely wrecked my ankle," she replied "This is Tim. He and his people looked after me."

Betsy glanced nervously at him.

"It's okay, Betsy," she said. "If you can believe it, I actually knew Tim before the Pulse."

She nodded slowly.

"I'm gonna tell everyone you're here," she said. "My goodness, people have been worried sick. Norah hasn't slept in two days."

Lucy's heart caved in at this. In light of their fight, it was difficult to remember that they were family, that they loved each other. Furthermore, it was confirmation that Norah had managed to make it home safely when Lucy herself had not.

"Ma'am, I'm actually gonna be headed out," Tim said to Betsy. "Just wanted to make sure my friend, Lucy, got home safely."

Strangely, he seemed anxious to leave and anxious to stay at the same time. He kept glancing off toward the center of Promise, as though he wanted to learn more about the place Lucy called home.

"Nice to meet you, then," Betsy said.

She turned back toward her post, leaving Lucy and Tim alone.

"You're really just gonna head back, huh?"

He toed down the kickstand of her bike and helped her down from the horse.

She hugged him hard. When she leaned back, there were tears in his eyes.

"I'm glad I got to see you again," he said. "Like Forrest Gump and Jenny when they were in D.C."

She laughed.

"Don't you want to see Norah?" she asked.

He frowned, scrunching up his face as he did so.

"You know, maybe that's not such a good idea," he said.

"Why?"

"You said she's doing well?"

"Yes," she replied. "Very."

"Seeing me, it might drag up some bad memories."

Lucy had not considered this. It reminded her of Jack's warning not to tell her about Emma. In both cases, the men had been advising her to keep the past in the past. For Norah's sake. But there was more to it here. Tim was telling her goodbye.

"Okay," she replied softly.

"Tell her I said hey."

"I will."

He leaned in as though he were going to kiss her. She froze, but she didn't turn away. Her eyes remained open, and at the last second, he changed course and pecked her gently on the cheek. He squeezed her arm gently.

"I hope we see each other again soon," he said.

"Me too."

He set a foot into the stirrup and swung the opposite leg over the saddle. He put a gentle heel into the horse's right flank and set her moving. Lucy watched as they receded into the distance, wishing he wasn't leaving but glad that he was.

15

On a Thursday night in mid-May, a massive line of thunderstorms swept across the region like a rolling locomotive. The day had started humid and hot; you could almost feel the air destabilizing. Shortly before sunset, the skies to the west darkened like a bruise. The wind picked up, blowing steadily across Promise. And when the storm finally blew, she did not mess around. It was a fantastic storm, one that Lucy stayed up watching. Slow moving, extremely electrified. Hundreds of lightning bolts fractured the night sky while sheets of rain swept across Promise. Lucy sat under the awning of the back porch of her medical clinic, absolutely mesmerized.

Her ankle was healing well, but a significant limp plagued her everyday movements. It had been two weeks since she had returned from her two-night adventure away from Promise. Upon her return, Jack had been none too pleased with either her or Norah. He had really let each of them have it, Lucy more than Norah. Lucy knew better; Norah, he was a bit easier on, his anger diluted by the stupid things teenagers did for love and the stupid things they did in general.

It had been a dumb thing to do, thought Lucy, looking back on it as the storm buffeted the James River. But it had been a necessary thing. She couldn't have Norah wandering off unattended. No, she should have not gone alone. Jack would have gone with her; in fact, his presence would likely have been a welcome buffer to the bone-on-bone experience that her relationship with Norah had become recently.

Not only that, but her solo mission had nearly cost Lucy her life. It would have been a stupid way to die, but people died for stupid reasons every day. She wasn't immune to such a fate. Some good had come of it, of course. The reunion with Tim Whitaker had been an unexpected and pleasant surprise. She found herself reliving the few precious hours they'd spent together. She lay awake at night thinking about him, and that was how it slowly dawned on her that she did want him after all.

Besides, there were worse ways to pass the time.

But alas, there was no time for that now or maybe ever. He had his people to look over, and she had hers. And Promise had a mighty big thorn in its side right now. At least they had a potential ally in their back pocket. Westerberg was a silent partner right now. She hoped it stayed that way.

The storm weakened over the next hour; the blowing downpours tapered off to a steady shower before stopping entirely. Lucy shuffled back to her room and went to bed. As the storm pushed off to the east, there was no way for anyone to know that that would be the last rain they would see for more than a month.

It easily escaped notice at first, and only when the grasses started to yellow a bit did they start to wonder when it had rained last. That sent them scurrying for their weather journals to check the precipitation log. Indeed, by the time they checked, it had been thirty-four days since their last measurable rainfall. And it would be a long time before they saw their next one.

Day after day, the sun broke from its nest and climbed hard into a piercing blue sky. No clouds in any direction. Even the stifling humidity failed to trigger the big storms that were normally frequent in Virginia in June. The sight of people craning their necks up, willing the skies to darken and bring the rains was commonplace. Then they would sigh, their shoulders sagging upon the realization that today wouldn't be the one for rain either.

Irrigation helped minimize the damage to the crops. It had been one of their earliest capital improvements—a complicated system of PVC piping drawing fresh water from the James River and to the fields. Without electrical power and bare knowledge drawn from old reference books in the country library, the system was difficult to operate and thus only used during the driest of spells. It impacted their output, costing them about a third of the expected June harvest.

And if the drought conditions had been their only problem, it might have been okay. They might have made it through the hot, dry summer unscathed. The first Friday of the month was close, but they just made their quota. But as they struggled to keep the crops hydrated, sometime around the second week of June, Promise was hit with an invasion of aphids. Lucy could not remember who'd first spotted them; they had been so careful, so careful. Mark Ellis, the farm manager, was particularly sensitive to pestilence and spent a good chunk of his time on watch for the slightest hint of invasion.

But aphids were particularly sneaky, and in this case, they had been particularly unlucky. They showed up in a sector of the farm that Jack had just finished inspecting the day before; by the time the next set of eyes hit that area, it was too late. Lucy walked the fields, her eyes filled with tears as she studied the mangled crops. Aphids suckled the sap from a wide range of cultivated plants, weakening them until they were barely clinging to life and compromising their ability to bear fruit.

They fought like junkyard dogs to curtail the damage, and only their yeoman's efforts prevented the insects from wiping out the complete harvest. But their early estimate, and this was being generous, was that they had lost fifty percent of the crop before bringing the infestation under control. Each of the next three weeks was a sphincter-clenching nightmare as they fought to meet the quota.

By the time the first Friday of July hit, Promise's cupboard was virtually barren.

They were going to miss their quota.

Lucy did not sleep a wink that night. She doubted many people did.

She was up at first light. Ironically, a heavy layer of clouds had moved in overnight, and it looked like a sure bet they would have some rain before the day was out.

The morning was more than a little symbolic. If someone had been writing a nonfiction account of their post-apocalyptic experience, of course it would be raining on the morning that they would fall short of their colonial obligations.

Her stomach rumbled. Like many others, she had contributed her meager rations to the children of Promise. She could manage a couple of days without food; the younger kids could not. Even they seemed to understand the pickle they were in. Not one said a word about the vegetables on their plate, slurping them down without complaint.

The morning dragged by interminably.

Part of her wanted it done already, even while another dreaded what lay ahead. They always said that waiting for the bad thing to happen was always worse than the bad thing actually happening. She wanted to believe that. But she had a terrible feeling that the bad thing was going to be much worse than the mere anticipation of it. She felt guilty for letting it come to this. Perhaps if they had worked a little harder, spent a little more time ruminating on it, they could have come up with a plan to come out from under the thumb of their mysterious overlords.

But that was wishful thinking.

Just because she was the hero of her own story did not make her invincible. There were bad people out there, and it was just their time in the barrel. She remained optimistic that they would figure a way out of this particular darkness, but it wasn't going to be today, and it might not be tomorrow or next month or even next year. But someday, they would find their way back into the light.

But before they could make it to any of those waypoints, first, they had to make it through today.

Today.

Just grant them a little mercy.

Already, the crops were recovering, and she was optimistic that they would have no problem meeting their next quota, even if they had to tighten their belts a little longer. They could do it. They would suffer, and it would be terrible, but things were trending in the right direction. Then they could focus on the fall harvest and pickling and canning. They could resume planning their independence from their oppressors.

Promise was extremely quiet that morning. People shuffled along without saying much to one another. Everyone knew that it was going to be a bad day, like a particularly bad trip to the dentist. Just get the tooth pulled and be done with it. It could only get better from here. In fact, a light sprinkle had been falling all morning. Not the purplish gray of thunderclouds, but better than the cobalt blue sky they'd been staring at for weeks.

Mark Ellis and Jack waited for the couriers at the main gate. Lucy lingered with another small group not far behind them. No need to draw it out. The dust cloud from the approaching horses harkened their arrival a good ten minutes before she put eyes on the Haven's crew. Right on schedule, the couriers arrived to pick up their weekly share. She hated how punctual they were. Promise was one of multiple tribute communities, and the fact they were always on time meant that the Haven had its shit together.

Three on horseback, accompanied by a fourth pulling the all-familiar wagon. Joshua was with them, as he always was. Lucy hated him and the way he fancied himself as some kind of ambassador. As though their familiarity with one another softened the monstrousness of their occupation of Promise.

He pulled back on the reins, a big smile on his dumb face.

"Well, don't I feel special?" he said, clapping a hand to his chest. "You two coming all the way up here to say hi."

He dismounted, spat on the ground, tucked his thumbs into his belt. He wore jeans, black boots, and a sleeveless, black leather jacket.

Why did everything have to be such a cliché in this world?

"How's everybody doing?"

"Look, Joshua, no point in beating around the bush," Mark said, "but we're short this week."

"How short?" he asked without a hint of emotion.

"We had a bit of a pest problem, but this dry spell really killed us."

"How. Short?"

"Really short," Jack said. "Maybe a quarter."

He clicked his tongue rapidly against his teeth. It sounded like a rattlesnake in the weeds.

"That is disappointing."

Lucy's heart was beating rapidly against her ribcage. They had never discussed the specific consequences of failing to meet the quota, but it was clear that it wouldn't be anything good.

"You know, we're hoping you can cut us a break this time," Lucy said.

The Council had agreed on this approach last night. They wouldn't beg, but there was no harm in negotiating. Promise had been a good producer, easily meeting their quotas every week. Even last week, when it had been a close call, and there had been empty tummies throughout Promise, they had delivered a complete share. Their luck had simply run out.

Joshua retreated to the rider on the horse-drawn wagons and exchanged a few words with him. The man handed him a slip of paper. Then he slowly approached Lucy and Jack, tapping his hands together, his lips pressed tightly together. Lucy watched him like a hawk. This was going to end badly.

"I'm disappointed," he said. "We've come to rely on you. You're one of our best producers."

"All the more reason to give us a break."

He lit a cigarette, smoked it quietly, crushed it under his boot. The quad had fallen quiet. The silence was almost painful. No one spoke.

"I wish I could agree with you," he said.

Another stretch of awkward silence.

"You see, our world is an unforgiving one," Joshua said, pacing around Lucy and Jack. "We fight against that with order. Without order, there is chaos. And if there is chaos, it all comes undone."

He paused when he'd come back face-to-face with Lucy.

"Undone."

Another silence.

"Do you want everything to come undone?" he asked. "Well? Do you?"

"No."

"No! Of course not. I don't know about you, but I don't want to go back to the early days when we were killing each other like dogs for a can of baked beans."

He disengaged from Lucy and Jack and addressed the crowd that had formed.

"Do you want to kill each other for baked beans?"

No one replied, but there was a smattering of unenthusiastic head shakes.

"See?" he said, refocusing back on Lucy.

"So what happens now?"

"Now we make it clear that there are consequences. So there is no misunderstanding. If I call your name, please step forward."

He rattled off five names.

Robert Finney

Esther Schwartz

Paul Poytress

Jacob Campos

Michael Lopez

The four men and one woman came forward. Lucy clenched her fists so tightly that the nails cut tiny crescent moons into her skin, leaving her with four bloody smirks in each palm. To be at such terrible mercy of another. But what choice did they have? They had yet to even locate the Haven. And when they came to Promise, they came in force. They were simply outmanned and outgunned. She could do the math.

Lucy had hoped to use the summer to gather intel on

the group and exploit their weaknesses. Jack was not as patient. If today was about to go sideways, and all indications were that it was indeed about to do that, he would be difficult to corral.

Joshua walked the chorus line of the terrified group, up and down, up and down, like a drill sergeant inspecting a new batch of recruits. Then in the blink of an eye, he placed a gun to the forehead of one Robert Finney, triggering a ripple of groans and murmurs from the crowd. He fired a single shot into the man's forehead. Finney's body dropped like a puppet whose string had been cut. A few screams pierced the silence, but only a few. As though what had just happened was expected.

As for Joshua, his summary execution of Robert Finney did not appear to faze him. He continued walking the line up and down. One of the remaining four, Paul Poytress, doubled over and vomited. Several were crying, but no one moved.

Lucy felt sick herself. This group's capacity for inhumanity was difficult to process. But they were a conquered people now, and this was how it was. You had your victors and your vanquished, and if the victors turned out to be like their occupiers, well then God help you.

Joshua paused once more before the line of potential victims. Finney's body still lay where it had fallen, leaving a noticeable gap between Paul and Esther. He stepped toward Esther and placed a hand gently on her shoulder. Her eyes cut to the ground. She did not look at him. She was an older black woman; she had remained deeply religious and led a weekly faith service at Promise.

"I'm sorry you had to see that," he said.

Her eyes remained focused squarely on the ground.

He tilted her chin upward so they were eye to eye.

"But it's important," he said. "In furtherance of something greater than all of us. This is the beginning of something wondrous. Do you understand?"

She nodded subtly.

Then he shot Esther in the forehead.

16

August.

Although the days were still long, they had grown noticeably shorter than the fertile days of early summer. In June, the light clung to the day like a baby to its mother, but now, like a teenager, daylight seemed ready to flee at the first opportunity. The warmth held on, however, even well after sunset. The air was thick with the heat that had built up over the day. All in all, Virginia's hottest month of the year had not disappointed. Sometimes Lucy pictured a red bulb of mercury at the tip of an old thermometer inflating and then bursting like in the old cartoons. The saving grace was that the long drought had finally ended. Every day or two, big thunderclouds fired up to the west and delivered a good soaking. They were lucky. Rain was normally scarce in August unless a mid-summer tropical system snuck ashore and sent waves of moisture a hundred miles inland.

After the summer they'd had, they needed a bit of

luck. Just something to get them through. The rain had helped. The crops had recovered, and within a month, they were close to their pre-drought output. The next couple of Fridays had been close, and there had been some tightening of the belts, but they had made it. But this week, everything had come together. A number of plants that they'd given up on had started to bear fruit. There was enough to meet the quota and plenty to eat. The couriers had left in the middle of the afternoon, their bizarre horse-drawn pickup truck chassis loaded down with the fruits of their labor, taking what did not belong to them. It physically pained Lucy to see them leave with their blood, sweat, and tears. Tonight, they had feasted. They sat around and filled their bellies with flatbread, roasted tomatoes, zucchini, and cheese they had made themselves. They got drunk on terrible moonshine fermented from potatoes. Afterward, they sat by the fire, despite the heat, and kept drinking. A few older teenagers snuck in a few nips at the bottle; no one seemed to care. They did not get away with it, as they believed. Teens never got away with it. Not from the first time that a teenager had raided their parents' liquor cabinet, back before they even had liquor cabinets. Wherever they stored beer back in the early days of beer making.

Fireflies pinged the fragrant air. In the absence of artificial light, they had made a huge comeback these past five years. Lucy recalled articles about the rapid demise of lightning bugs each year. The Pulse had taken care of that in a hurry. This time of year, they were ubiquitous in the evenings, a decidedly American version of the Northern Lights.

It was a delightful evening, but as Lucy sat near the fire, she remained troubled. It seemed as though everyone had just moved on from the horrific executions of Esther and Robert. This wasn't the case, of course. Everyone grieved in their own way. And life had to move on. She understood the need to celebrate when they could.

Fulfilling the weekly quota was a relief, especially after the horror they'd endured. Knowing they had a little time to breathe before the next pickup left them feeling good, like they had accomplished something. It was a dumbass thing to think, of course, to be proud of your new role as a supplicant. To be happy with the scraps. To be happy with the scraps of a bounty that you yourself had seen to.

The loss of life they'd seen was shocking. Promise had seen relatively little bloodshed during its fragile existence. These were people who still had full, clear memories of the old days, and it was hard on all of them to see such violence. That wouldn't always be the case as they continued to peel off calendar pages.

But they had been beaten. Lucy could see it in their faces. She could see it in her own face. Beaten. Much of it stemmed from the violent deaths of their fellow citizens. It was this kind of loss that inured you to the way the world was. It was the most depressing education one could imagine.

But still it nagged at her. The laughter, the merriment.

How could they enjoy themselves if they were just one bad step away from another bloodbath at the hands of the Haven?

Lucy stuffed her hands in her pockets and stomped away from the campfire. Her celebratory mood was fading, and she wanted to be alone. She wanted to see Tim. He would understand. He would not have participated in this folly. Together they would develop a plan, a strategy to take down the Haven.

Drink. She needed to drink. She went back to the campfire and asked for the bottle from Teresa. She took a long swig of the swill, recoiling as it burned her throat, but continued her long drink. Then she handed the bottle back to Teresa, her face hot and her head swimmy, and stomped off. Nothing mattered. It was how it was. Maybe she was the one who had it wrong, and her neighbors had the right idea. What was the central tenet of hedonism? A lesson from her AP English teacher, Mrs. Key, came back to her: *eat, drink, and be merry, for tomorrow we die*. Was it Shakespeare? No, she didn't think so. It was too harsh and not poetic enough for Shakespeare. Well, fuck off, Bill. Sometimes, clear and to the point was better than poetry.

Eat, drink, and be merry, for tomorrow we die.

She laughed.

There was no stopping what was coming.

They were like locusts, the Haven, and they would suck Promise dry. There was no wider community to be a part of. Like a Mafia capo, they would take all they could. Sure, you got your protection as long as you paid the piper, but once the goodies stopped flowing, they would burn it down. In the case of Promise, the outcome would be far worse. They would just die. Maybe not right away. When it became apparent that the end was near, the place would just fall in on itself like a deck of cards. No one would fight because there would be nothing to fight for. Why kill yourself when there was nothing left but a barren cupboard and empty bellies? You would take your chances out on the road. That's how it worked. Communities rose and fell every day. You weren't special. It was like the story of western civilization. Empires rose and fell, and now it was happening in miniature on a grand scale.

Despite the heat, a somewhat fresh breeze was blowing through the camp. A hint of fall hidden away in there behind the curtain of humidity.

They still knew very little about the Haven. Jack had tried following once, but each group was accompanied by decoys who took different routes, crisscrossing this way and that until it was impossible to figure out which horse or wagon was headed where. Jack abandoned his pursuit, worried that he might have been spotted.

Lucy shouldn't have been drinking so much.

She wasn't necessarily on call, as that was an anachronism of a time gone by, but she wasn't *not* on call either. And on a night like tonight, with many Promise residents good and lubricated by their moonshine, her services could well be in demand. Fights, overindulgence, accidental injuries sustained by ever more dangerous dares.

Despite the alcohol flowing through her veins, or perhaps because of it, Lucy was growing more agitated. Fall would be coming soon, the final harvest of the season. After that, the supplies would grow thinner than they already were. The summer had been fruitful, and in past years, they would have been canning their surplus for the winter. But the surplus had gone to Joshua's, so the winter cupboard was already close to bare.

"Do you people have any idea what's coming?" she finally snapped.

Her voice was thick and harsh and sliced through the banal conversations like hot steel through flesh. The remaining revelers fell silent, glancing at her, embarrassed.

"Y'all are celebrating like we got something to celebrate," she went on. "We're digging our own graves."

Lucy looked around the semi-circle of revelers surrounding the fire, but none held her gaze.

"Winter will be here before you know it," she said, climbing to her feet. She snatched the bottle out of Teresa's hands and splashed the liquid onto the fire. It triggered a large flash of flame, large enough to send people scurrying backward. A few people yipped in pain, singed by the bloom of fire.

"And we're not gonna have enough to eat."

"But—"

"But nothing!" Lucy shouted. "If we keep giving them such a big cut, we are going to starve. The rations we have left will be barely enough to keep the strongest alive. The older ones? They won't make it. Half the kids will die."

"They won't let us die, will they?" someone asked.

"They don't care if we live or die," Lucy said. "They will suck us dry. And if we all die, then they will just move on."

"We'll figure something out," someone said.

"Will we?"

She flung another splash of moonshine on the fire, triggering another bloom.

"Goddammit, we have to do something," she said. "We can't keep doing this."

The group fell silent as Lucy stormed off into the darkness. It was quiet but for the crackle and whoosh of the rippling blaze, embers floating off into the ether of the night. Jack followed her to her cottage.

"Luce?"

She ignored him, muttering under her breath as she looked for something.

"Lucy," he repeated, this time with heft in his voice.

She stopped pawing through her belongings, sitting back on her haunches.

"What?"

"What were you thinking?"

"Speaking truth."

He sighed and let it out slowly.

"I'm not sure that was the best way to go about it."

"And why not?

"You scared them."

"Good," she said. "Maybe they need to be a little scared. Hell, I'm scared."

"Scared of what?"

"That we've already lost."

"We'll figure something out."

"You think so?"

There was a fatalism in her voice.

Lucy's mood was as sour as she could ever remember. It had been since the executions two weeks earlier. Sure, they had gotten back on track, but it didn't mean much to her. What mattered was the loss of these two people she had lived alongside these last few years. Robert had been a librarian, Esther a church secretary. The murders had cast a pall over the community darker than the deaths accompanying their initial takeover. A harsh reminder that they were at the mercy of the Haven. Promise was no longer in charge of its own destiny.

That was what depressed Lucy the most – the sense that she was no longer in control of her own life. You didn't jump through their hoops? Too bad, here's another body for you to bury. They were like trained monkeys. No better than that. You just did what you were told, and maybe if you did it just the right way, you'd get a handful of peanuts.

They'd all been reduced to automatons. Get up, go through the motions of your daily life, the one you thought you once owned. But now those motions were dictated by someone else. All in furtherance of delivering the share that their masters had requested.

"We have to do something," she said, her words slow and slurred from the alcohol.

"We will," Jack said as she fell asleep.

Lucy started sleeping a lot.

It was strange. She had never been much of a sleeper. Even as a child. It had driven her poor mother crazy. For baby Lucy, sleeping through the night never meant more than a few hours at a stretch. This continued through adolescence, high school, and into college. Last one to bed, first one up. Her body just never demanded it. Of course, she knew about the health benefits of sleep and often wondered if she was driving herself to an early grave by not getting enough shuteye. It wasn't like she didn't try. She had knocked off the screens two hours before bed, she didn't have a television in her bedroom, all the things they told you were conducive to a good night's sleep.

And she didn't ever feel shortchanged on rest. Four hours for Lucy were like eight for the average person. She didn't nap, she didn't get tired in the afternoon. Even when she had worked the overnight shift early in her nursing career, she had no problem pushing through the graveyard hours. A cup of coffee every now and again, but even that was for the social aspects, something to do with the other nurses yawning, struggling to keep their eyes open at four-thirty in the morning.

When Emma had gotten sick, sleep was nothing but a nuisance, a thief of her time with her daughter. She didn't sleep when Emma was awake, and she sure didn't sleep when Emma was asleep. She sat with her for hours and watched her sleep. Even when the prognosis had been optimistic, Lucy took no chances. She didn't want to look back and think she should have spent more time awake.

Then the Pulse had happened, and she had gotten by on even less sleep than ever. Two hours at a stretch, maybe three after a long day, and she had really pushed herself. It was better to have both eyes open as often as possible.

Until now.

After her blowup at the group, she slept deep into the next day, even outsleeping the hangover. Conveniently, no one needed major medical care and no one came looking for her. What was the point of getting up if there was nothing to do? If there was nothing she *could* do.

And when she was awake, she began looking forward to when she could get back to sleep. Sleep was another world, another life, away from this terrible place. There was always the possibility she would see Emma in this otherworld. There was no seeing Emma here, no sir, Emma was dead and gone, and Lucy would be stuck in this mortal coil for God knew how long, separated from the thing she loved better than anything else that had ever existed in the universe. But in the darkness of her unconscious mind, Emma lived forever, Emma was eternal. And it didn't matter how weird or strange the dreams were, and it didn't matter that when she woke up, Emma would be gone because in that sliver of time, in that moment on that other plane of existence, she and Emma were together again.

It wasn't real, people would say, and that was why she didn't tell anyone.

Who were they to say what was real and what wasn't?

In this world, in the world they said was reality, they didn't have enough to eat, and there was no way to know if on any given Friday, someone would end the day with a Haven bullet in their head. Sure, sometimes, the horrors of the real world spilled over into her dreams, and sometimes she had to watch Emma die again. But that was okay, because there was always the chance that the next dream would find them eating ice cream on a hot summer day, the melting treat drip, drip, dripping on the sidewalk as they rushed to finish it.

She worried people would start to notice how much she was sleeping, so she began hiding in her clinic. She shut the door to her small office and started taking naps on her cot. The canvas was hell on her back, but she didn't care. Her excuse for spending so much time in her office was the development of a new records system for the residents of Promise. That was why the door was closed. *If you need me*, she would say, *just knock. I'll be here.*

It became a thing. She got to work at seven in the morning and saw patients. In between visits, she hid away in her office and slept. Around her, life continued unabated. There was so much to do. As long as she fulfilled her obligation to provide medical care, no one seemed to care about the manner in which she provided it.

But there was no new record-keeping system.

There was no point in it.

Promise was winding down. Promise was dying. You could almost hear it. The big seams holding their society together starting to split. She watched the others through the window, scurrying to and fro, and she wanted to yell at them to just stop, just give it up already. Better to cut bait now than to live this pipe dream that it was all going to work out. Close out the bar tab now and move on with their lives. If they waited until fall or winter, operating under the erroneous assumption that they would defeat the Haven, they would be left holding a bill they couldn't afford to pay.

It was early on a Thursday morning. She was treating Mark Ellis for a bad cut on his hand. She cleaned and debrided as best she could. Then she applied some antibiotic cream (old, expired, what was the point? She was going through the motions). As she finished bandaging his wound, her ears pricked up at the sound of the horses whinnying from the stable.

"Keep it clean," she said as he made his way out. "Keep an eye out for any sign of infection like we talked about. Redness, warmth, fever."

"Got it," he said. "Thanks, Lucy."

The clinic fell quiet once more.

She went outside, drawn toward the horses.

Drawn to the horses, drawn to the possibility of escape. That's what she should have been doing. Planning to get out of here. Preparing Norah for the inevitability of what was to come. Promise was dying.

Then she found herself at the stables. No one else was around. The animals had had their morning meal, and in the heat of the day, were left to rest in the shade of the stables. She knew better than going out again on her own, but she couldn't stop herself. But it was like someone else was controlling her. First her foot was in the stirrup and then she swung her leg over the saddle. There, in the quiet heat of the morning, she sat atop the horse, gently stroking its mane.

She hopped back off and opened the stable doors; then she remounted Pancake and sat before the wide open before her. She needed to stop this. She needed to climb back down and head back to the clinic. But even as she was thinking these things, she had quietly guided Pancake out of the barn and toward the woods on the southern edge of the settlement. She hugged the tree line until she made it to the main road, then turned northeast.

Eat, drink, and be merry, for tomorrow we die.

The refrain played over and over in her head. The voice of her English teacher echoing in her head. She had been a good teacher. Instead of constantly focusing on dry and stuffy short stories, she taught them poetry and song lyrics and novels and screenplays, all the media that combined and taught them the power of the written word.

Lucy wanted to believe that she was just out for a ride, that she didn't have a particular destination in mind. But as she drifted further from the borders of Promise, it was like another Lucy had taken control, a grown-up Lucy, a Lucy who did not lie to herself.

Even in the fog of pain, returning to Promise from Westerberg, she had committed the route to memory. It wasn't as if Tim didn't want her to know where he was. He could have blindfolded her after all. No, he wanted her to know. In case she ever found herself in dire straits, if she ever came to such a pass that she needed help that no one else could provide.

It was funny. Of all the thousands of hours of her life, she'd only spent about twenty-four of them with Tim Whitaker. Less than that, now that she thought about it. A few hours at the high school where they had first met. Another sixteen or so during the rescue of Norah from that psychopath, Simon. And yet she still felt close to him after all of these years. He had not become a memory, after all. He wasn't something tucked away in a dusty, old box that you looked at from time to time. He was bolted onto her soul.

There was something special about their connection. Every now and again, you would meet someone like that. Someone who made you feel like they should have been part of your life all along, that there had been a hole in your life in the shape of that person all this time. Fortunately for her, and fortunately for Norah, she had met Tim Whitaker when she needed him the most. Even if she hadn't realized it at the time.

She had traveled at least a dozen miles in her fugue state, somehow cleaving to the route to the warehouse. It was a warm day, and she was very thirsty. She hadn't even thought to bring a bottle of water with her. What was she thinking? Just giving a middle finger to the way the world was? This world didn't care; it would chew her up and spit her out.

Jack would go ballistic when he found out she had left again. She even had the perfect comeback for him.

At least I'm out of bed...

The joke wouldn't have gone over well. That alone brought a smile to her face.

A cloud drifted in front of the sun and brought her some much-needed shade. Her skin felt tight with sunburn.

All these years, she and Tim had been separated by no more than thirty miles. It made her sad to think about it. She'd been here, and he'd been there, and they might as well have been on two different planets for all the good their proximity had done. It was emblematic of their world now. You felt all alone because you were all alone.

They were embroiled in this terrible struggle with the Haven now, a struggle that meant nothing to no one outside their little bubble. Even if the Haven controlled all of central Virginia, that didn't mean a hell of a lot in the grand scheme of things.

After all, that was why she was going to see Tim.

Wasn't it?

For Promise?

Or was it for her?

She had been so ready to declare Promise dead. Was this little trip in furtherance of that, or was she looking for a way to save the patient? What could Tim offer? Her community had twice as many people as Tim's. She couldn't ask for supplies. He couldn't spare a single can.

Hell, even treating her to a meal had been an act of extraordinary generosity you really couldn't afford these days. But maybe he would want to join their fight. Maybe he wanted to join her fight.

She turned onto Route 245, the last turn before the access road to the distribution warehouse came into view. The trees thinned out behind her. Ahead was clear grassland, gently rolling hills in the Virginia countryside. It looked like a grand, green quilt of farmland. Corn growing tall and green, the silks and stalks rippling in the afternoon breeze. Whose corn, she did not know. Perhaps it was Tim's. He would be resourceful like that.

The outer gate of the warehouse was a hundred yards up the road.

Her heart was pounding in her chest. She was as nervous as she'd been on her first date so many years ago. Firing through her was a machine gun of emotions. Fear, anticipation, regret, anxiety, excitement.

She didn't even know what she would say when she saw him. Even though that was so unlike her. Lucy Goodwin was not one to improvise. She liked thinking ahead, having a plan. It gave her a sense of control, especially in situations where control was an ethereal thing, as easy to grab as a puff of smoke.

But the more she tried to come up with a plan, the more confused she became.

She drew back the reins of the horse, bringing him to a halt right in the middle of the roadway under the shade of a single great oak tree, its canopy curling oddly over the asphalt. The leaves rippled in the warm afternoon breeze.

Just turn around and go home.

You have no business here.

She froze.

She'd lost her nerve to continue, but she could not bring herself to turn around either. She would just wait here in the shade until she died of thirst. Yeah, that was the ticket. Lucy Goodwin, dead at age forty-four from paralysis and indecision.

Then the decision was made for her.

Out here in the open.

Someone was calling out to her.

It was Tim.

18

Tim began jogging toward her, a look of concern on his face.

Why was he running? she wondered.

Not that she minded watching him run toward her. He was still in good shape. Probably made it a requirement for anyone who lived here to stay in top physical condition. Not a bad idea, maybe one they should implement back home. Steel themselves. Become stronger and faster. It was a dog-eat-dog world after all. Survival of the fittest. The muscles in his legs, the way his chest filled out the dry-fit shirt he wore. Wow, Lucy Goodwin, just wow, you've really made contact with the horny teenager you were thirty years ago.

"Lucy, are you okay?" he asked upon reaching her. He placed his hand against her leg, not in a titillating way, more to stabilize her. Still, it felt good, the touch of his hand.

"I think so," she said, feeling faint even as she replied.

"Let's get you out of this heat."

Was it hot?

She hadn't even noticed.

She really should have brought a bottle of water with her.

She glanced down at her arms, which seemed redder than she recalled. The skin was tight and stiff. *Sunburn,* came a voice inside her head. *Your dumb ass is sunburned.* Suddenly, a wave of shame washed over her, and everything became clear. Again, she was here, brought to Tim's doorstep by her own misfortune.

He climbed up on the horse and took the reins as she sagged against his back. He guided the animal inside the gates of his community and led it to a shady corner of the property. He sent a young man for water.

The young man, his face pockmarked with acne, brought a bowl and set it on a low-slung loading dock. The horse drank immediately and hugely. The boy handed Lucy two bottles of water. It was lukewarm, of course, but cold water was a rarity in the summer. Wintertime, when the brooks and creeks and springs ran ice cold, when you wanted it least, you could have all the cold water you wanted.

As she drank, he led her to a new part of the facility, one she hadn't seen during her previous trip here. A series of prefabricated mobile trailers lined the back of the property, roughly a dozen. She followed him to the one on the end, at the very northwest corner of the property. It was cool and dark inside.

She smiled.

This was home. This was where Tim lived.

"I'm sorry it's such a mess," he said, flitting about,

cleaning up the clutter of everyday life. Books and plates and dirty clothes and such. There were three maps on the wall; one of the immediate vicinity, one of the state of Virginia, and one of the continental United States. She looked nostalgically at the names of the states, which sadly no longer had any meaning.

"Please, have a seat," he said, gesturing toward one of the sofas.

She sat down. It felt good to sit. She had drained one bottle and moved on to the next. Her folly was coming into clearer focus. She felt like a damn fool.

He sat next to her.

"How's that ankle?"

"Not bad," she said. "Stiffens up if I'm on my feet all day. Which, fortunately, only happens on days ending in -y."

This drew a laugh. It pulled attention away from the gigantic fool she'd made of herself on this little excursion. This was worse than what Norah had done. Even she had been smart enough to travel with proper supplies. Lucy had done it like someone with a death wish.

Hell, maybe she did have a death wish.

Maybe she would see Emma again. What was so bad about that? As good a reason as any to believe in God and angels and heaven and hell. It scared her to think these things, but she still thought them.

"What are you doing here?"

She scraped her forehead with the nail of her thumb. The sound was huge in the eerie quiet of the trailer.

Dear God, what had she done?

She had nearly gotten herself and the horse killed.

All of a sudden, it was very, very hot.

And that's when she understood that she had come here for herself. Not for Promise. But for her. Deep bolts of shame rocketed through her. Shame that she had given up on her family. That's what the people of Promise were, they were family. Likely the only family she would ever have. And she had turned her back on them. When they had needed her, she had scolded them like children. When they had tried to distill a little joy from the darkness, she had mocked them.

"I don't even know."

She was afraid to look at him. Afraid that if he saw her face, he would know she had made this trip, come all this way in the heat, so desperate to get here that she hadn't even bothered with a bottle of water, just to see him.

"Lucy," he said, leaning forward, elbows on his knees, his hands clasped together. "Look, I know we don't really know each other very well. But it feels like we do. You know? I so badly wanted to go back to the farm with you that day. I just couldn't."

"I know," she replied. "It was unfair for me to ask. I shouldn't have asked."

"I'm glad you asked," he said. "It told me a lot about you. I was basically a stranger to you. Still am, in a lot of ways. But we went through something that night, right?"

She nodded.

"Yeah. Yeah, I guess we did."

He chuckled softly to himself.

"You know what I'm doing here?" he asked.

She shrugged her shoulders.

"I mean, here, still in Virginia?"

She shook her head.

"I'm here because of you," he said, nodding his head. "It's true. I've been kicking myself for five years, losing that piece of paper. You're the bravest person I've ever met. The most amazing person I've ever met. What you did to save me, to save Norah, I've never seen anything like it in my life."

Tears welled up in her eyes. She didn't want to hear these things. She didn't deserve to have things like that said about her. She was a coward and a quitter. she doubted Tim would still think so highly of her once he knew the truth. That she had given up. That their time in Promise was over.

"It's over for us," she said.

"What do you mean?"

"We can't keep up. Meeting the Haven's quota. It's too much. We're gonna starve. Maybe not next week or next month, but certainly by this winter. They're just too strong, too powerful."

He leaned back in his seat, tapped his fingers together.

If she knew him like she thought she did, right now, he was thinking about absorbing Promise into his community. The way he had plied her, Norah, and her late friend, Manny, with pudding cups and energy drinks at the high school when he hadn't known them from a hole in the wall. Probably the most touching act of kindness she had seen in all the time since the Panic. He'd had no reason to help them other than to be kind.

"Don't even think about it," she said.

She wouldn't let him do it. She had to cut him off before the thought gained too much momentum in his generous little head. He had responsibilities and people to look after. They were his charge now, not Lucy.

"About what?"

"You're not taking us on."

"Just listen to me," he said.

"No," she said. "You don't want any part of this, and I won't let you risk these people's lives for us."

"Will you at least hear me out?"

"This isn't like back at the high school," she said. "Pudding cups and such."

"Maybe you and Norah can come here."

He said it with little authority because he knew what she would say.

"You know I can't do that," she said. "I already feel like a big enough coward. I can't turn my back on them."

"But if Promise falls, you'll need to go somewhere."

She shook her head and scoffed.

"I shouldn't have come here," she said.

"I'm glad you did," he said. "And I really think you should reconsider."

"It would be wrong," she said. She couldn't explain how or why it would be wrong. It was like a conflict of interest. If she had a landing spot already lined up, she might be more inclined to quit. Promise deserved better. Jack deserved better. Those who had already died, their memories deserved better.

He chuckled sadly.

"I know. I know you wouldn't do it."

Tim looked up at the ceiling, chewing on his lower

lip. They'd drawn closer together on the couch, their knees barely touching. Her heart was racing. She hated not seeing him anymore. She hated knowing that after today, she would likely never see him again, and that there would be a hole inside her for the rest of her days. How could she so desperately miss someone she barely knew?

She reached out and lay a hand on his knee. He glanced down at it intently, as though it were a grenade. Perhaps it was. Perhaps she wanted it to blow up. She didn't make another move, but she did not remove her hand either. She would leave it up to him. She didn't want to say goodbye without saying goodbye.

After what seemed like an eternity, he placed his left hand over hers. His right hand had slipped behind her neck and was drawing her face close to his. Their lips touched briefly before they drew apart once more, the pair taking a moment to process what had just happened. Electricity flowed through her, and she decided not to wait a second longer. She pushed him against the seat-back of the couch and straddled his upper thighs. She took his face in her hands and kissed him the way she had thought about kissing him for a long time. His hands snaked around her back as she paused to remove her t-shirt. His hands were strong and callused from the years of work since the Pulse.

He stopped for a moment, chuckling as he did so. He caressed her arms, her neck, tracing his finger around the swell of her breasts and down the flat of her stomach.

"Not bad."

She slapped him lightly.

"Glad you approve."

He gently rolled her off him, yanking down her jeans and underwear, pulling down his own pants, pushing up against her and then inside her. He kissed her deeply, and she closed her eyes, and it all drained away. Every terrible thing that had ever happened to her, for a brief, wondrous moment, simply vanished. Like some trick of an illusionist, if you turned your head just so, it was all gone, the loss of her Emma to the loss of their world to the coming collapse of Promise. He finished quickly, just as her orgasm burst through her, and a sharp cry emanated from her throat. It was as if this thing had to happen quickly because it was all this world would allow. Just a brief flash of happiness. Try to take more than that, and you would be punished.

He rolled off her, understanding this was a one-time event, that this was not the appetizer for a night of crazy sex. This had been two people telling each other without words what they meant to each other amid the horror the world had seen fit to unleash upon them.

After getting dressed again, they sat quietly on the couch, entwined in each other's arms. Neither said a word, the room silent but for their calm breathing until they fell asleep.

19

Lucy was at breakfast a month later when she began to feel ill. A wave of nausea, and then another, and then another. She blew out a shaky breath, hoping to steady her stomach. She sat at the table as long as she could, but eventually, the decision was made for her. She bolted outside and curled around to the back of the cafeteria just in time for her breakfast to make an unwelcome reappearance. Her legs were shaky, and she pressed a hand to the wall to keep herself up. A chill ran through her. Her skin was clammy and cool, and she wasn't feverish. Her bowels felt normal. A bizarre occurrence of emesis. She took the day off, carefully monitoring her vital signs. But everything seemed normal. Her temperature, blood pressure, pulse, respiration, all within normal limits.

Illness was their biggest fear. It had been months since the coronavirus scare, and they had been fairly lucky since. Granted, summer was a low point for the spread of disease, but as their caloric and nutritional needs went increasingly unmet, they were ripe for a new outbreak. And in a weakened state, they might not recover as quickly, even assuming they recovered at all.

She felt better the rest of the day and all the next day, but she experienced another episode on a quiet Sunday morning. This one struck her as she lay in bed, listening to an early autumn rain patter the rooftops. Again, she worked on her breathing, shaky and ragged, attempting to settle her stomach. It was the oddest sensation. She wasn't hungry, but she wasn't *not* hungry either.

The only other time she'd felt like this was--

She hopped out of bed like she'd been launched from a cannon. Her legs rocked under her, and for a moment, they started to buckle, threatening to send her to the floor. She eased her bottom back down to the bed as it hit her.

The only other time she'd felt like this was when she'd been pregnant with Emma.

It was early. the cottage was still quiet. Dawn was breaking, but full daylight was still an hour away. Probably around five in the morning. She laughed. Pregnant. She was not pregnant. She could not be pregnant.

But then it all came back to her, all at once. Her one and only time with Tim. She did the math. A month, six weeks at the most since she'd ridden up there for a booty call. That's what it was, Luce. It was a booty call, and don't you dare deny it. How quickly did morning sickness begin to manifest? Certainly four weeks was too soon. Wasn't it?

And besides, they'd used protection.

Hadn't they?

She wasn't on the pill anymore because there were no more pills to be on. They'd been one of the first medications to disappear in the aftermath of the Pulse. She'd had a three-month supply, and when those had run out, that had been that.

Certainly, as responsible adults, they would have used some kind of protection. At least one of them would have taken the time to... what? Run down to the convenience store for a three-pack of condoms? Come on, Luce.

They had not used protection.

Oh boy, would her health teacher not be impressed with her.

Her parents either.

At least with Emma, she had been on the pill. The pill had just failed her.

This, though, was her own failure. Her and Tim's together.

Wait, wait, wait.

It wasn't a definite thing yet. The clinic. She needed to get to the clinic. Although they were out of oral contraceptives, there was still a stockpile of pregnancy tests. She pulled on a sweatshirt and a pair of shorts, absently caressing her belly as she did so.

The sun was rising by the time she got to the clinic. There were only two inpatients currently. A dehydrated farm hand receiving intravenous fluids and a terminal cancer patient. Both were asleep. Terri, her nursing assistant, was on call, snoozing on the cot. She tiptoed to the stockroom and foraged through the supplies until she found the test kit.

She pocketed it and made her way out to the woods for some privacy. She did not want to risk being interrupted while peeing on the stick. There was a thick grove of trees about twenty yards in; it saw little activity, even among the kids. The brush was too thick. Confident that she was alone, she opened the kit and studied the instructions. It was one of the fancier ones—it actually displayed the words PREGNANT or NOT PREGNANT in the result window. She lowered her shorts and crouched over the stick, balancing herself against a tree as she peed. It would take about three minutes for the result to register. When she was done, she pulled her shorts back on and began to wait. The tree was huge but oddly shaped. Its trunk was massive; two people could hug it without their hands touching. Its thick branches were low to the ground. Lucy wedged her foot against a divot in the root and hoisted herself up onto the branch, the test stick clenched between two fingers.

It had been ages since she had last climbed a tree, at least thirty years. Checkpoints on the way to adulthood. She and Jack had grown up in a rural county. Their yard bordered a large forest to the south featuring plenty of climbable trees. There had been a last time, of course. One day, she had climbed down from a tree and she had never gone back. There were a lot of last times in your life, and you didn't even know it until the last time was well behind you. The last time you held your child's hand. The last time you played in a softball game. At forty-four, a survivor of a paradigm-altering disaster, her life was riddled with things she had done for the last time.

One of those things should have been getting pregnant.

Forty-four.

Forty-four-year-old women didn't get pregnant.

Well, of course they did, it just didn't happen that often.

Another emotion swirled through her.

Guilt.

She felt guilty.

Because of Emma.

Having another baby would be wrong. She'd had her chance to be a mother, and it was disrespectful of Emma's memory to be pregnant again. Wasn't it? But why would she think that?

Emma wouldn't care.

What a weird thing to think.

Many strange thoughts zoomed through her head as the three-minute clock ticked down slowly. She kept staring at the blank result window. No three-minute span in human history had ever taken as long as these three minutes.

What if it was positive?

What if she were actually pregnant? She would have to think about the baby.

It would change everything.

She would have to leave Promise.

She might have to take Tim up on his offer. They would be safe there.

They would be safe until the Haven set its sights on Tim.

Could she be a mother again?

Norah.

What would Norah think?

She would hate Lucy all over again. She would feel abandoned. Amid their fighting and conflict, she would think Lucy had done it on purpose, gotten pregnant out of spite. That she was replacing her with a new model. This made Lucy tear up, this irrational thought, because that's what pregnant women did. Their minds became fertile ground for irrational thoughts.

Three minutes.

It had to have been three minutes by now. She shut her eyes tightly.

The test stick trembled in her hand as she lifted it to eye level. Her whole body was shaking now, so much so that she had to steady herself with her free hand lest she tumble from the branch.

Down will come baby, cradle and all.

She opened her eyes.

The word floated in the window.

PREGNANT

20

She carried the stick back to her room, not caring that it was stained with her urine. She would want to check it again later, just in case she had been hallucinating. Maybe her eyes were playing tricks on her. Maybe she just wanted to be pregnant for some reason she could not fathom, a secret rationale or motivation hidden away deep inside her.

She floated through the rest of the day. And the next, and the next. Three days, she felt like she was outside her own body, looking down at the story of someone else.

She checked the stick twenty-six times.

PREGNANT

She was pregnant.

A symphony of emotions swirled through her. Fear, joy, terror, love, anxiety. It came back to her, the nine months she had carried Emma. The nuts and bolts of it. The morning sickness hadn't been terrible. It hadn't been a walk in the park either, mind you, but it was manageable. She hadn't started to show until near the end of the first trimester; if the same form followed, she would have some time to keep it to herself.

She was pregnant.

She had not given any thought to having more children. Emma's death, of course, had cast a long shadow over her life. It threatened to swallow everything that was Lucy Goodwin. But it hadn't. Not really. There had been room for Norah in her heart. And she loved Norah. Truly, she did, with her whole self. Of course there would be room for a baby.

Something inside her began to stir.

She went to see Jack at the end of the day. The cicadas were loud. Baby owls screeched in the woods not far from his tent.

"I need you to come with me."

"Where?"

"I need to go see Emma."

I T WAS a short ride back to the farm, and they were there even before the heat of the day had set in. The familiar valley stretched out below them as they peaked the final rolling hill approaching from the west. They led the horses to the old stable. Abandoned years ago, they smelled musty and dry. Days gone by. She wanted to tell Jack about the pregnancy, but she wanted to tell him in front of Emma. She wanted Emma to know first.

It sounded silly, but it made her feel better all the same.

Emma had been cremated. Lucy could not stomach

the idea of her sweet, beautiful girl decomposing in a wooden box. Her ashes had been sprinkled in a sunny corner of the farm, near a big, oak tree sporting a good, old-fashioned tire swing. She had carved Emma's initials into the trunk of the tree. Every year, on Emma's birthday, Lucy laid flowers at the base of the tree. Keeping track of that date was one of Lucy's primary motivators in being the keeper of the calendar. She would not dare lose the thread of the calendar, lest she lose the defining contours of the best day of her life.

It broke Lucy's heart to see the farm these days. Without constant attention, the fields had become overrun with weeds and wild grasses. Where before there had been orderly rows of crops, now it resembled an agricultural scrapyard. It wasn't a total loss, however. In high summer, mint and strawberries grew wild, and she and Jack would harvest as much as they could before heading back. Generally, though, the landscape reminded her of the movie *Titanic*, when the underwater cameras swept over the wreckage of the ship, the detritus that lay entombed within.

With the horses secure, they set out on foot for Emma's memorial. Jack had not inquired as to the purpose of the trip. He intuited that his sister's silence was intentional. She would speak when she was ready.

The gravel path curled around the perimeter of the farm; it too had seen better days and was mossy with weeds and grass. Weeds, nature's immortal beings. They grew in everything and nothing, even broken concrete. They grew in the heat and in the cold. They grew with water and without.

The memories came rushing back on the fifteen-minute walk, even the smells, or more accurately, the *memory* of the smells. The fecund aroma of fruiting plants, of chickens and sheep that had once lived here. The olfactory memories were powerful indeed, plugged into the mind's central processor, always there on boot-up.

The tire was still hanging from the thick branch. It swayed in the gentle afternoon breeze. Emma had loved swinging on it; she especially loved it when her uncle Jack pushed her on it. It had been one of her and Jack's favorite activities. They had come here often when she had been sick, at least when she had been up for it, in between treatments. She was often too weak to do what other kids did, but she could swing, oh boy, could she swing. Jack was content to push her for hours on end. Neither of them ever tired of it.

Lucy approached the tree reverently. It was a good tree. Thick and healthy and full. The sun was overhead now, but the oak's canopy provided strong shade from its broiling rays. She rubbed her thumb against the carving in the trunk. Emma's initials were a stark white against the trunk's brown bark. Behind her, Jack stood quietly, shifting his weight from one foot to the other. She knelt down and whispered the news to Emma. Then she stood up.

"I'm pregnant," she said.

The words hung in the quiet afternoon air.

He did not reply.

"Yep," she said. "You're gonna be an uncle again."

He laughed.

"A new baby."

"Yeah."

"Dang, Luce, I know the world has gone to shit, but did you forget everything they taught us in health class?"

She emitted a sound that was half-laugh, half-sob. Just like Jack. Making jokes. It was a little endearing. It let her know that even if she wasn't calm, he was.

"Can I ask who the father is?"

She wasn't sure how to answer. Jack didn't know Tim beyond the story she had told about Arlington. He was a ghost to her brother, nothing more.

"Was it this fella Tim?"

She nodded.

"Does he know?"

"No."

She had to tell him, of course. Tim had a right to know that he would soon be a father. Well, probably would be at least. These days, it was a lot to assume that either or both of them would still be alive nine months from now.

She couldn't tell him right now.

Because he would demand that Lucy come to his community, where she would be cared for. But that meant turning her back on Promise. She couldn't do that yet. She had things to do first. She had to fight to make this place a home. She didn't know what the future held.

"You okay?"

He wasn't asking her about morning sickness. He was asking if she was okay on an existential level, on a fundamental level. Whether she was okay with bringing a baby into a terrible world that didn't have much to offer and could often be cruel to its weakest and youngest.

A smile spread across her face.

That's when it hit her. She had to do it for the child growing inside her, for Norah, hell, she had to do it for Emma.

The Haven would not take this from her. They could not be allowed to have the last word. They would no longer bend the knee. There were times in your life you had to make a stand. No matter what the cost. In Promise, they had built a home, a community, a family. To let the Haven come in and take that? It couldn't be allowed. It could not happen.

It was time to sit down and figure out how to expunge the Haven from their lives. They would have a weakness. No one was perfect. No one was infallible. They would find it. Perhaps they had grown fat and comfortable. No one had made a stand. No one had punched them in the mouth. And Promise had been as guilty as anyone else of lying down. It had been easier to lie down. But that came with a terrible price. The price was their humanity. Their free will. Their reason for living. Their very happiness.

They should have fought back from the very beginning. They had made too many compromises. They had fallen back, and fallen back, and fallen back, always thinking this last compromise would be the one to keep the Haven out of their hair permanently. And as Lucy had finally understood, there would always be more to take from them. Maybe everyone was waiting for someone else to step up. No one wanted Promise to collapse. They all knew the score.

Was that the kind of world she wanted to bring this new baby into?

Hell no.

Could she die before the baby ever saw the light of day?

It was possible. Yes, it was possible. It was even likely. Fighting back against an enemy like the Haven would require sacrifice. It would demand it. Because nothing was easy, not anymore. But her baby deserved a mother who would fight.

Promise deserved people who would fight.

They were all children of Promise, but they were also its caretakers. They were child and parent to one another. They leaned on one another when they needed it, and they held each other up when they could. Promise was a living, breathing entity, as much a part of Lucy Goodwin as she was a part of it.

It was a thing she loved with her whole heart. It was a place that would be home to her new baby, where her child would grow and be loved and be happy. She could have another chance at happiness. She had waited more than a decade for happiness. Maybe she hadn't believed she could ever be happy again. But she could, she believed that now. There was love in Lucy's heart, love that she had let go dormant. She loved her brother, she loved Norah, and she loved this thing inside her that was no more than a kidney bean of tissue and blood. She would fight for them.

"Yeah, I think so," she said. "I am more than okay."

She turned to face her brother.

The look on his face was one of steely determination. She hoped it reflected the one in her own.

"This isn't gonna be easy," he said. "Just so you know."

She took a deep breath and let it out slowly. A wave of nausea washed over her.

"I know."

21

For the next two weeks, it was all Lucy thought about. It was all the Council discussed. If they were going to make a move against the Haven, it had to be perfect. There was no room for error. The consequences of failure would be vast, too horrible to contemplate.

It was terrifying because they may have ignited the engine of their own destruction.

It was freeing because it meant the status quo was coming to an end, and for the first time, they were the ones shattering the so-called peace with the Haven. It wasn't peace they had after all; it was bondage. It was peace built on a lie. Whatever happened, they would be the architects of their fates now.

Lucy was sleeping better than she had since the day the Haven had swept into their lives like a storm cloud. The morning sickness persisted, but it was manageable; it hit her every morning like clockwork. She developed a mammoth revulsion to eggs. Just the sight of Promise's few chickens made her stomach flip. It was a shame, as she normally enjoyed eggs, and they were a good source of nutrition for pregnant women. It was also very odd. With Emma, she had eaten scrambled eggs every morning for the entire pregnancy. She craved it like she had craved no other food in her life. No strong cravings this time around, which was for the best. It wasn't like she could pop down to the supermarket and grab a big bag of spicy Doritos whenever she felt like it. Without regular access to prenatal vitamins, she had to work very hard to ensure the baby got the nutrition it needed.

Meeting in secret, the Security Committee spent a week working out the details of their first move against the Haven. Every night after dinner, they met in the cafeteria, brainstorming and strategizing. Normally, there was alcohol, which made it easier to discuss their insane gambit. Because even in hushed whispers, it felt crazy, it felt like certain ruin. But the alcohol made it a little easier. Just enough to loosen your tongue a little and not be trapped by your fears. That was why they called it liquid courage after all.

"We could poison their share," Jack said in one of their early discussions.

Lucy considered the idea, the nuts and bolts of it. They could douse the produce in any one of several lethal toxins. This idea gained some steam before Lucy reminded the group that they knew little of the Haven's demographic makeup. The Haven was likely home to children and other innocent people who did not steal from others, who did not execute hard workers when they came up a little short. The idea was dead on arrival.

"What about an alliance with the others from the Market?" she suggested.

They spent the next thirty minutes discussing an alliance with the other Market communities; a federation could prove a formidable adversary to the Haven and force it to abandon its system of tribute.

"Possibly," he replied.

"None of these people want to be under the Haven's thumb," Lucy said. "Common enemy and all."

"No, it'll never work," he said. "You know why."

Lucy considered it as she took a sip of her moonshine. But a number of holes quickly appeared in the plan. Jack was right. It involved too many moving pieces and would likely collapse under its own weight before they made a move. But the primary flaw in the plan was that she didn't know if all the others could be trusted. She didn't know if *any* of them could be trusted. It would only take one to betray their confidence. Someone seeking to stay in the Haven's good graces. Rooting out uprisings, being rewarded for their betrayal. And their rebellion would be squashed in its crib.

"You trust any of those clowns?" Jack asked Lucy.

"Not enough of them," she said, sighing.

Then he laughed one of his big, bellowing laughs. She had forgotten what that sounded like; it made her feel warm, made her feel safe.

Despite Jack's gallows humor, a pall fell over the discussion. The sudden awareness that they were alone in this struggle. They would have to do it alone.

Jack sat up a little straighter.

"They're not totally useless, however."

She was intrigued.

"Go on."

"There's got to be at least one teacher's pet in the bunch," he said. "Someone ratted us out to the Haven. So they've got a line into the party somehow."

A chilling thought occurred to Lucy. What if the leak was coming from inside Promise? She kept her suspicion to herself for the moment.

"They know who I am," Jack said, "so I can't go undercover. But I could become a double agent."

"How would that help us?"

"We would find out where they're based."

The precise location of the Haven was indeed the holy grail. Without it, they would remain the boogeyman, the monster under the bed, the axe murderer hiding in the closet.

They had to find it.

Jack left at first light on Market Day. He wore a cloak and had shaved his beard. One of the women had used makeup to lighten his skin and smooth out the crow's feet around his eyes. He also wore a pair of reading glasses. Up close, the disguise wouldn't last long, but if he managed to avoid entanglements, he would be able to operate on the sly for a little while. The Council had finally settled on an espionage mission against the Haven.

The Market was in full swing when he arrived a little after noon. He'd spent a portion of the morning doing reconnaissance from the perimeter. He stayed mobile, unwilling to pin himself down. There were no scouts prowling the woods surrounding the Market proper.

He'd been spoiling to fight back for months. Lying down for those who took from him was not part of his DNA. It was like undergoing an organ transplant, one that your body sought to reject. Part of him wanted to punch the Haven right in the mouth, but even he understood that was not the smart play, at least not yet. No, this approach was best.

He would be found out; he was counting on it. He found it hard to believe that all their Market partners had fallen under the Haven's thumb, but he had to consider the possibility. Finding out would be instructive.

There had been a few changes to the Market since he'd last been here. Two armed men stood guard at the gate. They questioned each person looking to enter. They conducted pat-down searches, confiscated a few knives and other sharp objects.

Jack's heart raced a little as his turn in the queue drew near, but he was waved through with minimal hassle. They either didn't know who he was or they didn't care. There weren't as many booths as there had been in the past, but the crowds were decent. He suspected illicit substances had gained value as currency in recent months. People would be selling more than that, too. They would be selling themselves.

Jack approached Barrett's booth first, waiting until the man was alone. He liked Barrett. Found him to be a standup character.

"Good morning," Jack said.

Barrett eyed him with suspicion for a moment before he saw behind the weak disguise. Then he smiled broadly.

"Jack," he said, more in a whisper. "What are you doing? You know you're not supposed to be here."

"Hence the disguise."

"Man, I hate to be the one to tell you this, but it's not much of a disguise. Like, not at all."

"Don't sweat it," he said. "I have my reasons."

"Want a peach?"

Jack's stomach rumbled, but he declined. No need to draw Barrett into his poisoned orbit.

"No thanks," he said, waving his hand at the offered fruit.

"You guys holding up out there?"

"We'll be fine," he said. "You?"

Barrett sighed.

"I mean, it is what it is," he said. "You square with the house?"

"For now," Jack replied.

He leaned back, glanced around surreptitiously.

"Might be a long winter, if I'm being honest with you."

Barrett's community had less than thirty residents. Although their contribution to the Haven would likely be small, they had no chance but to comply.

"At least they let you have Market Day still."

"Yeah, no one knows why you were blackballed."

"We killed two of their guys."

Barrett's eyebrows rocked upward.

"Yeah, that would do it."

"But you guys are getting through it?" Jack asked.

"Look, as long as they get their cut, they're okay with us playing house."

This made Jack chuckle.

"Be safe, buddy," he said, gently rapping his knuckles on Barrett's table.

"You too."

Jack picked his way through the crowd for an hour, picking up on bits and pieces of conversation. Much of the discussion centered around their new overlords. Most, if not all, had fallen to the Haven over the past two months. Eventually, the sense that he was being watched started tickling at him. About damn time. He drifted to the edge of the Market, near a booth offering tarot card readings and fortune-telling. Hey, if she was finding buyers for her bullshit, more power to her.

"Want me to read your future?" asked the woman at the booth. She was older, in her sixties. Her thick, silvery hair was tied back in a long braid. She wore heavy eyeshadow. She was tall and thin.

"No thanks," he said.

"First one is free."

He glanced around. He could sense someone watching him, but he still couldn't locate the source.

"Okay."

She picked up an ornately designed deck of cards and lay down the one on top. It depicted three men standing over a fourth man down on his knee. The man in the middle held a sword at the nape of the man's neck.

"The Judgment card."

Jack yawned.

"You're experiencing doubt," she said.

"Incisive."

The next card depicted eight golden goblets arranged in a pyramid.

"You're not happy with your current situation."

"Really, is anyone these days?"

She ignored his barb and turned over the third card in his reading. Seven swords.

"Aah," she said, laying a long, bony finger against her thin, hard lips.

"Betrayal."

It was an illusion, a trick, but it still made his stomach flip a little.

"But not like you think," she said. "You must stay the course. You must follow through to the end."

The crunch of leaves and gravel behind him broke his fixation on the Betrayal card, on this strange woman. He turned to see two men approaching him. They were dressed like the two sentinels at the gate. He had not seen them during his reconnaissance of the Market's midway.

"Afternoon," Jack said.

"A word please?" said one of the men. He was young, blond-haired, handsome. The other one was a little older and a lot dumber looking. Jack could have both men's guns in his back pocket before the woman got through the next card.

"But we're not through with his reading!" she exclaimed loudly.

"Fuck off, hag," the second man said.

"It's terrible luck to interrupt a reading," she shrieked. "You cannot interrupt a reading!"

"I said fuck off!" he barked.

"That's no way to speak to a lady," Jack said. "Apologize."

The first man reared back to pistol-whip Jack, but he telegraphed his move. Jack's hands flashed like lightning, snatching the gun from the other man's grasp before he knew what was happening. Jack turned the gun on both men. One stared dumbfounded at his own gun pointed at him.

"Now apologize and I will come quietly," he said. "I'll even give you your gun back."

The two men glanced at each other, humiliated.

"Fine," they said, one after the other.

"Sorry, lady."

"I can finish your reading now," she said to Jack.

"Another time," he replied. He handed the gun back to the man.

The pair escorted Jack outside the Market to a small campsite on the northern edge of the town square. Three large tents sat near the tree line, six-man if Jack gauged their sizes right. In the center were the remains of a campfire.

"Sit down," the man said, pointing to one of the chairs arranged in a semicircle around the fire.

Jack complied.

"You're from Promise," the man said.

"I am."

"You're not supposed to be here."

"I know," he said. "But I needed to talk to you folks."

"Why?"

"I have information."

"What kind of information?"

"Valuable information."

"What kind of valuable information?" the first one snapped, a hint of annoyance in his voice.

They were getting impatient, which delighted Jack to no end. These two were like anyone else, anxious to get their paws on the newest juicy gossip. Their lives were boring, monotonous most of the time. This encounter with Jack was likely the highlight of their month. And he had just sweetened the pot.

"Where's Joshua?" Jack asked.

"Not here."

"Where is he?"

"That's none of your business."

"Who's his boss?"

"Joshua's the boss."

"The hell he is."

"What makes you say that?"

"Guys," Jack said, leaning back in his chair, spreading his arms wide. "Let's not dick around here."

Joshua was a lieutenant, no more. He was definitely superior to these two idiots, but he wasn't the man behind the curtain. Joshua was on the road more often than he wasn't. The Haven's operation was too big, too complex for its architect to be on the road seven days a week. There were probably ten Joshuas.

"How about you tell us, and we'll tell the boss?"

"How about no?"

The man who'd cursed out the card reader drew his gun and pointed it at Jack's head. Jack didn't even blink.

The man was not going to shoot him. Such a decision was above his paygrade.

"Believe me, your boss is gonna want to know about this," Jack said calmly. "But if you kill me, you'll never know it. Until it's too late, that is."

"Zach," the second man said. "We need to take this up the chain."

Zach huffed and lowered his weapon.

"You try anything, and I'll kill you."

"Fair enough."

22

Breakfast arrived early in the morning. He had no idea what time it was, as there were no windows in the cell, and the cell block itself may as well have been buried at the Earth's core for as much light as he had down here.

Calling it breakfast was a bit generous, but it looked to provide Jack with some minimal nutrition. A stale piece of flatbread and a mealy apple about the size of a baseball. He ate the food quickly, not wasting his time on the taste. Food was fuel, nothing more, nothing less. Before the Pulse, he'd never understood America's obsession with food. Taking pictures of meals and posting them online, dear God in heaven. That was one positive byproduct of the Pulse, he had to admit. Gone were the days of sitting in a restaurant and taking a picture of your food before you ate it. Amen, hallelujah.

He'd been in here for three days, and no one had come to talk to him. The cell was similar to the one they had back at Promise, albeit a little smaller and a little danker. Whatever. He'd spent many nights in holes far smaller and danker than this one. But the plan was still on track. The first phase had gone off without a hitch, as the thugs back at the Market had bought his story hook, line, and sinker.

After agreeing to take him back to the Haven, they had slung a blindfolded Jack onto Zach's horse like a sack of flour. They rode for several hours, although Jack suspected they had ridden in circles and retraced their steps to disorient him as much as possible. It was not a bad move, smarter than he would have given these two clowns credit for.

"How much farther?" Jack had asked. He'd wanted to test them.

Zach threw an elbow into Jack's ribcage, taking his breath away.

"Keep your damn mouth shut."

They rode through thick forest and across dry creek beds, the journey piercing late into the afternoon. A strong squall caught them during the middle of their ride. The sky blackened, and sheets of rain poured down on them. The horses remained calm, thankfully enough. Eventually, they came upon a small cabin in the woods. It appeared to be their final destination for the evening. Dammit. This was not their headquarters. It was more likely a place for them to torture him, find out if he was hiding anything.

No matter. Jack had been tortured before. He had never broken. It was part of his counterintelligence training in the Army. And these two didn't look like they knew the first thing about extraction. But as it turned out, this was just a rest stop. They stopped for a bathroom break, restocked their supplies, and kept moving. He was relieved. He could handle whatever pain these yahoos could inflict on him, but he wouldn't be able to kill them. Otherwise, the whole operation would be ruined.

They turned onto a two-lane road and followed that for a few more miles. Based on the steady clock of the horses' hooves on the pavement, the road felt fairly smooth. They crossed a bridge. Although he could not see it, Jack could hear the water flowing beneath them, the rush of the breeze across the bridge. The outskirts of a small town. Jack tried to picture it in his mind, aware that reality would match nothing that he imagined. Still, his mind fought to create a picture of a thing he could not see. Ruins of an abandoned strip mall. Perhaps it had burned in the hours immediately following the Pulse. A small fire that burned out of control when no firefighters had come to extinguish the blaze.

Now his mind drew a small downtown area fronted by empty ghost buildings. Maybe the courthouse or a dry cleaner or a local newspaper office. The storefronts would be missing their plate-glass windows, shattered in the chaos of the post-Pulse world.

They turned left and maintained that heading for another half hour, forty-five minutes. They had done a good job blindfolding him, he had to give him that, and he had lost total track of time. He was annoyed with himself; it was something he was normally good at. Oh well, even a blind squirrel found a nut from time to time.

Eventually, they reached their destination. They yanked him off the horse, losing their grip on him. He hit the ground hard, his shoulder absorbing the brunt of the impact. It was still sore three days later. After securing the horses, they took him straight to this cell. As they escorted him here, he used his other senses as best he could. It smelled clean and fresh. A large tract of land. He did not think he was that far from home as the crow flew. The cell was in the basement of a large building. They'd done a decent job of keeping him under lock and key. No sentinel to trick the way their prisoner had tricked their own guard months earlier.

Sloppy. So sloppy.

If they'd only managed to hang on to him, they might not be in this mess.

Woulda, coulda, shoulda.

The die was cast.

And this world didn't give you many second chances.

He was loath to admit that the good people of Promise might be in even more trouble than they realized. This was a professional operation; he had no idea who these men or women were, but they had honed their game in these last few years. This place hadn't been built overnight. He wouldn't have been surprised to learn that this new operation had been bolted on top of an already existing criminal enterprise.

He was, hard as it was to admit, an alumnus of such an organization. After leaving the military fueled by boredom and an appetite for danger, he had been drawn to cons and grifting. He suspected Lucy knew, but she was kind enough to keep her thoughts to herself. He hated disappointing her, though. He looked out for his little sister, of course, because he loved her fiercely.

He had started preying on bored, married women in the western suburbs of Richmond, Virginia. Tennis was his entry point. He'd been an excellent high school player, ranked thirtieth in the nation but had given it up when he joined the military. After his discharge, on the skids financially, he began offering tennis lessons for beginning adult players on weekdays, and wouldn't you know it, married women in their thirties made up most of his clientele.

It was a simple con, as old as the institution of bored housewives. After bedding them, he'd casually drop a hint that he was about to close a big deal with a ridiculous return on his investment. The deal itself came in many forms–cables for faster Internet, solar panels, local vineyards, any of which triggered significant tax rebates from the government. The money would come back to him threefold in a matter of weeks, and *oh, would you want to be a part of this?*

He didn't spring the trap unless he was reasonably certain the mark and her usually dopey husband would fall for it, but even still, the success rate was only about ten percent. That said, even one successful score out of ten could net him fifty or sixty grand in cash, money that floated him until the next score. He moved from city to city, changing his name, relying on fake driver's licenses and passports to keep him ahead of the law.

While living in Washington, D.C., he had nearly netted the beautiful and not very bright wife of a gangster, part of an Irish-American gang, who saw potential in the young grifter. So instead of putting a hole in Jack's head and dropping him in the Potomac River, he brought him aboard. Jack had been free to continue his scams with some muscle behind him in exchange for a third of his cut. Given the alternative of being left in a ditch somewhere, it was a pretty good deal.

It was a well-run operation and a ruthless one.

They ran drugs and guns and prostitutes, they provided protection to tough, working-class neighborhoods from rival gangs, and they laundered money. Eventually, Jack tired of the life and had to buy his freedom from his debt to his employer. It cost him everything he had, almost two hundred thousand dollars.

But he was free.

And he had gone home to the farm. Eight years in the military, posted to the most dangerous spots in the world, another ten on the wrong side of the law, and in the end, he found himself right back where he'd started. In a way, it had all prepared him for the world in which they now lived. It had prepared him for this mission, this moment.

The corridor fronting his cell lightened a bit, harkening the arrival of visitors. Several sets of footsteps. He was sitting on his bottom against the wall, his hands clasped around his knees. He made no move to get up. Two men appeared in the dim glow of a lantern. He saw Zach and a second man he did not recognize. Zach unlocked the cell and swung the door open.

The new man stepped inside and plopped down comfortably on Jack's cot. He set the lantern on the floor at his feet. It cast just enough light upwards to illuminate his features. He was a handsome fellow. He wore a clean but rumpled button-down shirt and khaki pants.

"Morning," he said cheerfully.

Jack nodded but made no move to speak.

"Strong, silent type," he said. "I like that. I respect men of few words."

He patted himself on the chest.

"Me, I'm a talker," he said. "Not sure why. I used to get detention all the time. Maybe I picked it up from my mother. Now she was a talker."

Jack held a fist to his lips and cleared his throat.

"So what is your name, my friend?"

"Jack," he said.

"It's very nice to meet you."

"And your name?"

"My name isn't really important," he said. "I've found that anonymity has quite a bit of value in this shitshow we call life."

Jack fought the urge to roll his eyes. These villains.

"Anyway, I trust you've been treated well."

"Well enough."

"Great. I understand that you've got information you wish to share."

"I do."

Jack's heart was pounding but in a good way. The game was on. Time to apply his tradecraft. They had worked out every last detail of his story, down to the heartbreaking twist at the end.

"Well, let's hear it."

"I need some assurances first."

"Like what?"

"I want my safety guaranteed. My safety and my sister's. We come live here."

The man scoffed.

"I could just torture you for the information."

He said it casually. He would do it, of that Jack had no doubt. And Jack could take it. But there was no need to suffer if it wasn't necessary. Besides, there was a larger plan at play here. Just a little freedom to figure out where they were and then get the hell out of here.

"Sure, but that's messy and can take a while," he said. "You may not have that kind of time. And I'm a big boy. I can take a lot of punishment."

"Hmmm," the man said. He scraped the stubble adorning his cheek. "So this information is time sensitive."

"Indeed."

"Fine," he said. "We have room here at the Haven. If we can corroborate your report, you have a deal."

This was exactly what Jack was hoping for. In fact, it was preferable. It would take time to track down this story, to confirm it, and that would give him the time to do what he needed.

"Okay," he said. "The other communities, they're planning an assault."

The man chuckled dismissively.

"Is that right?"

"One of your boys spilled the beans," he said. "Told a pretty lady at the Falls where your base is."

The man clicked his tongue against his teeth. It was a believable story, believable enough that it needed to be taken seriously. And the notion that one of his young henchmen had spilled the Haven's most critical secret during pillow talk was entirely plausible, albeit wildly disagreeable.

"Who?"

"I don't know," he said. "The mole's identity is not known."

"When did this happen?"

"Sometime in the last couple of weeks," he said. "Maybe a month."

The man was up and pacing the cell now. Jack had delivered just enough intelligence to rattle him. The Haven was powerful, but a battle against all its enemies at once would be costly.

"When is this assault set to take place?"

"Soon," he said. "In the next week."

"What are they coming with?" he said, kneeling down next to Jack. "Slingshots and bad language? We disarmed the communities."

"Look, I don't know, man," he said. "They've got a line on weapons. Unknown third party."

"Why?"

"Winter will be here before you know it," he said. "Some settlements have done the math. They don't think they'll survive."

"And here you are," the man said. "You're pretty high up in Promise. Why should I believe you?"

"Look, my sister comes first," he said. "Family's all that matters to me. I don't want anything bad to happen to the other folks, but she has to come first."

"So you don't support this assault?"

"I want to," Jack replied. "But let's just say I don't see a path to victory here."

The man gently patted Jack on the cheek.

"Smart man," he said.

"And that's not all," he said. "My sister is pregnant. She's due this winter. I can't take a chance that we've got nothing to eat when the baby comes."

"And the father?" he said. "Is he one of yours?"

"No," he replied. "He doesn't know about the baby. And he's not gonna know."

"It's a tough, old world out there, isn't it?"

Jack nodded.

"Indeed."

"And what am I supposed to do with you?"

"I need to get back," he said. "Otherwise, folks might get suspicious. They're in the early planning stages. Not many know about the attack. I'm one of them."

"Not a bad position to be in," the man said.

"What do you mean?"

"You're basically writing your own ticket out of here."

"Hey, man, your call."

"You're a good brother," the man said. "Most folks don't get along with their brothers and sisters. Seems like sibling rivalry never goes away. Always fighting for the scraps of the most important love there is."

"Yeah," he said. "I guess."

The man stood up and made his way to the cell door.

"To be honest, my sister's had it pretty rough," Jack said.

Time for the *coup de grace*.

Time to appeal to this man's humanity by making it clear how truly motivated Jack was to help, to buy safe passage for him and his poor, woe-is-me sister. He hated to do it, but they could leave no stone unturned.

"Is that right?"

"Yeah," he said. "She's already lost one child."

"Well, these are tough times."

"No, this was before. Cancer. Ten years old."

The man froze at the door, his hand on one of the bars.

"What did you just say?"

"My sister. She lost her daughter to cancer."

Something about the way the man responded made Jack's stomach flip. He didn't know why. The words had resonated with him somehow. Maybe he'd lost a child to cancer himself. It was possible. Often, as he'd found in his days with the syndicate, tragedy pushed people to deviant behavior. They'd lived good lives, and what had they gotten in return? Heartache.

"Yeah," Jack said, wanting to probe a little farther. He had connected with the man at some fundamental level. This could be good news, or it could be bad news. "Really makes you question things, seeing a thing like that. Seeing a child with cancer."

He rapped his knuckles against the bars. They twanged ominously in the strange acoustics of the cell.

"We'll speak again soon, Jack."

23

J ack had been gone for three days. Lucy told herself not to worry, but it was getting more difficult. Anything could have happened. Even if the Haven had bought his story, they could have just held him captive. Jack told her not to worry about this prospect. He assured her that he could escape; it was what he was good at. He was trained to do it.

Things were tense in Promise. No one knew about Jack's covert mission but Lucy and the other Council members, but there were other things to worry about. Like the coming autumn. The leaves were starting to fall. A good breeze sent the brown-tipped leaves fluttering to the ground like little messages from the future. A future of barren trees and barren cupboards.

The coming winter was going to be difficult, but the good news was that they'd be heading into it reasonably healthy. Folks were looking a little leaner in the face, but traffic in the clinic was normal. The day job was routine for once. Calm before the storm, she supposed. Before long, illnesses related to nutrition deficiencies would begin to crop up.

But that was a problem for Future Lucy. For now, she was worried about Jack.

And Norah.

Their relationship was mending. But today, Lucy was going to have to add another lash to its back. She had no choice. They were reaching a crisis point, and she couldn't function unless she knew that Norah was safe. She had continued to sneak out to visit her mysterious boyfriend. Lucy had looked the other way as they addressed the problem of the Haven.

But with no easy solution to that issue on the horizon, Lucy had to take charge. She had to be a mom. Lurking in the background, of course, was Lucy's pregnancy. Sometimes, it retreated from the forefront of her mind before storming in like a hurricane. A baby. She was going to have a baby. And seeing as she was the senior medical officer for their community, it would behoove her to make sure her charges were properly trained on childbirth techniques. If everything ran smoothly, it wouldn't be too difficult. If there were complications, well, that would be something else entirely.

There were other concerns. Autism and Down syndrome were very real risks in babies born to mothers over the age of forty. Mother Nature, she was a real bitch. She wanted women to have babies earlier than later. Lucy understood that from a biological perspective. And in the old days, it had been such a burden on women. Lucy was only twenty-four when she'd become pregnant with Emma. And the practice of nursing was well-suited for dealing with a new baby. She had worked three twelve-hours shifts a week, which left her four days a week with Emma. She didn't sleep much, but did any new mother, really?

She hoped Emma wouldn't mind a new baby. Because Lucy already loved the child more than she could have imagined. She wondered how Norah would handle the news; she'd been looking for the right time to tell her. Maybe tonight after dinner. Yeah. Worrying about telling Norah about the pregnancy would take her mind off Jack.

That wasn't the only item on the agenda either. Now that Lucy thought about it, it was going to be a difficult discussion. She had decided to bar Norah from leaving Promise for the immediate future; it was simply too dangerous.

Lucy was sitting under the awning outside the clinic. She had just finished the evening medication pass for the four patients that were in house. It was a nice night. A passing thunderstorm in the middle of the day had broken the vise of humidity. A cool breeze was blowing. A hint of fall in the air. In the old days, this might have been the week that Octoberfest beer offerings began dominating the beer aisle. She smiled at the memory. Good-natured arguments about which season of the year was the best.

Winter for all its fireplaces and hot cocoa and movie nights spent under a blanket. Summer for trips to the beach and frozen margaritas and catching a movie at the drive-in in Goochland County, not too far from where she now sat. She wondered what the place looked like now. The Pulse had hit in the middle of the day, so the place was probably empty. That would have been a freaky image. People hoofing it home from the theater; it was out in the middle of nowhere, and a walk home would not have been an enjoyable jaunt. As though that would have mattered in the grand scheme of things.

A noise broke her out of her daydream.

Speak of the devil.

Norah loped gracefully toward her. She had finally stopped growing, topping out an inch taller than Lucy. She was so achingly beautiful that it scared Lucy a little. She saw how the men looked at her, and even how they tried to *not* look at her. Like they knew better, but they still had to work hard at it. She kept her hair cropped close. The cut accentuated her high cheekbones and beautiful brown eyes.

Lucy hadn't seen her all day. The older Norah got, the less she saw of her. The less she was an extension of Lucy. More a full-fledged member of the community. She didn't even know what say she had over the girl anymore. What, just because she was under eighteen, Lucy had the right to dictate the contours of the girl's life? That was an anachronism of a world gone by. Norah had spent her formative years in the crucible of the post-Pulse world. She had grown up fast.

If Norah just decided to ignore her, Lucy really didn't know what she could do to stop her. In some ways, they were still running on the momentum of the old world. The way things used to be. Norah was used to the way things were, although that was changing.

Lucy lay an absent hand on her belly, now sporting the faintest of bumps. It would be invisible to anyone else, but Lucy felt it in the slight snugness of her clothes. Again, her thoughts drifted to her baby's life ahead. She (*she? Why did she think it was a she?*) would come into a world knowing nothing of their previous lives. Would she believe her momma when Lucy told her about cars and airplanes and even something as basic as electricity? There were so many things that would be nothing but history to this child. Lucy decided she would start a diary, a journal, to document all the things they had once had but had since lost.

Assuming, of course, they survived the coming war with the Haven.

"Hey, Mama," Norah said.

"Hey, yourself," she said. "How was your day?"

"Good."

"Hey, we need to talk," she said. "Can you sit for a bit?"

Norah rolled her eyes a little. Not a lot, just a little. It was automatic by now. Teenagers just rolled their eyes whenever an adult in their lives decided they needed to talk.

"Okay," she said with a breath of annoyance.

They sat for a bit in silence as Lucy wrestled with which item to begin with.

The lockdown. She could finish with the good news of the pregnancy.

"What do you want to talk about?"

"Couple of things," she said. "They're both pretty important."

"Is this a good news, bad news type thing?"

"Uh, maybe?" she said. "I guess you might prefer one over the other."

"Well then start with the bad news."

"So you're not gonna like this," Lucy began, "but I want you to stay inside the borders of Promise for a while."

"Why?"

Lucy clicked her tongue for a second as she considered her response.

"Things have gotten dangerous out there."

"Why?"

"You know we're struggling to keep up with the Haven's demands."

Norah nodded.

"And there may be trouble coming."

"What kind of trouble?"

"Not sure yet," she said. "It could get messy."

Lucy regretted the words as she said them. Talking about war with a child.

"Good," she said. "I hate that they take so much from us."

Lucy felt a tickle of relief. Maybe this wouldn't be as hard as she expected. Kids, man, they always surprised you. It was a mistake to underestimate them.

"That's the bad news?"

"I thought you'd be upset," she said. "With your friend and all."

"Actually, his dad gave him the same rule," she said.

"Sounds like a smart dad."

"Can I see him one more time though?" Norah asked. "We're supposed to meet up tonight."

"I don't think so," Lucy said. "Like I said, it's too dangerous."

Norah huffed but raised no additional objection. It was like negotiating a minefield. Lucy hoped she'd carefully made it to the other side without setting one off.

"So what's the good news?"

"So this is gonna seem like it's out of left field."

"Okay."

"I'm pregnant."

"What? How?"

Lucy raised a single eyebrow.

"Right," Norah said, looking away embarrassed.

Lucy had taught Norah about the birds and the bees not long after she'd become her primary guardian. She had known nothing about the business of men and women, and Lucy wanted to get that out of the way early.

"Who's the father?" Norah asked.

"Do you remember Tim?"

"Yeah, kind of."

Tim and Norah had only spent a little time together during their chaotic escape from Simon's clutches. Strange to think Norah had such little recall of a person from such a critical moment of her life. The beautiful amnesia of childhood.

"Well, he's the baby's father."

"So since you're tired of me, you decided to have your own baby?"

Norah's words were like a punch in the face.

"No, of course, not," Lucy said, reaching out and squeezing Norah's arm. "I love you more than anything, like you're my own flesh and blood."

"But I'm not your flesh and blood, am I?"

Lucy didn't know how to respond. And it was this delay that seemed to enrage Norah even further. This had gone off the rails so quickly.

"Yeah, you don't give a shit about me anymore because you'll have your own baby now. That baby will just do whatever you program it to do."

Lucy laughed at this. The idea that a baby she carried herself would be any more pliant or less difficult as a teenager was rich indeed.

"What's so funny?"

"Norah," she said. "This baby will need a big sister. That will be your job."

"I don't want the job," she snapped. "And I don't want you!"

She fled, leaving Lucy sitting alone on the stoop.

NORAH'S EXPLOSION had left Lucy shell-shocked. Her reaction had been totally unexpected. She had always wanted to believe that Norah had never viewed herself as some kind of consolation prize, good but not good enough because she wasn't Lucy's biological daughter. All these years, those feelings had been bubbling under the surface, and the pregnancy had been the perfect spark to ignite them. Maybe she should have told her about Emma long ago.

Norah did not appear for dinner, which was highly unusual. Her metabolism burned hot, and she never skipped a meal, especially these days as the food rations grew thinner. Lucy ate her cabbage and potato soup by herself and then got up to look for Norah. Knowing the girl, she had probably decided to defy Lucy and go meet her boyfriend for one last rendezvous.

But what could she do, short of locking her in their cell?

She had to trust that her lessons and the values she held dear had taken root inside her, that they were enough to keep Norah on the straight and narrow.

After dinner, Lucy went back to the clinic and worked on paperwork by lantern light. Ordinarily, it was times like this she really missed electricity. Even by computer, under the fluorescent lights of her old emergency room nurse's station, charting had been a gigantic pain in the ass. Now it was just a tedious nightmare.

But the mindlessness of the work was a welcome distraction tonight. It was mindless work that had to be done, and it let her focus on the blowup with Norah. She was at a loss of what to do; it was another stressor at a time she could ill afford it. So she continued working, cleaning up charts, looking for warning signs in her patients she may have missed at first blush. The work carried her late into the evening, until the last bit of revelry had died down.

That was why the sudden burst of shouting and screaming that came late, probably close to midnight, had been so alarming. Her heart racing, she set down the chart she'd been reviewing and picked up her lantern. Outside, the wailing continued.

She rushed outside, spotting a small crowd of people that formed near Promise's main entrance. A group had circled a skittish horse, its rider in obvious distress. The woman aboard was yelling and shouting unintelligibly.

As she got closer, she recognized the rider. Her name was Amelia. She was from Barrett's settlement. Initially, Lucy could not understand what she was saying. As Lucy drew closer, her words, choked with tears, came into a better focus. She was saying the same thing over and over. Then Lucy understood.

"They killed everyone," Amelia was saying. "They killed everyone."

"Everyone quiet!"

Lucy's sharp words cut through the chatter.

The group fell silent.

"Amelia, what happened?" she asked in as calm a voice as she could manage.

"They came this afternoon," she said. "The ones from the Haven. They started killing everyone."

Lucy's stomach flipped.

"Come on down," Lucy said. "You need to rest."

The woman's face, which had been frozen in panic and terror, illuminated by the dozens of lanterns swinging in the others' hands, suddenly relaxed. Lucy could only imagine the woman's terror-soaked midnight ride here.

"Okay," she said. "Okay. Okay."

She shimmied down to the ground. Someone took the horse by the lead and walked it to the stables for water and hay. Amelia crumpled to the ground, holding her head in her hands. Her shirt was splattered with blood. The sobbing restarted in earnest. She wailed.

That's when Lucy remembered Norah had not appeared for dinner. She grabbed Terri by the elbow.

"Terri," she said, her voice panicked. "See what else you can find out. I have to find Norah."

Terri nodded.

Leaving Terri to tend to Amelia, Lucy turned and sprinted for her lodge. She burst through the empty common area. She banged into the wall in a desperate sprint to reach Norah's room, praying she was in there, praying that she would see the dim glow of candles that Norah liked to burn while she was in her room stewing.

But the room was dark.

Norah was missing.

And the Haven was on the rampage.

She set the lantern on the bureau and began digging through Norah's belongings. She didn't love the idea of rifling through the girl's private things, but she had no choice. Norah was her daughter, and she had to do whatever she could to help her. And this invasion of her privacy could give her a clue as to the girl's whereabouts.

There was nothing on the top of the bureau. Norah was a fastidious girl, different in that respect from the average teenager. To be fair, Norah's teenage years were much different than they had been for any teenager of the last century and a half. Perhaps she found order in the upkeep of her room when her life and her world were wracked by chaos.

She next turned her attention toward the nightstand. Lucy opened its single drawer and began rifling through the contents, looking for anything that might shed light on where she'd gone. A note, a journal. Perhaps she had returned to the spot they had had their terrible fight, but she couldn't be sure. She couldn't afford a wild goose chase; she needed actionable intel, and she needed it now.

At the bottom of the drawer lay a thin stack of photographs, maybe half a dozen in total. These were new to Lucy. She set her lantern on the nightstand as she flipped through them. The first five were childhood pictures of Norah's boyfriend with a pretty woman, presumably his mother. He was young in the shots, no more than eight or nine years old. But he looked the same, even now. Some kids were like that. Even in adulthood, the face of the child they had been lurked just underneath.

The pictures were heartbreaking and wondrous in their ordinariness. A shot in the park. One from Halloween with Alexander dressed as a ninja. A third at the beach, his mother's hair whipping behind her in what must have been a strong breeze.

Lucy smiled. Just seeing these photos made her like the boy a bit more. He'd been like anyone else. A little boy with a mommy who loved him. Lucy wondered if she was still alive. She understood why Norah had them. These were a little slice of the boy she loved, and it was clear that she loved him.

Then Lucy flipped to the last photograph.

She froze.

It was another picture of the boy, but this time he was with a man who appeared to be his father. The man was handsome and young. Preppy-looking. They were standing in front of a very large Christmas tree like the one you would see at the mall during the holidays.

As she stared at the photo, her heart began to race.

Lucy recognized the man right away.

His name was Simon.

The man who had held Norah and Lucy captive so many years ago.

24

L ucy fell back onto her bottom, her gaze transfixed on the photo.

Simon.

A very bad man.

When the Pulse had hit, Simon had been in the business of human trafficking and had set his sights on Norah and Lucy. Only with a little luck and the help of one Tim Whitaker had Lucy been able to avert such a terrible fate.

The last time Lucy had seen Simon, he'd been trying to kill her, his plan to trade her and Norah completely foiled, his headquarters in flames. He was cutting the makeshift rope they had constructed to rappel to the first floor of the Ballston Mall from the skyway after she, Tim, and Norah had escaped his clutches. More specifically, escaping after she had badly burned his face to facilitate said escape. If he'd started cutting the rope a few seconds earlier, she would have plunged two stories to her death.

A million questions rippled through her like fireworks.

Most notably—how had he survived?

Lucy had always believed the man had died in the fire which ultimately had consumed the entire Ballston Commons Mall. Like her, Norah, and Tim, Simon had been trapped on the skyway; that was why they'd taken the extraordinarily insane step of rappelling down using a rope of belts and blouses. It was still the craziest thing that Lucy had ever done in her life.

Did Norah not recognize him?

There was no way to know. Lucy did not know how much interaction Norah had had with Simon when she had been delivered to him like so much human cargo. Even if she had spoken to him, it was hard to say whether she had ever gotten a good look at his face. And if she had, would she remember him five years later? Another question she could not answer.

And most importantly, was he the mysterious leader of the Haven?

She laughed bitterly.

Of course he was.

There was no other possibility.

He was a monster. When the end had come for their world, when the lights had gone out permanently, Simon had shown what man was capable of. He trafficked in human beings and planned to use Norah (and Lucy, if he'd had his way) as currency.

He was the man behind their ruin, behind the murder of her fellow residents, behind the apparent destruction of Barrett's community.

He was a monster.

Somehow, he had survived the fire at the Ballston

Mall. Somehow, he had risen from the ashes and now posed a threat not just to her, not just to Norah, but to so many more. An entire community had been destroyed. Wiped out because Lucy had failed to finish the job all those years ago.

How was she supposed to know?

She had done all she could.

One final terrifying thought raced through her head.

Had Simon and Norah met recently?

Had she been to the Haven?

No.

She didn't believe so.

Norah hadn't been to the Haven any more than Alexander had been here.

Their love was star-crossed, conducted in the shadows, on neutral ground because they had strict parents who disapproved of young love from parts unknown. The very thing that had probably made the relationship so alluring to Norah and Alexander.

Lucy took some solace in this.

Now finding Lucy and Alexander took on much more urgency.

If she could find them, he might lead them to the Haven.

Yes.

She would find them, and she would make him tell her where his father was.

Amelia.

She needed to talk to Amelia.

She climbed back to her feet, shaking her head clear of the shockwaves of the last few minutes. She hurried back outside, where Terri and Amelia were still deep in conversation. Lucy squeezed the small woman's shoulder. Amelia turned and threw her arms around Lucy. The woman wept silently, her body heaving. Lucy held her tight.

"They came in and just started burning everything," she said. "They didn't ask any questions. They didn't even tell us what we had done wrong."

"I'm so sorry," Lucy said. "I'm so, so sorry."

And she was sorry, sorrier than she had ever been in her life.

Because their plan had failed.

It had backfired spectacularly.

The Haven had taken its revenge on the community that they needed the least. By tomorrow, word would spread to the others that resistance would not be tolerated. And the thing was, they hadn't even planned to fight back. This was all on her, Jack, and the Council. It was their fault. She had not expected the Haven to inflict such terrible retribution. She had gambled on the notion that the supply chain was too valuable to disrupt. But the Haven had blown up her assumptions. Her gamble had failed.

It was a terrible oversight on her part, one for which she would never forgive herself.

imon Conway could not sleep.

It was late and it had been a long day, but he was still wide awake. Sometime after two, he got out of bed and dialed up the lantern on his nightstand. The kerosene hissed as the suite filled with sickly yellow light. He sat at the edge of his bed, took some deep breaths, but his heart continued to race. It was unlike him. Normally, he slept deeply. He only slept a few hours a night, usually between one and six a.m., but it was high octane slumber that supercharged him for another day at the helm of the rapidly growing Haven.

As he slid out of bed, Serena, who lay sleeping peacefully next to him rolled over and buried herself deeper under the covers. She did not stay over often, but tonight, her eight-year-old son was spending the night with the family of another boy his age. The light didn't bother her, and he wouldn't have cared if it did. Serena was young and beautiful. Ten years his junior, she was a welcome distraction from the stress of his job. She didn't say much, and that was fine with him. The sex was fantastic. She appeared to enjoy it as well. This cheered him up a bit.

Good to know he still had his fastball at forty-five. Her body was soft and firm at the same time, the way thirty-year-old women's bodies were. It wasn't love. It was more of a mutual aid agreement. They each got something out of it. He made sure the boy got access to the best teachers, the best medical care. He did not hold any illusion that she loved him, and he wouldn't have wanted her to.

He looked up at the flat-screen television mounted at the wall. This would have been a good night for an old movie to help him sleep. He wasn't much of a reader, but he had enjoyed winding down with a movie in the old days. A relic of days gone by. He still missed it though. Even after all these years, he had never quite gotten used to a world without power. He had learned how to thrive in such a world, learned how to make the best of a bad situation, but it was still a bad situation. He missed the finer things he had come to enjoy. He missed the fancy cars and the hotel suites and the five-star restaurants that his business successes had afforded him.

That wasn't to say that his life was bad.

Simon Conway had adapted quickly to the post-Pulse world. Within minutes of the event, staring at his darkened phone, understanding at a primal level that this was far more than a simple blackout, he had begun planning for the future. While others waited dumbly for the electricity to come back on, waiting for someone to come help them, he had operated as though it was never coming back. Because it was what the evidence was pointing to. It wasn't just electricity that had failed. It was anything requiring an electrical charge – including batteries. This wasn't some short circuit at an important relay station.

It had been a paradigm shift.

One he had been ready for.

He had come up as part of a crime syndicate outside of Washington, D.C. He was a bright kid but hated school with a blinding passion. He gave college a shot, enrolling at George Mason University. And he found success in college; it just wasn't in the classroom. He started a bookmaking operation, taking action on all sports. He was popular with the fraternities, even a few sororities. Some people made money, most lost money, but Simon Broome always ended in the black. The bookmaking was so successful, he dropped out of GMU after his freshman year to focus on the business.

His work drew the attention of a local crime boss named Sean Costello. He took Simon under his wing, buying out his client list for six figures. Simon rose quickly through the ranks. He became Costello's right-hand man, loyal to a fault. Simon added drugs, human trafficking, and prostitution to his illicit portfolio. The sky was the limit, and the money poured in.

Then one night, Lady Luck had kissed Simon.

He'd just finished a meeting with Costello at his condo and was on his way out the door when he remembered he'd left his coat on the sofa. Costello must have believed he was alone. He was on his speakerphone.

"Yeah, it's all on this flash drive," he was saying.

Indistinct chatter.

"Yeah, I'll be ready to testify."

Simon could feel his heart breaking as he stood in the foyer, his hand still on his coat tree.

Costello had flipped.

He was going to take them all down to save his own ass.

Simon was enraged. Panic threatened to overwhelm him. Costello could burn them all on about fifty different felonies. Murder, conspiracy, distribution, just to name a few. State and federal prosecutors would be tripping over themselves in half a dozen jurisdictions to send him to prison. But as he stood there in the foyer, listening to Costello betray him, he focused on solving the problem.

He wasted no time.

Abandoning the coat, he carefully slipped out the door and returned to his car in the condo parking lot. Later that evening, Costello took his Norwich terrier for her evening walk. That was when Simon had struck. He quickly pistol-whipped Costello into unconsciousness, binding his hands and feet together before dumping him in the cargo area of his sport utility vehicle. A slash of duct tape covered his mouth. The little terrier stood there looking up at him, confused, yapping at him. He couldn't bear to leave the small pooch to its own devices so he scooped her up and put her in the front seat. He drove home, parking in his garage, leaving the bound Costello in the trunk.

He stayed up all night, debating his next move. He sat on his couch, the little terrier on his lap. He couldn't call any of his associates; for all he knew to the contrary, others had flipped as well. He didn't have much time to act. They would be looking for him soon. It was the most surreal night of his life. An hour before dawn, he cooked the dog some chicken and rice. As she gobbled it down, it became clear what he needed to do. He went to the garage and gathered a dozen abandoned paving stones.

Before the sun rose, he carried the dog out to the car and drove out to his boat, the *Peacock*, at the Buckley Marina. He backed the car up to the dock and quickly transferred Costello onto the deck of the boat. The man flopped around like a fish. He fired up the engines and sailed deep into the Chesapeake Bay. It was a beautiful day for sailing, and Simon made the trip with tears in his eyes. He did not speak to Costello, he did not ask him why he had done what he had done. When they were ten miles offshore, Simon duct-taped Costello's mouth and nose shut; Costello became apoplectic as his oxygen was cut off. Three agonizing minutes later, Costello was dead. Simon secured the pavers to Costello's body and then wrapped him in duct tape. Then he kissed Costello on the forehead and threw him overboard. Costello's body sank instantly. It was over. The dog did not seem to mind.

When the FBI came looking, Simon told them he did not know where Costello was. He accused them of malfeasance. He went crazy. And the FBI's case against the gang had collapsed. The dog lived with him for another five years before succumbing to cancer. He named her Abby.

Success in the new paradigm had taken work.

He worked hard to run his organization.

The same work ethic that helped him succeed in the post-Pulse world.

He carried the lantern out to the living room and set it

on the table. The rain had picked up, now a steady thrum on the roof. Still anxious, he poured a scotch, two fingers worth, and opened the curtains. It was too dark to see anything. His suite overlooked the first tee box. Normally, it was a good view, but it was raining. The gentle susurration of rain on the rooftop should have helped him sleep, but it did not. Nevertheless, he liked rain. The way it cocooned the world. It gave a man time and space to think.

He propped his feet on the table and took a sip of his drink. It was warm and immediately helped soothe his nerves. His meeting with the prisoner from Promise the previous day was still on his mind. He had been tickled by the man's offer; Jack clearly did not know the Haven already had a spy inside Promise.

Simon had learned about the existence of Promise about two months before their takeover of the settlement. By then, the Haven had widened its territory north to Fredericksburg, establishing satellite outposts to consolidate the smaller communities that were cropping up in the wake of the cataclysm and were able to produce. These were small settlements, a dozen people, two at the most, and they fell in line quickly. They didn't have much to offer, so he brought them in as human capital. Some were starving, sick, and ready for anyone to come in and run the show.

That was how their man, Dixon, had been able to escape. Danny had been on guard duty. They recruited him at the Market, guaranteeing him his safety and future residence at the Haven, once Promise had outlived its usefulness. Danny had been a reliable source of information, and he had not mentioned any alliance between Promise and the other colonies. So the man was not there to betray his people. He was there looking for something. But then he had mentioned a little detail, virtually insignificant. He had a pregnant sister. She had lost a child to cancer.

Simon had come a long way since his bookie days in the freshman dorms at George Mason. Success in this new world had not come easy. Some days it had taken force. And some days, especially, in the early going, it had almost not gone his way at all.

A door in his mind suddenly opened. Locked up tight for years. His hand drifted to his cheek, still ridged and rippled like a relief map, the byproduct of a dangerous encounter in the early days of the apocalypse.

With a woman.

He never learned her name.

But he remembered everything about her. The way she looked.

She had tricked him. She had nearly killed him. To this day, it ate at him. He wanted nothing more than to skin her alive. But he had assumed that she was lost forever to the winds. They had spoken only briefly, when she had deceived him into thinking the girl he had captured was in diabetic shock.

What was it she had said?

Cancer.

Her daughter had died of cancer.

Like the daughter of Jack's sister.

Could it be the same woman?

He would not have been surprised. Very few people

had ever pulled one over on Simon Conway, but this woman had. He'd been a bit panicked at the time, and the girl was an incredibly valuable asset. It was a monstrous thing he was doing, he understood that, but it was not personal. He didn't do anything to the girls himself. He was just a vehicle, a waypoint. Perhaps a minor distinction, but an important one. Things were rapidly deteriorating in Arlington, and he made a mistake. He had fallen for her ruse.

Then she had escaped with the girl, all but leaving him to die on the skyway.

But now he knew where she was.

And he would make her pay for what she had done.

26

Alexander was hungry and exhausted. He had been working with the blacksmith all day, learning how to forge new tools and weapons for the Haven. It was tedious, backbreaking work, not typically his wheelhouse of interest, but he had grown to like it. Okay, maybe *like* was a strong word, but there was something deeply satisfying in working a piece of metal into something useful. In finding structure and order where there had once been none.

Jesus, he was starting to sound like his father.

He stopped by the kitchen after his day had ended. He'd been at it since sunup, and dinner was still a couple of hours away. His stomach rumbled at the smells emanating from the kitchen. Maybe there would be a scrap of something he could snack on. His appetite had been voracious lately, the boy caught in the middle of a rapid growth spurt, perhaps the final one of his adolescence. He had shot up three inches just this summer alone. He was even taller than Norah now, which delighted him immensely. Now she had to tip her head up to kiss him, and that felt right. It felt natural, the regular order of things.

He missed her terribly. She had missed their last scheduled rendezvous a week ago. He did not know where she lived. Neither would be welcome in the other's community. Besides, the idea of introducing her to his father horrified him.

The kitchen was hopping when he arrived. The Haven had two hundred mouths to feed. Its kitchens were its busiest production centers. Keeping the Haven fed and healthy was a massive undertaking. It encompassed large growing fields, which were its most important resource. His father's main priority was to ensure the Haven was always self-sufficient. It was, he had explained to Alexander, why he chose to do things the way he did. It was why he could seem cruel and uncaring for others. Simon had said that he did these things because he loved the Haven so much.

But still, Alexander struggled with it. There had to be a better way. That wasn't how the old world had worked. The United States had made what it needed and traded with other countries. They could do the same thing.

Alexander lingered by the entrance as Jorge, the head chef of the Haven, barked orders at the half dozen assistants tasked with kitchen duty. He was in his early fifties, of Puerto Rican and Cuban descent. Many of their meals had a decidedly Latin flair to them. The kitchen, which Jorge had spent years upgrading to his tastes, occupied the first floor of this building. He had even constructed a brick oven in the back. The cooking instruments ran on propane, one of the key raw materials the Haven sought to secure. For now, his father had reached a deal with a supplier up north near Fredericksburg. An enterprising sort who had figured out how to bottle propane even in the absence of electricity. It was tricky and complex work. The Haven kept a strong security presence in residence at the propane facility.

"Hey, kid," Jorge called out. "I see you over there."

Alexander waved timidly.

"Come taste this," he said, stirring the contents of a large cauldron. He ladled out a portion into a small bowl and popped a spoon into it.

Alexander crossed the room, drawn to the oven by the heavenly smells from Jorge's pot. He lifted a spoonful of the steaming mixture from the bowl, blew on it, and took a bite. It was some kind of bean stew. Probably something his mother had made for him. He'd learned how to cook from his mother.

It was spicy and delicious.

"Really good, Jorge."

The man beamed. He poured his heart into his work. Alexander hoped he could find something equally rewarding in his future. He just didn't know what that would be. Would he just spend his years working in the smithy? Or in here, as a sous-chef? Maybe he'd end up in waste management, the horrifying job of disposing of the vast amount of human excrement the Haven generated each day.

"Jorge, did you always want to be a chef?"

He nodded as he stirred the stew. Then he turned and barked at one of the assistants working at the large counter in the center of the room. The man was chopping vegetables on a large cutting board.

"Smaller pieces, Daniel!" he yelled. "You'll choke a horse with pepper chunks that big!"

He muttered something in Spanish before turning his attention back to Alexander.

"Since I was a little boy, I loved to cook. Why do you ask?"

"I don't know what I want to do."

Jorge chuckled.

"No need to worry about that."

"Why do you say that?"

"Oh, your dad has big plans for you."

"What do you mean?"

Jorge laughed again.

"What, you think you're gonna be making tools the rest of your life?"

Alexander was confused.

"Look kid, I've known your dad a long time, and there aren't many people he trusts," he said. "He wants people he can trust around him. Who better than you?"

Alexander stood dumbfounded while Jorge attended to some chore. His father wanted him to help run this place? He knew Jorge was trying to make him feel better, but now he felt more depressed than ever. He didn't even know what he wanted to do with his life, but his father had already decided that for him?

Jorge returned carrying a tray of food. A small bowl of the stew, the steam curling out of it, and a piece of bread. Then, to Alexander's surprise, he worked up a loogie and fired it into the bowl. He stirred it in with a thick finger.

"Do me a solid, Big A, take this down to the prisoner."

ALEXANDER CARRIED the tray to the cell, Jorge's salivary deposit not far from his mind. The man needed to eat. Throwing it out wasn't an option. Besides, the man probably suspected they adulterated his meals in some way. It happened all the time. Once, he'd read a comedian's autobiography in which the man had recounted a friend's tale of masturbating into the soup of the British prime minister while working for a catering company serving a state dinner.

The guard on duty nodded as he opened the exterior door to the prisoner's cell. He locked the door behind Alexander, who was familiar with the protocols of serving meal trays to prisoners. The man, who'd been lying on his bedroll, heard Alexander approach and swung up to a sitting position.

"Hey, kid," he said.

Kid.

Why did everyone call him kid?

"Dinner time," Alexander said. "You know the drill."

This was the fourth or fifth time he'd delivered this prisoner his meal tray. Today was the first time he'd said a word. The prisoner stood up and moved to the back of the cell. Alexander removed the bowl and bread from the tray and set them on the floor just inside the bars.

"Smells good," he said. "What is it?"

"Some kind of bean stew."

He wasn't supposed to talk to the prisoner.

"Any special additions from the chef?" he said with a hint of sarcasm.

"Uhhh," Alexander replied.

"Don't sweat it, kid," he said. "I'm sure the heat killed the snotrocket or whatever he spiced it with. Beggars can't be choosers, after all."

"Okay."

"Have a seat."

"I'm not really supposed to."

"I get the feeling no one's gonna give you too much grief on this," he said.

He dunked a piece of the bread into the stew and took a bite. He was clearly starving, and the prospect of a foreign substance in his food didn't dissuade him in the slightest. The man's comment intrigued him.

"What do you mean?"

"You look like your old man," he said.

Alexander did not reply.

"Am I right?"

Alexander dropped to his bottom and pushed up against the far wall.

"What's your name?"

"Alexander."

"Nice to meet you," he said. "I'm Jack."

Alexander's heart was racing. He felt guilty and exhilarated at the same time. His father would be furious if he caught him shooting the breeze with their prisoner, and that made him want to do it even more.

"How old are you?"

"Seventeen."

"Almost a man."

"My dad doesn't think so."

Jack guffawed and scratched the days-old stubble on his face.

"You've got to remember, parents always see their kids as kids. No matter how old they get. I had a friend, almost fifty years old, his mom calls him one night, and he happens to be at the office catching up on paperwork. His mom freaks out that he's by himself. Six feet tall, two hundred fifty pounds, and his momma thinks he's gonna get kidnapped or something."

Alexander hadn't looked at it that way. That said, he wasn't sure he agreed with the man. Simon was many things, but sentimental was not one of them. He didn't have a loving bone in his body. Fear and control were the most oft-used tools in his parenting toolbox. It was how he ran the Haven.

"Maybe."

They sat in silence while Jack finished his meal. He cleaned the bowl out with the last bit of stale bread and then set it back near the bars.

"So what's it like around here for a kid like you?"

The man was obviously pumping him for information, but Alexander found himself not caring. He was easy to talk to, and he seemed to listen. Hell, that bit about how parents looked at their kids was more insight into his relationship with his father than Simon himself had provided in the last decade. So he was getting something out of it too.

"It's okay," he said. "I guess. We have it good here."

Alexander danced around this issue carefully; he often felt guilty about their bounty. He knew he was eating off the backs of others. The bodies of others. But what could he do? Starve himself to death?

"I miss school though."

A surprised chuckle emanated from deep inside Jack's throat.

"Really?"

Alexander nodded and braced for the mockery. The others at the Haven teased him for his bookish ways. But he didn't care. He loved to learn. He made weekly trips there, exchanging one backpack full of books for another. His father did not always approve of his book choices, but he gave him wide discretion as long as he read the books his father chose for him. Recently, he had read *The Prince* by Machiavelli and *The Art of War* by Sun Tzu.

"That's good," Jack said. "Can't say I would've felt the same if I were in your shoes, but this world's gonna need smart people if we're gonna make it."

"You don't think we'll make it?"

The corner of Jack's mouth turned upward in a sad half-smile.

"I guess I don't have a lot of faith in people anymore," he said. "Can't say I ever did."

If only you knew the truth, Alexander thought. *You wouldn't have any faith at all.* His father had been the architect of many atrocities these last few years, and the people here just went right along with it. He didn't understand.

"So, you got a girlfriend?"

An embarrassed smile spread across his face, which Jack noticed immediately.

"You dog," Jack said. His tone was teasing but warm. He wasn't poking fun.

"I don't know if she's my girlfriend."

"Hey, it's okay, bud," Jack said. "You love her?"

A slight nod of the head.

"Good for you," he said. "You hang on to that if you can."

Jack stood up and approached the bars, looking left and right conspiratorially.

"You know about safe sex right?"

Now his whole face flushed with embarrassment. Alexander did know. They had just started teaching it in school when the power went out. He'd been intrigued, of course, as all boys of twelve would have been, and he finally found a good book about it in those early days. Indeed, he knew all there was to know and then some. At least in theory. His father sure as hell hadn't taught him a damn thing. In fifteen minutes, Jack had imparted two important life lessons in him, which put him two ahead of Simon over the last decade.

Alexander and Norah had not had sex; he wanted to, very badly, but he had no idea how to broach the subject with her. He was afraid to do anything to scare her off.

"Does she live here too?" Jack asked. "Must be convenient."

Alexander's face fell as he thought about Norah. He was starting to worry he would never see her again. They always arranged the next meetup at each of their rendezvous, but since she had missed it, he didn't know how to get in touch with her. He'd just have to hope she showed up at the next Market day.

"No," he said. "She lives in one of the other communities. I don't know where it is."

"What's her name?"

"Norah."

Jack's face went blank.

"Norah, you said?"

"Yeah."

"Black girl, about your height?"

Heat shot up Alexander's back. Did this man know Norah? Were they from the same community? Terrified and hopeful all at the same time.

"Yes," he said. "Short hair."

Jack clicked his tongue as he took in Alexander, as though he was really checking him out for the first time.

"You know her?" Alexander asked hopefully.

"She's my niece."

27

A lexander could not sleep. It was late, probably closer to dawn than midnight, but he had been lying on his back, his hand under his pillow, cradling his head just so. He'd been staring at the ceiling, thinking about Norah, Norah, Norah. He and Jack had not spoken much longer, but long enough to confirm it was the same girl. A connection! A way to see her. Excitement rippled through him.

But how?

Then he remembered that he did not ask Jack where Norah lived.

He laughed.

How could he be so dumb?

He should have asked.

He could be on his way there the next day.

Then something else occurred to him.

The prisoner wasn't going to part with that information. It was valuable information. Of course, Simon and his top advisers knew the locations of all the settlements under their thumb, but that information was closely guarded. He had even asked his father later that evening, but when Simon had become suspicious about his motivation for asking, Alexander had abandoned the line of inquiry. He could not risk his father knowing about his relationship with Norah. That wouldn't be good for anyone, least of all him.

He slipped out of bed and pulled on a pair of pants and a jacket. He cracked open the door to his room, looked up one end of the dimly lit hallway and then down the other. As he stepped into the hallway, the door to his room closed behind him and latched shut quietly. Candles flickered in the sconces mounted near the crown molding. A single guard was perched at the door to the stairwell leading up to his father's suite.

His footfalls along the carpet were silent, and he reached the main staircase without incident. Lanterns at each landing illuminated his trip down. On the first floor, he casually walked past the two guards on duty. They paid him no mind. He was known to wander the grounds at night, and besides, he was the big man's son, even if he was a bookish little prick. They would give him no trouble. Although he was free to roam the Haven, getting access to the prisoner would be a different matter. It was one thing to deliver his evening meal to him. This was something else entirely.

The cellblock was housed in the basement of the golf cart garage. Alexander looped behind the clubhouse, crossing past the first tee box, the staging area for a tricky par four. It was one of the three holes on the course in use. They had converted the other fifteen into farmland.

Alexander had always hated golf; he never understood the purpose of wasting so much prime real estate on such a ridiculous sport. But even he had to admit, the three-hole course was a welcome diversion for the troops.

He paused at the corner of the pro shop, giving him a direct line of sight toward the garage. One guard on duty tonight, a guy named Bill. He was a weird dude, kept to himself mostly. The garage featured a small basement that they had retrofitted into the detention area.

What was he doing?

He had already made it this far without a conscious idea of what he was planning to do.

Or did he?

If he were being honest with himself, the plan had been formed the moment he'd learned Jack knew where Norah lived. That was all the motivation he needed. And now he had something the man would want. He had leverage. For the first time in his short life, he had leverage.

Bill was lounging in an old beach chair, smoking a homemade cigarette. Its smoke was pungent, its acrid tang reaching Alexander's nose from fifty yards away. His father probably would not have approved of such a casual approach to prisoner security. He looked around for inspiration.

There.

A series of golf bags lined the porch fronting the pro shop.

He crept onto the porch and selected a driver from the bag closest to him. It sported a massive, oversized head, the ones designed to forgive even the most amateur golfer's horrific golf swing. He took a few practice swings, relishing the swoosh as the driver cut through the air. He flipped the club upside down and pressed the head against his lips.

He was really doing this.

His whole life, it felt like he'd been waiting for something. Like he was marking time for something important. Especially since the Pulse. Especially since he had seen what kind of man his father really was. It wasn't right, what they did at the Haven. Taking from others. It would be one thing if he tried to lead these people, to encourage them all to work together. But he didn't. He was a taker. He'd been a taker for Alexander's whole life, and of course, for much longer than that. He would free Jack. Jack would take him back to their community. He could live there. He and Norah could be together.

Alexander did not want to be a taker. He did not want Jack to die.

He wanted to see Norah again.

Keeping the club close to his body, he stepped off the porch and edged closer to Bill. His back was to Alexander. He obviously was expecting no trouble.

A twig snapped underfoot, and Alexander froze, holding his breath. He waited for the big man's head to pop up, to process the signal that he was in danger. But the sentinel did not move. He sat, smoking his cigarette. Alexander was no more than ten yards away now, just a few more steps.

He could call it off.

He could stop right now and go back to bed.

No one had seen him.

He would find Norah another way. If she felt about him the way he felt about her, then she would look for him too. It was the way love worked, the way it was supposed to work. And if she didn't feel that way, then all this was for nothing. His body quaked with fear. Fear of making the wrong choice.

But which choice was the wrong one?

If he woke up in his own bed tomorrow, the driver back in its bag on the pro shop porch, would he regret having done nothing? He could be with Norah by this time tomorrow. His heart soared at the prospect. She wanted to see him too. Her mother had stopped her from seeing him. He recalled the incident at their picnic.

And the truth was, he didn't begrudge her those feelings. She wanted to keep Norah safe, and she had every reason to believe that there was danger out there. How could you not respect someone like that? He wished he had someone that cared about him like Norah's mother cared about her.

His own mother had loved him like that. How much he missed her. He never understood how she'd ended up with a man like his father. Perhaps she saw the broken things inside him and believed that she could fix them.

This was about more than just seeing Norah.

It was about starting a new life and living a life like his mother had.

His grip on the club tightened as he drew closer to Bill, a snake ready to strike. Just a few more steps and he would be within range. Then he was there. He drew back the club, exhaling ever so softly as he did so.

His soft exhalation was enough to alert Bill of the

imminent attack. He leaped out of his chair like a cannon just as Alexander stepped into a mighty swing. It struck Bill squarely in the back, drawing a howl of pain, but it was not enough to drop him.

Oh, shit.

Bill's hands clawed against his battered back as he staggered around in pain, still unclear what was unfolding. He turned just as Alexander readied another mighty swing. This time, he parried to his left, allowing only a glancing blow to strike his midsection.

Now Alexander was terrified. He was unskilled in combat, and Bill was a beast of a man. He was rapidly running out of time to put the man down for good. Bill charged at his attacker, his hands scrambling for a weapon lodged just so in his waistband.

Fear roared through Alexander as Bill's shoulder connected with his own. Bill stumbled, and the pair tumbled to the ground. No words were spoken; it had become an elemental struggle for life and death. Alexander was in big trouble now. Tears of panic and terror flowed down his cheeks. He was going to die here. His stupid, juvenile plan had blown up in his face because he was not a fighter. He was not his father's son.

Bill pushed himself up to his hands and knees. He pushed up onto one foot, breathing heavily, one knee still on the ground. Perhaps the initial strike had done more damage than Alexander had realized. Owing to his youth, the boy was on his feet quickly and recovered the club he'd dropped as Bill had tackled him. He loaded up another swing just as Bill regained his footing.

This third swing connected solidly with the side of Bill's head, resulting in a sickening crunch from the fracture of the periorbital bone around his eye; Bill dropped back to a knee, completely dazed now. Afraid to hit him again with the club, Alexander finished the job with a foot under Bill's chin. It flattened him on his back, and he lay still.

Alexander's legs buckled underneath him, and it took all he had to remain upright. He still had so much work to do, but he couldn't focus on it. He staggered around in a circle, dizzy, his eyes unable to focus. Bill lay unconscious at his feet. Or maybe he was dead, and Alexander was now a murderer. Alexander didn't know, and he was too afraid to check.

Norah.

Norah.

Norah.

That brought him back to center.

Immediately, his heart rate slowed, and his legs steadied underneath him. Crazy what love could make you do. He laughed, and had he heard himself, he would have been troubled by the manic, screeching sound of said laugh.

Step two.

Keys.

He needed the keys to the cell. They were clipped to Bill's belt loop. Finally, something had gone Alexander's way. He grabbed them and Bill's lantern and slipped inside the garage. The access panel to the basement was in the back corner of the garage, catty-corner from the entrance. He made his way around the dusty carts. The garage was still redolent with the old smells of oil and gas.

He unlocked the access panel and climbed down the short ladder descending to the basement. Time was of the essence. He approached the cell and was surprised to find the prisoner awake and waiting for him.

"I wondered when I'd be seeing you," he said.

How could the man be so calm? Alexander's heart was beating so quickly, it felt like it might strangle him.

"If I let you out, you'll take me to Norah," Alexander said as firmly as he could. He wanted assurances. He wanted guarantees.

"You got it, boss," Jack said.

"I mean it, no funny stuff."

Jack held up his hands in faux surrender.

"Wouldn't dream of it."

Alexander was flying on blind faith now. Once the cell was open, there was no guarantee that Jack would live up to his end of the bargain. He looked to be dangerous. The kind of guy who could snap Alexander's neck without breaking a sweat. He hesitated, but then he remembered he couldn't turn back now. He was past the point of no return. The attack on Bill alone probably warranted a date with his father's hanging tree. And nepotism wouldn't save him, either. His father would probably slide the noose around his son's neck himself.

Because without order, there was chaos.

"We go right now," Alexander said. "Right now."

"It probably wouldn't be wise to wait until after breakfast," Jack said in a slightly mocking tone.

Alexander's cheeks flushed with shame. It was a

dumb thing to say. Of course the prisoner would want to go right now. He slid the key into the lock, pausing before he altered the course of his life forever.

"My dad will kill me," he said softly. "Literally murder me."

Jack didn't reply. It was not hyperbole. If they were caught, there was a good chance that Alexander would pay for this transgression with his life.

"Well, let's get on out of here then."

He turned the key slowly, feeling the tumblers turn, the lock disengaging.

The first act of his life was now ending. Everything up to now had been pointing toward this moment in time. And it felt right. It felt like the best, truest thing he had ever done.

The cell door drifted ajar.

It was done. Jack wouldn't allow the cell to be locked again with him in it. It didn't matter. Alexander didn't want to undo it. He had no regrets. He had done a good thing, perhaps a great thing. Even though there was something in it for him.

"Thanks," Jack said. "I owe you."

"I just want to see Norah."

Jack nodded.

Alexander took the point, leading the way up the stairs. Jack held Bill's gun. A hostage ruse might buy them a few moments if things went sideways. The garage was dark, silent as a mausoleum.

They crept between the dead golf carts. The full moon shining through the garage window tracked thin lines of silvery light across the concrete floor and the heavy canopies of the carts. They paused at the doorway for a peek through a window. Bill was stirring, struggling to climb to his feet.

Jack slipped out the door and came up behind Bill, striking him in the back of the head with the weapon. As Bill crumpled back to the ground, Jack caught him under his arms and dragged him toward the garage. Alexander was deeply impressed. Bill was a big man, and Jack was carting him like he was a sack of groceries.

"Grab his legs," whispered Jack. He was calm, so much so that Alexander could scarcely believe it.

They quickly moved him to the access panel and down to the basement. Jack eased the unconscious man over the edge, guiding him down as far as he could before letting go. Bill's body slid down to the floor. Jack and Alexander followed it down. They moved Bill into the cell.

Behind them, a rustling sound. Then the faint sound of a click.

Jack's trained ears identified it instantly, and he dove to the ground, his hearing muffled by the sudden discharge of a weapon. Everything was happening very quickly. A high-pitched squeal of pain. The boy had been hit, but he didn't know how badly. Jack dropped low and charged at the shooter. In the small space, he covered the ground in a fraction of a second. His shoulder drove into the man's midsection and drove him against the door behind him. The man's head rocked backward, smacking the wall and disorienting him. His gun rattled to the ground. Jack grabbed the man's head in his powerful hands and wrenched it sharply, snapping the man's neck.

The tiny cell block was quiet once more.

But for the pained moaning behind him.

The boy was on his back, his hands pressed to his sternum. Blood was spilling rapidly between his fingers, pooling on the ground underneath him at an alarming rate. In the light of the lantern, the boy's face had gone a milky shade of pale.

There was nothing Jack could do for him.

He knelt down at the boy's head, cradling it gently. Alexander struggled to speak, but he could only form a few whispery bubbles as the life drained out of him. Jack's heart broke. This was a good, brave boy who lay dying here. It was awful to witness. Awful how this world chewed up and spit out the very best it had to offer. With the last of his strength, he reached up to Jack's collar with a bloody hand and pulled him close.

Jack leaned in.

"Norah," whispered the boy.

A few moments later, his breathing slowed to a crawl before stopping entirely.

Alexander was dead.

28

Lucy was administering an annual checkup to seven-year-old Hailey when an animated discussion erupted outside. The girl was healthy enough. Like all the kids, like everyone in Promise, she could use a few extra calories each day. Otherwise, she was in good shape.

"She's looking good," Lucy said to Chris Johnson, the girl's father, once the checkup was complete. "Heart and lungs sound good and strong. Make sure she looks after those teeth." Dental hygiene was a problem for many people in their post-Pulse world. Commercially made toothpaste had long since vanished, and they were left to develop their own products to keep their teeth clean.

"Thanks, Lucy," Chris said. Then he turned to his daughter and said, "What do we say, sweetie?"

"Thank you, Miss Lucy," the girl said.

Lucy smiled and tousled the girl's hair on her way out the door. After making a few notes in the girl's chart, she went outside to investigate the commotion.

It had been four days since Jack had left, three since Amelia's arrival on horseback with her terrible message. Lucy was starting to give up hope. You took a chance. Sometimes your bets would pay off, and sometimes they didn't. Even in times of war, she still had work to do. Life went on. Fortunately, Norah was safe. She had not even left Promise. She'd been out for an evening walk when the photos in her drawer had been revealing their secrets to Lucy.

Terri was rushing toward her as she stepped outside, calling out Lucy's name.

"It's Jack," she said. "He's back."

Her brother was limping toward the clinic, a pained look on his face. He was alive. Instinct had her scanning his body for obvious signs of injury or trauma. That look on his face, however, concerned her. Behind him trailed Carol and Jon, two members of the Council.

She hugged him. Neither had ever been much for excessive displays of affection. Even as she hugged him though, she was palpating his arms and back, looking for injury. The nurse inside her never took a minute off. She didn't know what she would do if something had happened to him. He had filled in the gaps in her life like caulk.

"They'll be coming soon," he said to the others. "We need to evacuate Promise."

Lucy's mind was on overdrive. It was something they'd planned for in the event of an attack on their settlement. There was an abandoned church about four miles east as the crow flew. There they had stashed weapons and nonperishable foods to float them for a few days.

"Jon, Carol," Lucy said, "start rounding everyone up. We need to be on the move in an hour."

They nodded their assent and then left Lucy alone with her brother.

"You're not hurt?" she asked.

"No," he said. "Where's Norah?"

"She's in her room," Lucy said. "Why?"

"I need to talk to her," he said.

"About what?"

"Come with me," he said. "You'll want to hear this too."

She had to tell him.

"Listen," she said. "There's something you need to hear first. This boy she's been seeing. His father is the leader of the Haven."

"I know," Jack said.

"And that's not all," Lucy said.

Jack's brow furrowed, a puzzled look on his face.

"Remember the man who held us right after the Pulse?"

Jack nodded.

"Simon."

A look of understanding swept across his face.

He sighed.

"The past is never past," he muttered.

"What?"

"Nothing."

They fell silent for the balance of the walk to Norah's room. Jack had been dreading this moment. It was all he'd thought about since his escape from the Haven, which had been paid for with Alexander's sacrifice. The death of a child.

He had made sure that Alexander's sacrifice had not been in vain. After killing the man who'd shot Alexander, Jack had moved his body into the cell with Bill, who was slowly coming to but still quite loopy. He locked them in the cell together and left them there.

It was still an hour before dawn. It bought him some time to make it back to Promise. The coast was clear when he returned topside. He hated leaving the boy's body down there, but he didn't have any choice. Alexander deserved a hero's funeral. If they survived this, he would make sure Promise honored him as one.

He spent another thirty minutes or so surreptitiously exploring the expansive grounds of the resort. It was big, obviously home to a sizable population. The use of the golf course as farmland was smart. This was fertile ground and had been carefully maintained up to the moment of the Pulse. Plus, it was well-marked and featured multiple water hazards that provided for easy watering. Clever indeed.

He still didn't know where the golf resort was, however. It was a gap in his knowledge he needed to rectify immediately. He circled back to the first tee and followed the access road back to the resort entrance. On the way, he passed a makeshift stable. The horses slowly waking up. Soon, the sleepy-eyed stable hands would emerge to begin the morning feeding. He saddled the gentlest one he could find and rode her out to the main road.

The sky was lightening ever so faintly to his five o'clock, putting him on a southeast heading. He turned left and pushed the horse up to a trot until he spotted a road sign. The sun rising in the east served as his beacon. Route 402. He rode the horse hard for an hour until he recognized a highway intersecting with 402. He was about twenty-five miles from home. He left the horse near a creek, preferring to make the rest of the trip by foot. It made moving in stealth much easier. He figured he had until sunrise before his escape would be detected. That would give him a head start of several hours.

"He didn't make it, did he?" Lucy said.

Jack shook his head.

"No."

Lucy closed her eyes. At the threshold of Norah's room, he squeezed Lucy's hand.

Norah was sitting on her bedroll, a journal open in her lap to a blank page. She was twirling a pen in her hand. In the dim light of the lantern, she looked stunningly beautiful to Lucy, in that gray area between childhood and adulthood.

She smiled when she saw Jack. She jumped out of bed and hugged him tightly. Regardless of her issues with Lucy, her love for Jack was deep and strong. They had a strong bond, perhaps stronger recently than Lucy's bond with either of them.

"I was starting to worry," she said.

"I'm fine," he said morosely.

The tone of his voice shook her.

"What?" she said, easing out of his embrace and stepping backward.

"Sit down."

She did, looking up at Lucy for help. Lucy held her gaze but said nothing. She wanted Jack to tell the story. He'd been there. He could tell her everything she wanted to know, as awful as it was.

"I met Alexander," Jack said.

"You did?"

"Yeah."

"Is he okay?"

His failure to reply told Norah everything she needed to know. Norah was already shaking her head in denial.

"He helped me escape."

Norah covered her mouth with her hand.

"And?"

"Someone tried to stop us."

"No," she said, her voice cracking.

"I'm so sorry."

"No!"

Lucy's eyes watered at the news of the boy's death. Her heart was breaking. It was almost as painful as the grief she had felt after Emma's death. Grief was a funny thing. That she could grieve for this boy she had only met for a few moments as she had grieved for her own daughter, the great love of her life, was a strange thing indeed. Because it was going to wreck Norah. It was going to destroy her.

"Honey," he said, "I want you to know how brave he was."

This caught Norah's attention. She looked up at Jack, her eyes wet.

"He loved you a lot," he said. "Getting to you was all

he could think about. And because of him, we know where the Haven is."

Norah nodded.

It was at that moment Lucy understood that Norah was an adult now. Seventeen but older and wiser than any seventeen-year-old should have been. She couldn't treat her like a child anymore because the world they lived in had stolen that from all of them. Norah's face looked hard and full of resolve. This boy had sacrificed everything for her, and in doing so, he had given them all a chance. A chance to push back. A chance to fight back. A chance to end it.

And the craziest thing was that Norah seemed to understand this. Lucy understood why she had loved the boy. She regretted the way she had treated him during their sole meeting. If she could take it back, she would. But she couldn't. She could only be there for Norah now. She could comfort her. Because even if she understood at a rational level what he had done for them, the grief would be there. Always.

If Norah lived to be a hundred years old, she would grieve for Alexander.

THE COUNCIL HAD GATHERED the entire population of Promise in the cafeteria to announce its next steps. The day they had long feared had arrived.

They were going to war.

And they were going to war today.

There was no time to waste. Jack may have gotten a

head start of a few hours, but no more. And the Haven's secret was out. Its hidden location had kept it insulated from even the threat of a counterattack. Now that was gone. Immediately, the Council dispatched scouts to the other settlements to let them know the Haven's location and inquire whether they could count on their support for a first strike.

"Effective immediately, an evacuation order is in effect," Councilman Schlosser announced after he'd called the meeting to order. "All citizens deemed non-essential are to depart immediately for Promise's backup location. You are to remain there until given the all-clear."

Terri Packard, who led the Evacuation Committee, stood up and began directing dozens of residents out of the cafeteria. The evacuation plan had been on the books for some time. It was chilling to see it put into effect. Lucy watched with a heavy heart as scores of her fellow residents left the room. She hoped to see them all again soon.

Within minutes, there were only about two dozen people remaining, all members of Jack's Security Committee. After Jack shared his intelligence, he begged off the meeting to begin gathering Promise's arsenal. The Haven had confiscated many of their weapons, but he had stashed a few in a silver case buried in the woods behind his tent. No one had known about them until now. They could not take a chance that someone's loose lips would reveal their existence. Especially knowing there had been a traitor in their mix.

They debated attack strategies. A number of ideas

were discussed and quickly dispatched. A frontal assault was out of the question. They simply did not have the numbers, and even if they did, Lucy was not sure they'd want to send so many to certain death. For better or worse, they were not like the Haven. They would not be cavalier about the loss of their people, as the Haven surely was. It was how places like the Haven could thrive. The needs of the many outweighing those of the few and all that. The bottom line was that they did not have enough bodies or weaponry for such a strike.

Still, some argued for such an attack, buoyed by the insane belief that right made might. That the morally superior position would somehow carry them to victory. Lucy scoffed while the man, Ethan Shea, made the plea to the council. Had he not been privy to what had been happening here for the last several months? He even offered to lead the attack, which made Lucy laugh out loud.

This enraged Ethan.

"You've got a better idea, I suppose?" he bellowed.

As a matter of fact, she did.

He waved his hand mockingly toward the podium. She got up just as Jack returned to the room with the case. At last count, it had contained four nine-millimeter pistols and one semi-automatic assault rifle.

"We take a small strike team," she said. "Five people. We sneak into their compound and destroy it. If they're going to come here, their place may be not well-defended right now."

Murmurs from the group.

"But we have to go now."

29

A dozen people volunteered for the attack on the Haven. Jack selected Lucy, Julio Loaiza, and Kelly Dale. All were young, fit, and strong. All had shown skill with weapons. Two had some experience with martial arts, which could come in handy in a stealthy attack on the Haven. Lucy readied her gear. They agreed to carry two bottles of water and a little flatbread each. No more. Truth be told, they wouldn't need more because by this time the next day, they would be either victorious or dead.

As Jack had said, the past was never past.

Once again, she was preparing to go to war with Simon. But this time, she was going in as a soldier, as a fighter, rather than as a decoy. The last time, they had been extremely lucky to get away with their lives. She would count on no such luck this time. She took Norah aside to bid her farewell.

"No need to say goodbye," she said. "I'm going."

Lucy smiled.

"No, sweetie, you can't," she said. "I can't let you."

"I'm not asking," she said with an angry heft in her voice.

"And I don't care," Lucy snapped back. "I am not risking your life. I don't know how this ends."

The girl's shoulders sagged as the finality of Lucy's decision settled in on her.

She was looking at something over Lucy's shoulder, a blank look on her face.

"I have a confession," she said.

"What is it?"

"I remember Alexander's father."

Lucy's eyes widened in surprise. She had not mentioned remembering Simon.

"His face was burned on my brain that day," she said, referring to the day Simon had held them both hostage and planned to trade them for supplies.

"I didn't know if you remembered," she said. "It was dark, and you didn't spend much time with him."

"You don't forget a man like him."

Lucy had no reply to that.

"Anyway, it was about a month after I met Alexander," she said. "He was really sweet, you know. Not a mean bone in his body. He didn't even like killing bugs. He would move them. No matter how ugly or creepy-looking. He would just pick them up and move them."

Norah shuddered; it brought a smile to Lucy's face. The girl had a pathological fear of insects and bugs. Sometimes, it was a real problem in their rural lives.

"Anyway," she continued, "one day I asked him about his family, and he told me his mother had died when he was little and that his father was a hardass but that he took good care of everyone."

"Did they get along?"

"I think they just stayed out of each other's way," she said. "Alexander knew how to keep his father calm. He didn't hate him, he didn't love him, he was just this guy who had raised him."

A flash of memory. During their sole conversation, Simon had told Lucy that he had a son. She couldn't believe a man who was so cavalier about other people's lives could be a parent to a child, but that, of course, was silly. Anyone, no matter how evil, could be a parent.

"Did you ever go to the Haven?" Lucy asked.

"No," she said. "I wouldn't have kept that from you."

Lucy nodded.

"Anyway, that day you followed me," she said. "Alexander brought some pictures with him. Mostly of him and his mother. But the last one in the stack was one of him with his father. It was like a punch in the face. I wanted to scream. I started shaking. Alexander asked me what was wrong. I told him I had just gotten chilly, which was a dumb thing to say because it was like eighty degrees out."

She paused.

"But he believed it."

"Yeah," she said. "He believed anything I said, the big dummy."

Her eyes watered at the memory of her sweet, naïve boyfriend.

"I asked him if I could have the pictures. I told him

how cute he looked with his parents. It would have looked weird if I asked for just the one with his father."

"Why did you want it?"

"I don't know," she said. "I guess I couldn't believe it was really him. I needed to look at it some more. Part of me didn't want to believe it. I kept looking at the picture, looking for ways to convince myself it wasn't him. But I never could. It was him. The father of this boy I loved."

Hearing the lament in her voice broke Lucy's heart even more, if such a thing were even possible.

"And that, Mama, is why I want to go with you."

"Listen to me, Norah," she said. "You've already lost too much. If this goes badly, Promise is going to need you to lead."

"Okay," she said. "Will you be careful?"

"You know it."

"One more thing," Norah said.

"What?"

"I know about Emma."

Lucy's stomach flipped. She looked for something to say, but the words would not come. She did not know how Norah had known about her. At this point, it probably did not matter.

"It's okay," she said. "I wish you had told me about her."

"I'm sorry," she said. "I just didn't want you to feel like you had to compete with her. With a ghost."

"When you come back, will you tell me about her?"

Lucy's heart soared.

"You bet."

Thirty minutes later, the group of six was ready to go.

They had one stop to make.

Lucy did the math as they rode. Tim's community was ten miles to the north. According to Jack, the Haven lay another fifteen miles to the northeast. It would cost them a few hours, but it was worth the side trip. Tim would have weapons. And he deserved to know about the baby.

The trip was risky, and the outcome was uncertain. But not doing anything was dangerous, too. Perhaps even more so. Especially now that Alexander was dead. Now that the Haven would be coming.

Now that hell was coming.

They would have to be first.

The sun had begun its slow descent toward its nest. They had a few hours of daylight left. Lucy liked the way this was shaping up. The side trip to Westerberg would bring them to the Haven after dark, which was exactly what she wanted.

As they rode, her thoughts were focused on the baby growing inside her.

A baby.

It was still hard to believe.

Her best guess put the pregnancy at about ten weeks. This tracked toward a late winter or early spring delivery, assuming she lived that long. Her mind drifted. To another time, another world. She pictured herself holding a newborn, wriggling and grunting, unsure of anything other than everything it had ever known, to the extent a newborn could know anything, had been destroyed.

Perhaps this time, she would get a happier outcome as a parent. She had suffered so badly. The trauma had never healed. And she had to let it heal. She would always be Emma's mommy, and she would always love her more than anything in the world. But she couldn't stay in the shadow of the past.

As it was, the odds would be stacked against this baby. She would be born in a world much different from the one in which Emma had arrived. Two siblings, separated by time and worlds. She wondered how Tim would react. Probably be thrilled, knowing the guy. This would be his first. He would be a good dad. She could see that. He gave of himself. He put the well-being of others ahead of his own. He would find a way to make the kid's life normal.

It was an admirable trait, one that didn't get you far in their world. But the world needed people like Tim. Otherwise, it would continue down this path toward brutishness, toward survival, toward baseness. The world needed fathers like Tim. Fathers who would raise their kids to be kind and generous, raise kids to work together to solve their many problems. It couldn't go on like this, this constant state of war.

Then she wondered how they would manage raising a baby. She couldn't leave Promise any more than he could leave his community. But the baby would need both parents. She put the issue aside for now. They would cross that bridge if and when they got to it. There were so many other bridges to cross between here and there, and some of those bridges were going to be rickety indeed. If those bridges were even there at all.

Someone sneezed, breaking her out of her daydream.

They were less than a mile from Tim's distribution center. It was late afternoon. As they drew closer, the butterflies in her stomach multiplied. They would be dropping a lot on the poor man. He'd probably been planning on a routine day, an ordinary day. There was something to be said in the ordinary. It meant that nothing terrible happened, that no one died, that you had enough to eat, enough water. An ordinary day was a beautiful one indeed.

"Hey Luce," Jack said.

"Hmm?"

"Was that trailer burned the last time you were here?"

They had drawn near the western edge of the warehouse complex. A small trailer south of the main warehouse had been consumed by fire in the not-too-distant past. Black soot covered the roof where it had caved in, making it look like a ruptured abscess. A flutter of anxiety rippled through her. This damage had not been there.

As they turned onto the access road, more evidence of some dramatic event revealed itself. The anxiety tickling Lucy's stomach was now morphing into fear. She slowed the horse's pace; the others followed suit. The guard station had been destroyed. No guard was on duty, as there had been during her two previous trips here.

Something had happened here.

Something terrible.

The group's chitchat started, pulling back the cloak on the immense silence pressing down on them. There were no muted murmurs, no sounds of life drifting from beyond the fence. An owl hooting in the trees was the only sound. The group froze in unison, all sensing trouble. Lucy feared the worst. The Haven had found this place. Lucy removed the field glasses from her pack and surveilled the area. Nothing was moving. A number of the buildings bore signs of damage, both fire and firearms.

"What do you think?" Jack asked.

"Not sure," she said, her voice a whisper. Her thoughts raced to Tim's wellbeing. She was not ready to lose him. Not now.

"Should we check it out?"

"Yeah," she said. "There's no one here. Safeties off though."

The group drew their weapons as they made their way down the short access road to the perimeter fence. The main gate hung loosely from its hinge like a bird's broken wing. There were tracks here. Tire tracks. She put that to the side for the moment.

Jack took the point, Lucy behind him. Kelly brought up the rear, keeping an eye on their six. They found the first body near the trailer. Shot in the chest. The body had swollen in the heat as it decomposed. It was a man, maybe in his early thirties. The stench was stronger here.

"Holy Mary, mother of God," muttered someone behind them.

Dozens of canned goods were strewn about the ground. More bullet-ridden bodies dotted the perimeter. If Westerberg had only been home to a few dozen people, they would have been outmatched and outgunned by an enemy like the Haven. The deep stench of death hung over the place like a cloud.

Near the back, Lucy spotted movement. There was a small fire burning. A woman was seated by the fire, her back to them. Lucy cleared her throat. The woman jumped, badly startled. Upon seeing Lucy's group, she scrambled for her pack, presumably going for a weapon. Jack and the others drew their guns. The woman froze, as though she were resigned to her fate.

Lucy held out her hand in peace.

"Take it easy," she said. "We're not gonna hurt you."

The woman was Asian, middle-aged, perhaps five or ten years older than Lucy. Her hair was mostly white, but her facial features belied a woman closer to Lucy's age. Hell, they all had aged a lot these last few years. She crumpled back to the ground and broke into tears. Lucy approached her gingerly, careful not to show aggression. A survivor of the attack could tell her what had happened here.

Lucy kept her hands up and open to indicate that she came in peace. She gestured toward the open space next to her.

"Can I sit here?"

The woman nodded. She was filthy and smelled terrible. Her clothes bore old, dark stains. Probably blood.

"Are you okay?"

"Do you have food?" she said, her voice raw and raspy. It had been some time since she had spoken. She was staring into the distance, not really focusing on anything.

Lucy retrieved the flatbread from her pack and handed it to her. The woman devoured it greedily.

"I'm Lucy," she said. "What's your name?"

"Margaret."

"Margaret, what happened here? Where's Tim?"

She shuddered.

"They came while we were at dinner," she said. "There must have been a hundred of them. They killed everyone."

Exactly what they had done to Everton. The decision to evacuate Promise had been the correct one. She could only hope they had not left a trail for the Haven to follow. She would worry about that later. She could only deal with this problem now. Destroying the Haven was the only way through this nightmare.

"Why did they do this?"

"I don't know," Margaret said. "I never saw them before."

"Did they take anything?"

"No."

They hadn't even taken the food. This was just a massacre. A show of force.

"Did anyone else survive?" Lucy asked gently.

"I don't think so."

She nodded her head tightly.

"How did you survive?" Lucy asked.

"I hid."

"Maybe some others are hiding?"

"No," she said. "I've looked."

"What happened?" Jack asked sharply.

"Jack, give her a second."

"No, it's okay," Margaret said to Lucy.

She turned back to Jack.

"I was at dinner, and I got chilly. I went back to my trailer to get a sweater. On my way back, I heard gunfire. I thought someone was taking target practice, but then I saw them pouring into the cafeteria. There must have been fifty of them. I guess they didn't see me. I watched through the window on the side of the building. Tim tried to surrender, but they just shot him where he stood."

She paused and closed her eyes, the trauma flooding back to her.

"I didn't know what to do, but then I heard them calling out to search for anyone else," she continued. "I was so scared. I ran back to my trailer and hid under my cot. I thought for sure they would find me. They even came in the trailer, but they didn't find me. They moved on. I didn't come out until the next day. I had no idea who had lived, who had died. It took me the rest of the day to figure out I was the only survivor."

She wept a little. Lucy gently closed a hand on the woman's forearm.

Tim was dead.

"I'm so sorry," she said.

The woman looked up at her and wiped tears away from her face.

"You're Tim's friend, right?"

Lucy nodded.

"I'm sorry," she said.

Lucy's chin dropped. Absently, she pressed her hand to her belly. Tim was gone. The work of the Haven. They were making their final move now. Consolidating control over the region. She could only hope their gambit worked. Before it was too late.

"What do I do now?" she asked.

Lucy chewed on her lower lip as she considered her options. She quickly came to a decision.

"We're gonna send you back to our place," she said. "Our community is about ten miles from here."

Lucy motioned for Kelly and Julio to join her and Margaret.

"This is Margaret," she said to the pair. "Take her to the rendezvous point."

Julio nodded.

"Listen," she said. "We're on our way to finish this thing. But you need to go back with these two nice people."

Margaret nodded.

"You know who did this?" she asked.

"I've got a pretty good idea."

Lucy rose to leave. Margaret grabbed her tightly by the arm.

"There were children here," she said with fire in her voice. "There were children here. You get them for what they did."

Lucy took the woman's face in her hands.

"I swear on my life."

30

K elly and Julio left with Margaret first. She had calmed down quite a bit, relieved that she would have a safe place to lay her head that night. Well, as safe as any place was these days. Safety was a relative thing.

She and Jack continued on a northeast heading. It was like riding through a nightmare come to life.

Tim was dead.

She could not believe it. Just like that, a huge void had opened up inside her. Scaffolding that had been keeping her afloat these last few weeks, perhaps even since she had met him five years earlier, had collapsed. This good and decent man was just gone. Her body was numb. Her hands gripped the reins tightly. She found herself struggling to breathe. As though it was a function she had forgotten how to execute. She didn't bother wasting time on the abject unfairness of it all. Everything was unfair now. Everything. Instead, rage swelled inside her. Rage that the world had been deprived of Tim Whitaker. Rage that he would never know about the child that was growing inside her.

She would get justice for Tim, and she would get justice for her unborn child, who would now never know the father that would love her so much.

A heavy rain began to fall about an hour after they left the warehouse, soaking them to the bone. It fell in sheets, buffeted by strong winds whipping across the road. A strong cold front harkening the approaching autumn. Behind it loomed a winter they would be lucky to survive if they did not defeat the Haven. The rain spattered her parka. The world was quiet but before the susurration of raindrops showering the blacktop, dancing across the foliage in the trees flanking the roadside.

"You okay?" Jack asked, pulling up alongside her.

"No."

He chuckled sadly.

"No, I guess you wouldn't be."

"We're gonna get these guys, right?"

Jack nodded.

"You're goddamn right."

"I want him to pay for this," she said. "I want them all to pay."

Lucy had never been one for revenge. She supposed it didn't matter if this mission was rooted in revenge. What she knew was that Simon and the Haven were a cancer. A malignancy that had to be extricated from their world. Unless they were stopped, it would continue to grow, spread its fingers into anything that was pure and good and ultimately destroy it.

"I'm sorry about your friend," Jack said.

"You would've liked him," she replied.

Jack did not like many people, but she was confident her brother would've liked Tim. He would have liked Tim because Tim was the kind of man that Jack knew he wasn't. Jack believed in the worst in people. He believed that most people were like him, and this world had done nothing to disavow him of this notion.

They rode in silence for a while.

"How much farther?" Lucy asked.

"A couple of hours."

They rode in silence, the metronomic whopping of the hoofbeats lulling her to sleep. She napped off and on, but every time she fell asleep, her dreams generated a replay of what she imagined the massacre at the warehouse must've been like.

"Let's go over this again," Lucy said.

"Big golf resort," he said. "There's a main hotel and a number of smaller cottages lining the course. They've converted most of the course itself into farmland. Which, I have to admit, was a pretty good idea."

"Where do we find Simon?"

"The kid said there's a penthouse on the top floor of the main hotel," he said.

Just the reference to the boy twisted Lucy's heart.

"Let's go over the plan again," she said.

Jack took a sharp breath.

"I'll create the diversion," he said, gently patting the saddlebags holding the ten sticks of dynamite they had brought with them.

It wasn't a great plan, she had to concede, but it was the best they could come up with. In the absence of a full-throated attack on the Haven, the best alternative was to create as much chaos as possible and force Simon to show his pretty face. At the very minimum, they could inflict enough damage to the Haven's infrastructure to create a truce between them.

"And I go after Simon."

"You know that this may not work, right?" Jack said.

"I know."

"You really want to take this chance?"

"Do we have a choice?"

Jack didn't reply.

"I don't want to do this," she said. "But our hand is forced. We won't make it through the winter. This way, we control our own destiny."

"And the baby?"

"I'm doing this for the baby," she said. "As long as there's a Haven, this baby has no future."

She was prepared to die today. She was prepared to die because it would have been in furtherance of a cause greater than herself. Even if it meant her life, the life of her baby. They would go down fighting together. Sure, they could have stayed home and hoped for the best. Hope that they produced enough to fend off starvation this winter. But it was false hope. The only choice was to stand and fight. Simon had made his choice. There had to be consequences for his decisions.

She was drawing a line in the sand.

If they didn't stop the Haven now, there wouldn't be another chance. Even if they bided their time, made it through the winter. Simon would grow too powerful. She wished it hadn't come to this, but she wished against many things about this world that had still come to pass.

A highway mileage sign ahead marked five miles to the Firethorn Golf Resort. Their current approach to the resort was too direct; the situation demanded a stealthier approach. Jack took the point, edging down an exit ramp toward an access road, separated from the main road by a long line of evergreen trees.

They decided to loop around to the back of the resort. There would likely be less activity than near the front, thus facilitating a stealth entry onto the property. They followed Route 238 for a few miles, passing a small lake to their right. Ahead, Lucy could make out the odd-looking farmland, cut to the design of a golf course that had once drawn duffers for a hundred and fifty bucks a round. Lucy conceded it was a good idea; golf courses had eaten up so much land. When they took over this place, she would make sure to maintain the farmland.

In the distance, farmhands worked the land, harvesting the late summer crops. They looked like little ants from this distance. She felt exposed and looked forward to the cover of the coming twilight. They decided to break for a snack and water while they waited for night to fall. A creek paralleling the road made for a good break point; they guided the horses there to drink. The horses would wait here while they executed their raid on the Haven. Left unsaid was the decision not to tie them up. If she and Jack both died, the horses would be trapped, condemned to death by thirst or starvation. She would not allow that.

"Okay," she said. "Remind me how many sticks we have?"

"Ten."

"Good," she said. "Can you set them up to go off at intervals?"

"Yep, I can manage."

"Once they start blowing, I'll go after Simon."

"You remember what he looks like?"

Lucy nodded.

"Do I ever."

Simon had been handsome in a classical sense. She didn't deny it, nor did it change the fact that he was a monster. She was reminded of a documentary she'd watched about Ted Bundy, the notorious serial killer. He was handsome, charming, intelligent, witty, and a complete psychopath. Simon was no different. No respect for human life. People were commodities. Freight to be bought and sold. With Bundy, it had been bought with his own murderous desires. With Simon, wealth and power.

And he had to be stopped.

THEY RESTED in the cover of the deep brush as the afternoon wound down and evening fell. The moon rose over the eastern sky, first a shiny dinner plate breaking above the horizon before climbing into its perch and shining down on them like a gigantic spotlight. They shared some flatbread and salted meat from their pack. It wasn't much. Enough to curb the hunger pangs but not so much as to weigh them down. They wanted to feel light and agile.

Using a stick, Jack sketched out the Haven's layout in the dirt while Lucy finished her snack. He pointed to a corner of the crude drawing.

"These are the stables here," he said, marking the spot with an X. "The tree line behind them is pretty thick. It smells terrible here. They don't do a good job cleaning the stables, so it's pretty unattended except at feeding time."

"We'll come in here, then," Lucy said.

Jack nodded.

It was a calm night, overcast. Clouds ran across the sky like ghost trains, silent and foreboding. Rain was in the offing.

The horses whinnied when Jack and Lucy eased by, but not loudly enough to alert anyone. They took position behind the resort. The main hotel rose up into the sky. Candles and lanterns illuminated dozens of windows, making it look positively medieval. That was where Lucy would find Simon. The grounds were relatively deserted at this hour, although a couple of sentries were on patrol.

"Weird being back here," Jack whispered.

Lucy felt good. Taking action felt good. Just being here made the Haven seem less scary, less formidable. An enemy to be taken seriously, but one that could be defeated. They reached the edge of the stables. It was time to go their separate ways.

"Ready?" she asked.

"Yeah. You?"

She nodded. Her heart was racing, but she felt strong and full of purpose.

"Take care of that baby," he said.

Her hand covered her belly instinctively. For her. She was doing this for her.

"Never piss off an angry mama," she said.

It was meant to be a joke, but there was a tremor in her voice. She was nervous. Well, of course, she would be. She thought about Emma. Lucy wished so badly that she was still with them. In her, Lucy could see the future. In her, she saw the good that people were capable of.

And when she had died, it reminded her that the world could be a terrible place full of terrible people. The Pulse had distilled that world down to its very essence. Day in and day out, a flood of terrible people doing terrible things to one another. But perhaps tonight, they could change that a bit. Nudge them toward a different destiny. It wouldn't be perfect. But it would be better.

"You sure about this?" he asked, perhaps detecting the shimmy in her voice.

"Yeah." Now her voice was firm again.

"Okay," Jack said. "The kid said his dad rarely leaves the penthouse. Helps build the aura, make him more myth than man."

"Gotcha."

They bumped fists.

"Be careful," she said.

"You too," he said. "You've got the harder job."

"Take out as many as you can."

He winked and shot her a finger gun before moving

on. She took cover in the shadows of the stable, waiting for her moment.

JACK RAN SILENTLY for the first building, going over the route they'd mapped out. Ten sticks of dynamite. If he could get them all in place, they might actually have a chance. Good old-fashioned dynamite. Even in this dead world, it was still there for them, ready to ignite, to bloom, to become the thing it was meant to be.

The pro shop was his first stop on this tour of destruction. He carefully removed two sticks of dynamite and placed them at the center of the store. He affixed the fuse to the blasting cap and made his way to the exit. By the door was a small propane tank, the kind you'd see on a backyard gas grill. It gave him an idea. He opened the valve, triggering the faint hiss of the release of gas.

This was the slowest-burning fuse. It would take about fifteen minutes to burn its way to the ordnance. He lay the end of the fuse on the outside of the door and set a match to it, birthing a tiny corona of flame creeping toward its destiny.

The clock was running now. He had just minutes to set the final five sets of charges. The golf cart garage was next. A few carts were likely gas-powered and would still be clogged with stale, useless fuel, but they would likely light up just the same.

From the porch of the pro shop, he scanned the vicinity for the sentries. Seeing none, he made a beeline for the garage where he'd been held hostage. It was a short jaunt to the garage. He leaned against the wall, risking a peek through the window, but it was too dark to see anything but the dim outline of the golf carts. He edged around the corner to the door just to the left of the garage bay. He turned the knob slowly and pushed it open. The peppery tang of burning marijuana filled the air. He froze. Someone was in here.

"Hello?" came the call.

He didn't reply. Footsteps headed toward him, coming from the corner.

"Lewis, is that you?" said the frightened voice. "Don't mess around."

"Yeah, it's me," Jack replied in a harsh whisper.

"Cool, cool," the man said. "You scared me, you asshole."

"Sorry."

The man appeared in between two golf carts. Jack could only see his silhouette in the dim light cast by the gibbous moon.

"Hey!" the man called out, his voice suddenly firm and sharp.

Shit.

Jack rushed at him; the man, quite high from the weed, reacted slowly. Jack plowed into him, driving him squarely into the concrete flooring. He snaked his arm around the man's throat, cradling his throat in the crook of his elbow. Before the man could even make a sound, Jack had snapped his neck, violently torquing his head over his bicep. Jack eased the man's body to the ground. He waited a moment for his breathing to stabilize, for the adrenaline rush of this deadly encounter to subside.

When he felt calm again, he set two more sticks of dynamite on the driver's seat of the centermost golf cart. Then he lit the fuse, this one about three minutes shorter than the first.

He made shorter work of the remaining three buildings, a storage shed, a dining hall, and a larger, nondescript warehouse, but time was becoming an issue. The encounter with the man in the garage had really slowed him down.

He finished unspooling the last fuse, a short one that would blow in less than thirty seconds. Sweat slicked his body as he worked, and his hands were trembling. He was really cutting it close.

He lit the final fuse and ran into the darkness.

31

Lucy's mind was blank as she waited for her brother to shove her toward her destiny. If Jack's gambit had been successful, the buildings would start to blow any minute now, and it would be time. Her brother would come through. He would not back out or lose his nerve. He was like a machine, a program that once you executed could not be stopped. So this was it. Their last stand.

Perhaps it was always destined to end like this. In this world, it was hard to imagine growing old and happy, sitting on your porch, sipping lemonade. Like most everyone else, she found it hard to believe that their powerless status was not permanent. Perhaps in the early days and weeks and months, it was reasonable to hold out hope that whatever needed to be fixed would be. Even if you still were, the lemonade was likely to be piss-warm and unrefreshing. A reminder that there were no more cold drinks to be had except in wintertime, when you might remember to dunk a six-pack in an icy stream for an hour.

No, this world was brutish, one that was going to do its best to chew you up and spit you out. And it was likely to get worse in the coming years. That was why you had to get while the getting was good. You couldn't sit around waiting for things to be good. You had to make them good. And if a place like the Haven, if people like Simon tried to take it away from you, you punched them right in the mouth. You bloodied them, or you went down fighting because life wasn't worth living unless it was worth living. And a life spent in bondage, subservient to another, was no life at all.

She would not stand for it.

Not for her.

And not for her unborn baby.

She was doing this for her child.

Even if it cost her everything, even if it cost them both their lives, it would be worth it. To die on her own terms. Not plucked out of a line, forced to her knees and then shot in the back of the head.

No sirree, Bob.

Lucy Goodwin wasn't going out like that.

She would fight to the last.

So would Jack.

She and her brother were as different as any two people, much less two siblings could be, but an innate belief in justice was the thread that tied them together. Their father had instilled in them an understanding that you had to fight for what was right at all costs. He'd fought in Vietnam, saw terrible action, took a bullet in the lung that had nearly killed him. Quickly, he had understood the war was a lost cause, a terrible cause at that. But keeping his brothers and sisters in arms alive, that was right. And so that's what he had done from 1970 to 1972, keeping them alive, giving lip service to command, going through the motions of the specific missions. The experience had scarred him permanently, driving him to relief in a bottle of whiskey and then to an early grave, but even at the end, it had been his prime directive. Their father would be proud of them today. His son and daughter were standing up to true evil, true tyranny because it was the right thing to do.

As the minutes ticked by, she grew increasingly anxious. Her jaw was clenched, her head starting to ache. Imagined scenes of Jack meeting disaster rippled through her mind like a horrific home movie. He had to succeed, he had to succeed, he had to--

The pro shop exploded first. A sudden burst of orange-hot light bloomed in the eastern side of the resort and expanded into the night sky. The sonic boom reached her ears a moment later. Thick, black smoke curled into the night sky, obscuring the moon shining down on them. The detonation was ear-piercing, even from where Lucy was standing. Her ears felt like they were stuffed with cotton balls.

WHOOSH!

The second building exploded, and chaos ensued. Three more explosions followed, one after the other, like a galaxy of stars unexpectedly going supernova. Even though they weren't synchronized, the effect of the sequential explosions was quite dramatic.

Haven residents began reacting to the sudden attack on their home base, pouring from the various residences in droves. As the size of the crowd grew, Lucy used the chaos to emerge from her hiding spot. She bolted straight for the hotel. In the confused darkness, no one paid her a second look. It was what she was counting on. She ran hard, the stress and exertion threatening to fracture her heart. She was dizzy with adrenaline.

One hundred yards became fifty. Then twenty. Then she was there.

She hid near the front door, behind a large, potted plant, as a steady stream of people exited the building. She quickly lost count of the number, but there were dozens, perhaps as many as a hundred people who flowed by her. She kept an eye peeled for Simon; he might be the type of leader to be the first on the scene. If he was, then she would be ready.

No sign of Simon, just a consistent flow of his underlings. She hazarded a peek into the lobby. The traffic had slowed considerably. A few more men were loitering in the lobby; they were armed, they looked nervous, their grips on their weapons tight. It was dark at this hour but for a single lantern flickering at the check-in counter.

Where was Jack?

Perhaps something had happened to him after setting the last charge. Perhaps he had been caught in the blast. It was not out of the question. The success of this gambit was far from guaranteed. She began sketching out a plan to storm the lobby by herself. If she timed it just right, if she targeted the men in the right order, she would have a chance.

She would wait another minute before making her move. One more minute for Jack to make it to the rendezvous point. She gritted her teeth and began counting to sixty, one Mississippi at a time.

She got to *fifty-six Mississippi* when a hand fell on her shoulder. It took all she had to stifle a terrified cry. She turned, her gun up, and found herself staring right into Jack's face. He pressed an index finger to his lips. She breathed a shaky sigh of relief and then punched him in the arm.

"You scared the shit out of me," she whispered.

"Sorry."

"Four of them inside."

Jack studied the scene, forming a plan of attack; as he did so, an idea occurred to Lucy.

"Follow my lead," she whispered.

She calmly stepped clear of the shadows of the planter and opened the front door to the lobby.

"Hey, you!" she called out as firmly as she could, drawing the attention of the four gunmen. They immediately responded with weapons up. She could only hope the darkness would conceal her identity.

"They've got them pinned down by the first tee," she yelled. "They want all hands on deck!"

"We're supposed to cover the hotel," replied one.

"This is straight from Joshua," she said. "They've got heavy weapons and he wants them neutralized ASAP."

This galvanized the group. As Lucy turned to lead them to the front lines, the one closest to the door motioned with the barrel of his weapon for the others to move; they started for the door, one at a time, right into

Jack's kill zone. With Lucy safely behind him, he burst from the cover of the planter and opened fire. The men were too stunned by the sudden attack to mount a response. It was over in seconds. They didn't even have time to duck. As ambushes went, it could not have gone better.

Jack took the point as they entered the now-unguarded lobby. It was large and spacious. To their left was the reception desk. To the right had been a high-end steakhouse called Tony's. There was a bar fronting the dining room, still stocked with bottles of liquor. Beyond was a long corridor leading to the elevators and the stairwell.

"Next stop, penthouse," she said.

Jack nodded.

They quickly crossed the lobby, moving deeper into the belly of the beast. Outside, the chaos generated by the explosions was still in full swing, but in the corridor, it was disturbingly quiet. The stairwell was pitch black. Jack quietly opened the door and gave Lucy cover as she stepped onto the first-floor landing. She froze, listening for sounds of activity. None.

"It's gonna be a black hole in there," he said. "Be careful."

She nodded.

She pressed her back against the handrail and edged her way upstairs, one step at a time, Jack trailing her. Behind them, the door quietly clicked shut. The stairwell was silent but for their quiet breathing and footfalls. There was no light. It was an absolute void, more than just darkness, an absolute absence of light.

She slowed at the first landing, carefully curling around and reaching out a toe for the next set of steps. Jack was just off her hip. She slid across the stairwell, again leaning up against the handrail, keeping her gun pointed upward. They reached the second-floor landing without issue. One more floor to go. As she placed her foot on the first step, a door above them slammed open. Dim lantern light spilled into the stairwell. She froze, waiting for her eyes to adjust.

"McDowell should've checked back by now," a voice said. This speaker was in the frame of the door, silhouetted by the light of his lantern.

Indistinct chatter in reply. A deeper voice, although unidentifiable. Lucy could not tell if it was Simon's voice. It had been five years since she'd last heard it.

"Find out and report back."

"You got enough guys up here?"

"I think we can handle it," the voice said. "Now go see what the hell is going on and report back. Three quick knocks."

The door shut, but the dim light remained as the sentinel made his way down the steps, carrying his own lantern. Jack gently pushed Lucy into one corner and crouched low in the other. In his rush, the man likely would not see them until he was almost on top of them. He took the steps two at a time, lantern in one hand, the gun in the other.

Jack pounced just as the man reached the landing and turned to head down the next flight of stairs. He grabbed the man's head and wrenched it violently counterclockwise; the man's body instantly went limp. Jack caught him under his arms and eased him to the ground, grabbing the lantern on his way down. The gun clattered harmlessly onto the steps and bounced down the steps behind them. Jack started to go up the stairs but doubled back and retrieved the dead man's gun.

Lucy set the lantern in the corner, but she did not extinguish it. Their eyes needed to adjust before they exited the stairwell onto the third floor. They finished the ascent without further incident. Jack reached for the door lever, but Lucy grabbed his hand midflight.

"Remember, this door might open directly into the penthouse," she said. "When we go in, we have to be ready to boogie."

"I'll go first," he said. "You cover me."

Lucy hesitated.

"Listen," he said, gesturing toward her abdomen. "You've got to make it out of here. It was dumb for you to come on this little adventure. I mean, I get why you did it, but it was still dumb."

He hugged her quickly.

"Let's get it on," she said.

He held the lantern up over his head and studied the doorframe.

"Door swings in," he said, gesturing toward the lack of hinges on this side of the door. "Small miracles."

They waited a few minutes. Enough time for the man to make a quick round trip.

Jack rapped sharply on the door three times.

She held her breath.

The door opened.

Jack fired four times directly into the chest of the poor

bastard unlucky enough to open the door. He barreled into the room, wrapping his arm around the bullet-ridden body and careening to the ground. He kicked his way free of the body and opened fire again to his left. Then, keeping low, he rolled across the corridor and took cover behind a large island counter separating the entrance foyer from a galley kitchen.

Lucy stole a peek down the weak side corridor to her right. Fortunately, the corridor ended just a few steps on the other side. It was a dead end, terminating at the penthouse's exterior wall, meaning they would only have to fight this insane battle on one front.

"Lucy, now!"

She barrel-rolled across the narrow hallway and scampered around to the safety of the island as Jack continued to return fire. Lucy crept around to the far side of the long counter and risked a peek while the shooters focused on Jack's latest fusillade. The corridor ran about twenty feet long and opened up on a large living area. There was no way to make it down the hallway without being cut to pieces.

There was a second hallway behind Lucy's position, running perpendicular to the main corridor, and bracketing the far side of the kitchen. It ran away from them into darkness. There appeared to be no activity on that side of the penthouse.

"Keep them busy," she told Jack.

He flashed her a quick thumbs-up, trusting her judgment. Staying low, on her hands and knees, she crawled out from her hiding spot, exposing herself for a brief moment. But the shooters were still focused on Jack. She ducked back out of range and down the far corridor. The hallway led to another wing of the penthouse; she counted three bedrooms here. It was quiet and appeared devoid of activity.

Jack's battle raged on. She needed to come up with something soon, as his ammunition would not last forever. Their opponents would wait a bit before making a move on him, but they wouldn't wait forever. She had five minutes to make something of this at most. She climbed to her feet, her heart pounding, the gun trembling just so. Two of the doors were open. The third one in the center was closed.

She touched her hand to the knobs of the two open doors. They were cool to the touch. She touched the knob on the closed door. It was warm and slick to the touch. Someone had just opened this door. She dove for the floor just as the door opened and a barrage of gunfire erupted; the rounds went right over her head. She returned fire, catching the unseen assailant in the legs. He fell to the ground, writhing in pain and howling. She fired once more into his head, and he went silent.

The master bedroom.

A lantern burned atop the chest of drawers, giving her a decent look at the massive room. A fireplace anchored one end of it. An extremely large television was still mounted on one wall. There was a small bookcase built into the opposite wall. A sliding glass door on the far side of the bed opened up onto a balcony. She slid the door open and stepped outside. It wrapped around the entire perimeter of the penthouse. She moved silently down the balcony, carefully negotiating the corner, and following it back down the east side of the building. It led her directly to the far side of the room where the remaining attackers had hunkered down. Down below, half a dozen fires continued to burn thanks to Jack's handiwork.

She had outflanked them.

There were three of them, each hiding behind one piece of furniture or another. The one in the middle drew her eye; her stomach fluttered. It was Simon. Excitement rippled through her. They might make it out of here after all. She checked her weapon. She had five more rounds left. Enough to take them all out.

Quietly, she crept to the sliding glass door and pulled it open, ready to face her destiny.

32

She took aim at the closest target and fired. The bullet struck him in the back; the other shooters were unloading their weapons down the hallway and did not notice the new fly in their ointment. That wouldn't last long, however. Quickly, she aimed at the second man and fired again. This bullet missed, shattering a television screen over their heads and drawing their attention.

Shit.

She fired again. This round killed the second man, laying him flat on his back.

The surviving bandits now understood a new front had opened up behind them.

"Jack, now!" she screamed, hoping he would make a move in the lull.

A howl that could only be described as a war cry filled the penthouse. Jack was charging the hallway now. Simon and the other man abandoned their positions, making a beeline for a doorway in the corner of the living room. She gave chase as Jack fell in behind her.

"That door, that door!" she yelled.

Jack kicked the door open but paused before venturing any farther. He ducked his head quickly in and back out again.

"Another staircase," he said, shrugging his shoulders.

"Roof?"

"Maybe," he said. "Possibly a fire escape."

Commotion back at the front door. Reinforcements, almost certainly. By now, the bodies they'd left in their wake would have been discovered. Footsteps down the hallway.

"Simon!"

They were pinned in.

"Hang on," she said, looking around the room. She grabbed a vase that had survived the gunplay from the table and tossed it into the stairwell, waiting for a response. It shattered, filling the stairwell with a tinkling cacophony. But it quickly fell silent again.

"Nothing," she said.

"They may be trying to escape," she said. "They don't know how many of us there are."

He winked at her.

She poked her head into the stairwell. Empty.

She bolted up to the steps. Jack was hot on her heels. A sign reading *Roof Access* was mounted at the top of the steps.

"You cover me this time," she said.

"Not a chance," he replied.

They posted on either side of the door, plotting their

next move. Down below, there was more commotion, but Lucy's barrier was holding. The door cracked open, but not enough for anyone to squeeze through. Lucy fired a shot down the stairwell, pushing their pursuers back. The door slammed shut, leaving them alone for the moment.

"Only way out is through," he said. He kicked the door open, blazing through his last few rounds as he did so.

She followed him, trying not to think about how insane all this was. Smoke from the fires had enveloped the rooftop in a hazy fog. Directly across from the door was a rooftop bar centered right in the middle of the roof.

The attack came from the left, a hard roundhouse right to Jack's chin. It staggered him, but he quickly regained his bearings. A massive specimen of a man, Simon's sole remaining guardian, drove his shoulder into Jack, taking both men to the ground.

With Jack occupying the big man, she focused her attention on finding Simon. The fires from Jack's bombing attack continued to burn, coloring the scene in a smoky orange. Visibility was poor and worsening by the minute.

"Simon!" she called out, keeping an eye on Jack's tussle with the larger man.

Silence for a moment.

Then his voice, still familiar and recognizable after all this time.

"So it is you," he replied from the smoky darkness. "Small world."

She stepped carefully, keeping her gun up at the

ready. The smoke was her friend now, keeping her concealed. She just needed one look, one glimpse of his perfectly chiseled face, and she could put an end to this. Around her, the sounds of Jack's desperate struggle filled the night air. Grunts of pain and exertion.

"Never thought I would get this chance," he said. "I've literally dreamed about it. Dreamed about peeling the skin from your body. And then your friend here mentioned you losing your daughter. I remember when you told me that back in Arlington. Weird how certain things just stick with you."

"Come and get me, you asshole."

A deep, bellowing scream filled the air; its tone was strange, like the sound of a car passing by.

"I got'em, Luce!" Jack called out. "You hear that, Simon? Your buddy just took a dive off the edge. You're all alone."

Silence fell over the rooftop again. The smoke continued to thicken. Lucy had drifted near the large HVAC system that lay dormant like a sleeping beast. She poked her head around the edge, looking for movement in the swirl of smoke. She made a complete loop of the large duct feeding into the building.

She was back near the long bar top, unable to see more than a few inches in front of her face. A flash of movement back near the ductwork caught her eye, and she hesitated. She did not want to hit Jack. She tracked the movement, trying to identify it before it disappeared back into the smoke. She eased up her pressure on the trigger of her gun.

The cat-and-mouse game continued for another

minute; then she heard a loud thwack, followed by the sound of a heavy load hitting the floor. Either Jack had gotten Simon or vice versa. She held her breath.

"Jack?"

Silence.

"Jack?" she called out again.

Nothing.

She struggled to keep her focus on Simon while dread about Jack's fate poured into her like concrete, threatening to paralyze her. She stayed low, under the line of the bar. Her knees cracked and popped as she crab-walked along the wooden paneling. Near its edge, she stumbled over something. It was Jack, down for the count, lying on his side. He was breathing, but he was not conscious. She would have to leave him for now.

It was just her and Simon now.

It had all come down to this.

Months under his boot. She was so close to throwing off the Haven's yoke. Already, the Haven lay in ruins below them. This could be the death blow.

Careful now. Don't blow it right at the goal line.

She curled back around the front of the bar, the HVAC system now to her right. She moved slowly, praying she had at least one more round in her weapon. In the chaotic fracas of the last few minutes, she had lost count. Her breathing was shallow and ragged. It was hard to hear anything over the din from the ground level as the Haven residents struggled with the multiple fires burning.

Near the roof's western edge, Simon struck from the right, kicking the gun free of her hand. It flew over the edge and down into darkness. He'd fallen short of a direct hit, however, giving her just enough time to spin around and away from his follow-up hit. He was within striking distance, though. She threw a desperate left hook, but she caught nothing but air. As she tried to pinpoint his location, she eased back from the edge of the roof.

A fist collided with the side of her head, briefly dizzying her, but giving her the intel she needed. Simon's location. She leaned to her left side and delivered a strong kick to the ribcage. He grunted and staggered backward. She moved in on him quickly, catching him with a solid jab to the throat, calling on all her Army hand-to-hand combat training, hoping her skills were still sharp enough to see her through this.

He countered with a sharp hook to her left flank, a direct shot that took her breath away. He was much stronger than she was; too many more of these shots would incapacitate her. She held her ground, steeling herself for one more shot before she executed her final gambit. He hit her again, this time with a hook on the opposite flank. It was harder than the first and left her doubled over in pain.

He grabbed her by the collar and pulled her close until their faces were inches apart.

"Look what you did to me," he hissed at her, rage dripping from every word. The right side of his face was badly scarred from the burns he had suffered at her hands five years ago.

"I'm going to enjoy this," he said, rearing back for another blow.

"And when I'm done, I'm going back to get that girl," he said. "Payback for my son."

She'd gotten him to square up against her, which was what she had wanted. She delivered a mighty kick to his groin, driving her knee square up into his midsection. He howled in pain and let go of her collar. Then the secondary pain set in, and he staggered past her, back toward the roof edge.

Now, Goodwin, now!

She rushed at him, driving her hands into his back and pushing him toward the edge. He tried to stop their momentum as her gambit became clear, his arms flailing like windmills, stomping his feet into the ground, but it was too late; she'd built up too big a head of steam. She kept going as far as she could before delivering one final shove. He disappeared over the edge, his scream filling the night air as he plunged three stories to his death.

Lucy stumbled and tripped to her knees at the edge. Her forward momentum kept her going as well, and she felt herself starting to go over. She curled her body into a ball and tried to direct herself away from the edge. Her body pinwheeled to a stop right at the edge; the rough concrete gouged deep scrapes in her arms.

But she was alive.

She rolled onto her back.

She was alive.

It was over.

∽

JACK. She had to get to Jack now. She did not know how much longer the barrier would hold up. She knelt by him and shook him by the shoulders. This was no time to be delicate.

"Wake up, Jack," she said. "We have to go."

It took a minute or so, but he finally started to come around.

"Did we win?" he asked groggily.

"Yes."

"Cool."

"Come on, we need to get out of here."

She helped him to his feet.

"How do we get out?" he asked dully.

"There has to be a fire escape."

They followed the perimeter of the roofline, nearly giving up hope before the metal staircase came into view.

"There!" she called out, picking up the pace.

On the northeast corner was a narrow ladder descending to ground level. Behind them, the door to the rooftop access blew open. A handful of armed men streamed onto the rooftop, slowed by the thickening smoke.

"Can you make it?" she asked.

He coughed.

"Yeah, I think so," he said. "But maybe I'll wait 'til you're at the bottom."

She scrambled down the ladder and was on the ground within seconds. She shielded her eyes and looked skyward as he took his turn coming down. He was wobbly and took several breaks, but eventually, he made it down.

They hugged tightly.

"You did it," he said.

"We did."

Around them, it was sheer chaos. Throngs of Haven residents were intent on fighting the still-burning fires, dazed and stunned at the sudden attack on their once impregnable fortress. The smoke and commotion were welcome companions as Lucy and Jack made their way to the exit.

It was almost dawn. They had a long journey ahead of them.

But soon, they would be home.

EPILOGUE

It was December 23. The day before Christmas Eve.

Lucy watched as Norah hung the last decoration on Promise's Christmas tree. It was a chilly afternoon, but they had a large campfire burning. The clouds were thick and low, and it looked like it might snow. Lucy didn't mind a little snow, especially at Christmas, but she did not want a big storm, not so early in the season. Snow was a potentially deadly threat these days.

The residents of Promise cheered loudly as Norah took a bow. They retreated to the warmth of the fire, sipping hot cider. Lucy would have loved to cook up S'mores, but chocolate was a luxury item they rarely saw anymore. No matter. They had full bellies and a safe place to lay their heads.

It was an astonishing turn of events. Lucy and Jack's stealth attack had triggered a total and complete defeat of the Haven. The memory of their terrible battle on the roof loomed large, as fresh in her memories now as it had been when they had made it back to Promise later that morning.

By the time they arrived, close to mid-day, the Haven had all but been abandoned. The place had risen and fallen with Simon at the helm. The fires had largely dissipated; Jack's sabotage had been extremely effective. Every single building he'd attacked had collapsed.

Lucy's pregnancy continued unremarkably. It was too early to feel the baby move, but thankfully, there was no sign that Simon's blows to her midsection had caused any damage. No spotting, no bleeding. She wouldn't know for six more months, and the waiting would be terrible, interminable.

Norah was still mourning Alexander's death and probably always would. Lucy could not blame her. The boy had been instrumental in the defeat of the Haven. Lucy had finally told Norah that; she still felt guilty for coming down so harshly on her that keystone day she had confronted them. Inadvertently, she had stolen a little of Norah that day. Ruining what was one of their final times together.

But time was healing many of the wounds. They were close again. They mourned together. She missed Tim terribly. She had not yet begun to process his loss. It was still too fresh. Too raw. For now, she kept herself afloat by remembering that part of him now grew inside her.

As she finished her cider, Lucy spotted movement from the corner of her eye. A man was staggering toward them from the woods. He looked disoriented, stumbling to and fro on anything but a straight line; he seemed to have locked in on the campfire as a beacon. Lucy drew her weapon, as did several others who'd noticed his arrival.

But the man did not seem put off by the bevy of weapons suddenly pointed at him.

"Hang on there, friend," someone called out.

The man froze, as though he had just noticed them. Then his legs buckled, and he collapsed into the snow. Lucy and several others moved toward him gingerly, keeping their weapons drawn. He was emaciated, his face scratched to hell. He was Black, but his skin had taken on an ashy tone. She pressed the back her of hand to his head. He was not feverish, and he did not appear to be ill. He did seem dehydrated, starving, exhausted to the point of collapse. He was almost certainly hypothermic.

Lucy and three others picked him up and carried him to the clinic. He began shivering once they placed him in the bed, so they covered him with a number of blankets. She took his temperature. Ninety-one degrees Fahrenheit. They got to work stabilizing him, bringing his core temperature back up slowly. They couldn't do it too quickly, lest they trigger a shock response that could kill him. They helped him down a few ounces of a salty broth, which he was able to keep down. It would do him no good if he couldn't keep it down. As his condition stabilized, he fell into a deep sleep just after sunset. Lucy monitored him for the rest of the evening. She slept on the cot in the office, wanting to be nearby in the event his condition changed.

He was awake and sitting up in bed when she went to

check on him in the morning. He still looked extremely thin and weak, but his color was much improved.

"Good morning," Lucy said.

"Morning," he said. He was glancing around the room as though he could not quite remember how he had gotten here.

"How are you feeling?"

"Better," he said.

"What's your name?"

"Solomon Tigner."

"I'm Lucy," she said. "I'm the chief medical officer here."

"Is Jack here?"

The question took her by surprise.

"Jack?" Lucy replied.

"Jack Goodwin."

"You know Jack?"

"I do," he said. "Are you his sister?"

"I am," she said.

"You look like him."

"How do you know Jack?"

"Is he here?" Solomon asked. "I have to speak with him. I've been looking for him."

"How do you know him?"

The man clasped his hands together as though in prayer.

"Please. Is he here? I've been looking for him for a long time."

"Okay," Lucy said. "I'll get him."

Terri had arrived and was doing inventory in the storeroom. Lucy asked her to fetch Jack from his tent.

They returned a few minutes later. His breath caught ever so slightly when he saw the man in the bed.

"Jack, do you know this man?"

"Yes," he said cryptically.

"How you been, buddy?"

"What are you doing here?" Jack asked, his voice small and strange. There was a hint of fear in his voice.

"Jack, listen to me."

He motioned for Jack to draw closer. Jack took a hesitant step toward the man.

"What?"

In a whisper, just loud enough for Lucy to hear:

"I know how to turn the lights back on."

Click HERE to order DAYBREAK, the thrilling finale of the American Midnight series!

AVAILABLE NOW!

The Finale of the American Midnight Series

Daybreak

Sign up at davidkazzie.com to stay up to date on new releases

AFTERWORD

I wrote NIGHTFALL over a ten-week span between May and July 2020, as we all came to grips with the new reality of our pandemic lives.

Writing the book was a welcome distraction from the increasingly bad news regarding the coronavirus, which continues to rage virtually unchecked as of November 2020.

The pandemic has been catastrophic. By the time the year is out, more than 250,000 Americans will have died, part of the one million-plus worldwide who have lost their lives to this terrible disease. It is an unimaginable tragedy and the defining moment of not just my lifetime but of the last century.

But good news is on the horizon. As of this month, there are two vaccines that appear extremely effective in combating the virus, and by the time you read this book, hopefully the vaccine will be flowing through the veins of millions of people.

Sometime in 2021, the third and final book in the AMER-ICAN MIDNIGHT series will be published, and my fervent hope is that by the time that installment is in your hands, the pandemic will be receding from view.

Until then, stay safe.

David Kazzie
    November 2020

ACKNOWLEDGMENTS

To my Advance Reader Team, thank you for your feedback, support and encouragement. We make quite the team.

To Dave Buckley, thank you for standing on the front lines of my first drafts.

To Ali Funk, thank you for your careful and meticulous work proofreading the final draft.

All errors are mine alone.

ABOUT THE AUTHOR

David's first novel, *The Jackpot*, was a No.1 bestselling legal thriller. He is also the author of *The Immune*, *The Living*, *Anomaly, The Nothing Men*, and *Shadows*.

His short animated films about law and publishing have amassed more than 2.5 million hits on YouTube and were featured on CNN, in *The Washington Post*, *The Huffington Post*, and *The Wall Street Journal*.

Visit him at his website or follow him on Facebook (David Kazzie, Author).